D1562642

in winter I get up at night

Books by Jane Urquhart

FICTION
The Whirlpool (1986)
Storm Glass (short stories) (1987)
Changing Heaven (1990)
Away (1993)
The Underpainter (1997)
The Stone Carvers (2001)
A Map of Glass (2005)
Sanctuary Line (2010)
The Night Stages (2015)
In Winter I Get Up at Night (2024)

NON-FICTION
L.M. Montgomery (2009)
A Number of Things (2016)

POETRY
I Am Walking in the Garden of His Imaginary Place (1981)
False Shuffles (1982)
The Little Flowers of Madame de Montespan (1985)
Some Other Garden (2000)

AS EDITOR
The Penguin Book of Canadian Short Stories (2007)

in winter I get up at night

JANE URQUHART

McCLELLAND & STEWART

McClelland & Stewart and colophon are registered trademarks of Penguin Random House Canada Limited.

Library and Archives Canada Cataloguing in Publication

Title: In winter I get up at night : a novel / Jane Urquhart.
Names: Urquhart, Jane, author.
Identifiers: Canadiana (print) 2023047523X | Canadiana (ebook) 20230475256 | ISBN 9780771051999 (hardcover) | ISBN 9780771098314 (EPUB)
Classification: LCC PS8591.R68 I5 2024 | DDC C813/.54—dc23

"Between Walls," by William Carlos Williams, from *The Collected Poems, Vol. I, 1909-1939*, copyright © 1938 by New Directions Publishing Corp. Reprinted by permission of New Directions Publishing Corp and Carcanet Press.

This is a work of fiction. Names, characters, places, and incidents either are the product of the author's imagination or are used fictitiously. Any resemblance to actual persons, living or dead, events, or locales is entirely coincidental.

Jacket design by Kate Sinclair
Jacket art: Christmas Eve by Joseph Hoover & Sons Co. Original from the New York Public Library. Digitally enhanced by rawpixel.
Typeset in Bembo Book MT Pro by Natalie Shefler
Printed in Canada

McClelland & Stewart,
a division of Penguin Random House Canada Limited,
a Penguin Random House Company
www.penguinrandomhouse.ca

2   3   4   5   28   27   26   25   24

In memory of Tony Urquhart 1934–2022

"He had much to give."

To Robert Gardner, who listened carefully and
spoke thoughtfully when I needed it most.

L ate last night I woke when the prairie moon slid into the upper mullion of my window, then reached inside and touched my face. I rose, flung off the eiderdown, and stood shivering by the sill for a few moments, looking at the blue-tinted snow with fury and sorrow inside me from a dream I couldn't recall. Then I pulled the curtains against the view, went back to bed, and lay on my back trying to manufacture sleep. The ghost of Harp came and went in an uncharacteristically mild way. Affectionate, attentive. So this time, it wasn't the loss of him that caused my anger. I assumed, then, that my heart would stop hammering against my ribs and I would fall asleep.

But sleep did not come. Instead, I found myself mentally walking through the rooms of one of my mother's houses. Not the family home we left behind in Ontario, or the ruined house in Saskatchewan, but rather, that other less geographically specific but more persistent house—the imaginary one she built inside her mind and furnished with whatever images she could seize from the narrow corridor of life allotted to her.

My own mind became taken up, as it often is, with keeping this other house of hers in order, or perhaps with attempting to establish order, for I have not completely—even now—solved its puzzles. Why a room filled with laughter on one day? Why all that anger and weeping on another? What were the most prized secrets of a kitchen, a bedroom? Did my mother understand what she had agreed to while walking from porch to parlour? Or was the contract unreadable? What does her complicity mean exactly? The storm occurs. Weather attacks the physical, everyday house. And suddenly there are no more decisions to be made, no more complicitous behaviour.

But even so, the bulbs near the stoop of the imagined house push their green spears up towards the light in spring, frost develops on the window in January, and some nights a moon and stars navigate the winter sky above the roof.

This morning, however, I have more pragmatic things to think about. The question of whether the schools will have a piano is one of those things. If the answer to this question is yes, I hunt up sheet music for songs the children might like to sing. If it is no, I make sure to pack a tin whistle or recorder along with my tuning fork. And the triangle, of course, with which I open and close the class. I also consider whether the teachers are interested in having their pupils study visual art. Some of the men are not, believing that art is a sort of game to be played once school is dismissed and the homework is finished. But some of them are keen. When I am working in those schools—and there are three of them on Fridays—I take along a fistful of brushes, jars of powdered poster paint, and five manuals of fuzzy grey photos like those shown to my class by a significant teacher when I was a child. They depict important works of art from the public galleries of the great capitals of the world. I must confess that I myself have not visited these capitals. Nor have I seen the artworks in their museums, though now that we have entered the 1950s, colour reproductions of such treasures have occasionally come my way. I have only one book with colour reproductions, but I always carry it with me to the schools where I am able to teach art as well as music. I pack everything I will need, along with my lunch, into the case I take with me. Only one case. The other hand is for my stick.

I was born twice, you see. Once gently, and once violently, which is why, although I am not yet old, I have the stick.

Waiting in the shed behind the house is the Ford that Harp gave me years ago. The car is almost twenty years old, and yet, summer and winter, it growls and then shudders into wakeful attentiveness at the turn of the key. I was too timid to accept the car at first—because of the light that such a gift shone on what could only be described as my weakness of character. But eventually, these comforting words appeared in the local News from Muenster column of the *Middleburg Messenger*: "Good to see our gadabout sometime music teacher and occasional abbey organist put the money from the sale of her father's farm to good use. She is now to be seen flying out of town in a brand-new Ford coupe painted robin's-egg blue!"

It is true about the colour. When I finally allowed the gift, I did so with an attempt at wit. "All right, all right," I had said. "But only if it is painted Virgin Mary blue." I had paused, then added, "Not red."

I hadn't once thought about the colour being that of robins' eggs.

I step tentatively out my back door early on these winter mornings, testing the path for ice or raising my feet carefully if there has been snow. My lameness makes the going slow in all seasons, but sometimes a schoolhouse will be set some distance back from the road and I must struggle through drifts to reach it. And of course, the driving is slower if it is winter. Often the road itself has been erased overnight by powdery snow, and then I won't be able to venture much beyond the town limits before I am forced to turn back. But this winter morning is precise and still and clear. Calm, and oddly bright, in the quiet darkness.

In stiller Nacht, I think. Remembering the child, Friedrich. His voice singing—not the carol but the song of broken-hearted Brahms.

I am very fond of winter dark when the world is still sleeping. I can hear a train approach from miles away, and if I stand on my back stoop for a few moments, I can see the locomotive's cone-shaped beam of light and the lit windows of passenger cars far out on the prairie. Closer are the illuminated windows of the monastery, where the brothers, including my own brother Danny, will have been up for a couple of hours. Will have sung matins, will have had breakfast, and will be now beginning the labours of the day. Danny will have already said a prayer for me, as he has every day since I was damaged by weather as a child, and then even more fervently once he knew about the man I loved. Dear Danny, after his own great passion, he became a practical soul, really, much concerned with the administration of the abbey and his own teaching. But he never forgets me in his prayers. I wonder which fact of my life, to his mind, needs the kind of revision most asked for in prayers: An improvement in my character, or an improvement in my gait? The former, I expect. Because after the big wind, the simple act of walking could only be seen as a God-inspired improvement.

Today, when I am a mile or two beyond the town, I begin to trust the snow tires enough to shift into fourth gear. The old blue car would be picturesque gliding through such Soviet surroundings, I think, knowing there is no one to see it. I recall the only Russian I came to know when I was a child: a girl called Tatiana who—without speaking—came very close to me when we were both wounded children. She was a miracle of sorts in her tented cocoon. So calm. So still.

I have driven into the full prairie now. The morning star is the only detail; otherwise, just empty space, with the odd snow ghost drifting absently through my lights. The three schools I will visit today have sylvan names—Aldergrove, Maplewood, and Oakdale—and yet, out here, there is an almost complete lack of trees. Perhaps the earlier settlers named their schools and churches and towns after all that was absent in their new lives. Everything they had left behind.

Years after the big wind came and destroyed our farm, Danny would tell me that in the immediate aftermath, he had found himself standing beside a small apple tree that—incredibly—had sustained no damage. While staring at the tree, stunned by weather, he tried to unpeel what he described as a sort of green fur that had wrapped itself around the thin outer branches. He managed to remove a piece the size of a postage stamp. Two eyes, he told me, a nose, and a partial moustache revealed themselves on the end of his finger. A few seconds later he recognized the eyes and the moustache as belonging to King George, and soon after that, he unpeeled a number 1 that he quickly realized was from a Canadian dollar bill.

When our family had taken the train to the northern Great Plains, that tree was just a sapling in a pot, and my mother had cradled it on her lap most of the way, leaving my not-yet-two-year-old twin brothers, Patrick and Timmy, to play in the aisle. After the house was built on the new land and fields broken open by my father's plough, she planted the tree in the front yard and nurtured it to the state it was during the spring when the big wind came. It was a bit taller than Danny, I remember. And like him in other ways—in the length, and the thinness of its branches, for example—for Danny is an awkward, lanky person, much given to throwing his arms around in the air to make a point. As I am myself. Any one of my acquaintances and all my students could tell you that.

Harp informed me that I resembled a broken windmill whenever I became enthusiastic about a subject. He told me that with fondness, and he was not one to express his fondness for me, ours being such a difficult union, and he the one—in some ways—to take the most discomfort from it. Later, I realized he liked me best at those moments of self-absorption because he could see me whole—a separate entity.

Not someone presenting herself for his inspection and sympathy. Or for his approval.

Whatever the case, approval, like fondness, was not something he would have put into words. He was exaggeratedly discreet: his conversation included neither compliments nor insults.

He once told me about Harpocrates, the Hellenistic god of silence and secrecy. A cautious finger placed lightly against the lips was the gesture this god had brought with him from antiquity.

After that, rather than use his actual name, I called him Harp. He was delighted. Not just by the pseudonym but by the combination, he said, of classics, music, and comedy (Harpo Marx), with no connection to science. His magnificent scientific discovery fascinated me, of course, and had done so ever since I was a child. It was as if he had glided through the children's ward and paused at each of our bedsides. I would know his ghost before I knew the man himself, so he might as well have stepped out of antiquity and into my life. He broke my heart often, but wasn't this partly what I wanted from him? That shattered cage that lets the anger out.

It wasn't until relatively recently, long after Harp's final absence, that I discovered Harpocrates was also known as the Hellenistic god of hope.

As a child on that broken morning, my brother Danny had gradually come to realize that there were hundreds of one-dollar bills wrapped tightly around the twigs and branches of the tree. My mother's handbag lay nearby, completely empty. Where had the money come from? What was she was saving it for? Even her coin purse was gone. It was as if she had been assaulted and then robbed by the wind.

In winter my mother had wrapped that tree against the prairie cold with whatever came to hand; a tablecloth, a sheet, and in the early days—and despite his protests—one of my father's flannel shirts. I think of that tree sometimes and wonder what became of it once we were all gone, and my mother was no longer there to protect it. Sometimes I imagine it in full bloom, though I have no memory at all of its blossoms. There must have been some in early summer, but I cannot recall them. Sometimes I imagine the tree, broken by winter and dried out by summer, serving as kindling for a prairie wildfire. Whenever, wherever I think of it, it always brings me pain.

Unlike my brother Danny, I did not see the little tree my mother loved sprout leaves that were dollar bills. I did not see the piles of broken boards that were—moments before—the house and the barn of the farm we had come to call home.

I did not see my mother's body abandoned, like rags and dust, by the wind that stole her.

On winter mornings such as this, there is a moment when as the darkness fades the world turns hundreds of shades of blue.

As previously mentioned, I have a six-inch nickel-plated triangle in my bag, along with the silver-coloured beater that I prefer to call a wand. I will stand at the front of the class in the first school of the day and hold the triangle in front of my face. The sounds that emerge from it will be bright and cold and as complex as the shades of blue in the remnants of the prairie night.

Towards the end of the class, I will select one child to come to the front and ring the triangle, which signals the end of singing. Full sunlight will often have entered the room by this time. I swear the sound the triangle makes is fuller and warmer. Perhaps it rings differently in a child's small hands.

I am the change that occasionally occurs in the midst of routine. Even the most tone-deaf among the children sit taller in my presence because they know that only a child can make the sound of children singing. The saddest, coldest schoolroom and then that piercingly beautiful chorus of life.

Like Harp, the only man I loved, I always go away again before the energy leaves the room.

I said that my father had chosen to homestead in Saskatchewan, but that is not entirely true. In fact, after heated conversation, and eventual raising of hands, he was chosen by the extended family for this adventure. In the Ireland of his ancestors, one son per family was required to become a priest. In the rural Ontario of my father's early twentieth century life, one son per family was instructed to go west for the land that was being made available there. His whole family would have to be uprooted; his Ontario farm would need to be sold. My father was not a young man, so this enforced change must have risen terrific and dark in his mind. But all we saw on the surface of him was calm, steadfastness, and an ability, inherited from his family, to adapt to, and then stick to, the plans of others.

It is true he came from a long line of land-grabbers, and that inclination may have been just as alive in him as his adaptability. My family, whose ancestors had endured the outlawing of their language and religion, the imperial takeover of their land, and the peril of famine, could never free themselves from property hunger. They gobbled up land in Ontario, field by field. Then they sent my father out to feast on the prairies in a similar fashion. All this without giving more than a passing thought to those who had for millennia inhabited the geography my family coveted. One tribe, forced out of its homeland by imperial dominance, war, and scarcity, migrates across the sea and forces another tribe out of its homeland.

The tragedy of this.

And then there is Brother Danny, who, like me, will have no children to take over whatever kind of farm, symbolic or otherwise, that he may have wanted to own. No farm at all for that matter. He shows absolutely no aptitude for greed, and now that I think about it, never did, even when he loved and wanted the attention of another. I myself was unable to overcome the sin of covetousness when it came to the attention of the man I loved. In some ways very different than territorial expansion, it's true, but similar in its doggedness and hunger.

I recall Danny running into the Ontario kitchen at least four decades ago, full of energy, screen door banging behind him. He and my father—who made a more sedate entry into the room—had been to the railway station in the town of Colborne to see the Western Agricultural Car. I could hear my father telling my mother that there were posters and crop samples from the northern Great Plains on that car, an exhibition of them.

"And, Emer," Danny shouted across the room to me, "we will all get rich there. You should see the pictures of the sky and all that wheat. There's always sunshine. And the station master says they'll give us a free ride, for sure. The railroad will do that. They'll take us there for free!"

My mother, who had been mockingly waving a wooden spoon above her head as if conducting while he spoke, pivoted away from the stove at this point. She was stirring a stew, and she had been silent and intent on it until now. "I am not about to travel in a colonist car," she told my father, quickly and firmly. "If we must go, then we will pay for something better." She turned slowly back to the stew but was reluctant to let go of her point. "I've heard," she said, with her back to us, "that they carry disease with them in the colonist cars. Those foreigners who come from God knows where." She lifted the wooden spoon to her mouth to taste the sauce. "And," she said, "what with the babble of those foreign languages! We'll never get any sleep. We'll not be fit for anything when we arrive, is what I say."

It was rumoured that my mother's own mother, my grandmother, had been so in love with my grandfather that when he told her he could not marry her for want of a white shirt to wear to the wedding, she had taken off her own petticoat in her parents' kitchen, where this discussion took place, searched for scissors and her needlework box, and created a good shirt for him right on the spot.

My mother was not like that. Not cold, exactly, but without passionate spontaneity. She kept hold of herself. Sometimes her face would redden with emotion while her expression remained impassive.

And so, my father booked a better class of train car, probably paid for by the extended family, loaded some possessions on a wagon, and rounded up his wife and children to walk the five miles, hill by hill, towards Lake Ontario. We passed through what we called our own village and paused at its war memorial, a small granite affair with a couple of dozen familiar names engraved on it. My father was proud of that memorial, having been on the committee that was struck to build it. (He himself had taken the farmer's exemption, and in any case, it was unlikely that, since he had children and was older, he would have been called up.) When we arrived in Colborne, where the CPR station was situated, we passed the more sophisticated war memorial there, as well. It had a stone soldier on the top of it who looked very alive to me. But my brother Danny told me he was likely just as dead as all the rest of them.

The spring roads were a mess, and our wagon was up to its axles long before we reached the town with the stone soldier. Danny and I—him twelve and me nine—were spattered by mud, and my father as well (my mother sat on the wagon with her tree and Patrick and Timmy). There was a swampy stretch where hunted criminals were rumoured to hide. As we passed through it, I couldn't help but think of the legendary highwayman from the poem we had been taught in our Ontario school, even though a man "with a bunch of lace at his throat"—in the ditch or otherwise—was practically impossible to conjure in these surroundings. Still, I moved towards sadness when the poem came to mind, not because of the content, but because of my temporary but important dark-haired schoolteacher, who had taught it to me. Called the Master, by his pupils respectfully, and by the populace ironically, he was much talked about in the community—sometimes with disdain—because he had already completed graduate work in the School of Pedagogy at the University of Toronto. This higher education of his was thought to be a ridiculous waste of time by most in the township. And because his family had, for a few years when he was a schoolboy, lived out on North Street in Colborne, the people of our riding felt they had a right to their opinion of him. It was said, for example, that the Master was further wasting his time by trying to write a book about foreigners and the education of their children. No one approved of this; not because of the subject matter, but because of the exemption from physical labour the very idea of writing a book implied.

The Master was to be with us for only a half-year. Neither Danny nor I had the full effect of him: we left Ontario in early May and his term didn't finish until late June. He was spending his time in such a pedestrian schoolroom because of something my mother called research. He was much too educated to be just an ordinary teacher, she explained, adding that he knew the schoolhouses, however, because—years before—he had been sent to examine teachers such as her for the third-class certificate. "This was when his university education was just beginning," she said. "And I had known him even earlier than that. We spent one year of high school together, before his family moved to the city."

"Would he not have gone to a one-room school himself, then?" I asked once I knew he had gone to the local high school.

"No," my mother said. "He went to the better school in the town."

She was combing Timmy's hair as she said this. And looking intently into his small face. The child was almost asleep because of the pure pleasure of it, and the warmth of the attention. "Still, I've known him a long time," she said, about the Master.

...

We stood near our belongings at the station. When the baggage man eventually came to take our trunks and bundles away, my mother held firmly to her little tree, saying that she wanted to attend to it on the train. "Looks like you've got your hands full already," he said, eyeing the twins. But he let her keep the tree anyway.

Danny and I watched the locomotive slowly approach and were beside ourselves with wonder at the chaos: noise, steam, wheels, pistons! For several moments, I thought the platform was moving, not the train, and I felt overwhelmed and light-headed. Then, like a great beast dying, the engine came to a halt. Iron stairs were thrown down, and some passengers emerged to take the air, walking back and forth on the platform; no one's destination, it seemed, was Colborne. Danny and I stood stupefied in the mist, and then, as the mist lifted, we saw the foreigners who had come down the iron stairs of the supposedly free colonist car, which was situated towards the rear of the train. Once they were on the platform, the men dug in their pockets for pipes, then lit and smoked them. But it was the women who held our attention. They were like bundles of rags. We said such things about them once we were on the journey and the shock had worn off. Everything about them was covered up by large, untethered sheet-like garments. They appeared to carry their clothing like a burden, as if there were sofa cushions and footstools concealed under the fabric. "It was like they were completely covered with laundry," Danny whispered to me after we had settled into our own part of the train. And then he asked, "Do you think they had hair?"

Their babes in arms were likewise swaddled, as were the children, so I could not reply to his question. I didn't know if they had hair. I had never seen anyone like them.

The train that took our family westward in the "better" car was propelled by the most extreme velocity that I had ever experienced, with farmhouses and herds and flocks hurtling by in an alarming manner, followed by the smudge of a vanishing grey barn. It was as if everything we had ever known was being blown away from us by a noisy industrial wind.

And all night long there was the sway and lurch of that train, for it is a long distance from Ontario to the northern Great Plains, and as our father chose to sleep on what he called the ground floor with Danny, and my mother and my two little brothers slept in the lower berth across the aisle, I was alone in an upper berth that was made up for me by a man in a dark blue uniform and cap. He joked with Danny and me, told us that his name was Abel and that he was the porter. Then he gave us each a peppermint. And when we asked him, he said he lived in two places; one of those was a house beside the sea, and the other was the train. "I *live* on this train," he said, putting emphasis on the word "live."

On the epaulettes of Abel's uniform were four brass buttons polished to such a degree, they caught the beams of the night light in my sleeping compartment. I thought the buttons must have been gold and said so to him. He threw his head back and laughed. Then he told me to hop into bed before the conductor came on duty. I said that I couldn't go to sleep because everything was coming and going too quickly on the other side of the window.

"You have to look far into the distance," he told me. "All that stuff flying by the window is just chatter and clutter. If you look far away, the things you see move by you at a stately pace." He yanked up the bedrail on the aisle side of my mattress. "I'm not sure if what's out there in the distance is the past or the future. But it is more important and longer lasting than anything that is right in front of you."

The sheets were stiff with starch, and I was not entirely sure I liked the feel of them. There was a heavy pleated curtain, and when it was pushed to one side, it revealed a night sky thick with stars. They were very far away and not moving at all. As I was trying to go to sleep, I thought of my new friend as Mister Porter. I wasn't comfortable calling him Abel, even in my mind. My mother had taught me that to call an adult by his or her first name was disrespectful.

The stars are important, I decided, recalling what Mister Porter had said, because of the distance between me and them. I wondered if Danny in the lower bunk saw the same faraway stars. I concluded that he did. The possibility that he might have been looking at a completely different set of important stars was too disturbing for me to contemplate.

...

My mother was not friendly during our days on the train. She sat stiffly in the seat with that one little tree on her lap, and if she spoke to us at all, it was only to admonish us for some aberration in our behaviour. Day after day she had the same basket over her arm, out of which she took handkerchiefs, nappies for Timmy (who, unlike his twin, Patrick, was not quite ready to do without them). Now and then she dug frantically in this basket and lifted the top part of a letter—one she had already opened sometime in the past—over the rim so she could see it, and know it was there, though she never read it.

Our father was much happier than she was. He took one or sometimes both of my smaller brothers on his lap and showed them things out the window. He talked about a new house with new beds and dressers for everyone. At one point my mother put the plant down on the floor and brought her hands up to her face and wept. My father turned to her with a look of great concern and kindness. "Are you unwell, Laura?" he asked. "What is making you so unhappy?"

Mister Porter had just walked down the length of the shuddering car, whistling a complicated tune. He had transformed the whole interior of the train from beds back to ordinary seats. This had involved a great deal of snapping and unsnapping and bouts of important buckling, along with the whistling. I could tell that he had noticed the beginnings of my mother's tears, but that he had decided not to embarrass anyone by asking what was wrong.

She did not answer my father's inquiry—just wiped her face with her handkerchief and bent down to lift the tree back to her lap. But then she closed her eyes tight and turned her face towards the window, and I could see her mouth moving. You might have thought she was praying, but I knew better, having seen her like this before. The noise of the train was such that no one could hear her whispers and yet I saw what she was saying. "You are a disgrace," she mouthed, "and a sorrow to yourself and others." She whispered this over and over on the train, just as she had in the kitchen at our now abandoned Ontario home, when she thought no one was looking or listening.

...

My mother's parents were known to be Catholic in origin, which would have been a mark against them in an Ontario Protestant township such as the one we were leaving behind. They attended the village Protestant church, therefore, in order to fit in. My mother would have been educated in a thoroughly Protestant schoolhouse; the family had no choice, really, there being no Catholic school, or even a Catholic church, in the vicinity. She got her leavings and ultimately undertook two months of teacher training. But she would never have been anywhere near a university like the one at which my dark-haired teacher was doing important postgraduate work. Though it may have been her fondest wish to miraculously wake in a world where she was able to attend, she would never have confessed this desire. It would have been considered wildly irregular—almost vulgar—for a woman to entertain such ambitious thoughts.

There were no women in her circle of relatives who had even considered further education. One aunt, a spinster, was deemed to be both musical and clever. Sometimes she sang in the evenings, my mother had told us, sad songs from the area, with morals attached. One, my mother remembered, was about a proud girl who out of vanity wouldn't wear a woollen cloak to a ball, only a silken shawl. "It was a long way from our parts to a ball," my mother confided, "she would have had to go ten miles to Barnum House in Grafton." My mother always paused in this part of the story to tell us that Eliakim Barnum was the only soul in the county who had "more than two pennies to rub together." Then there would be two or three moments of silence during which Danny and I prepared for the wonderful horror of the song's conclusion.

"That girl's horse and trap returned to the house some hours after she set out," my mother assured us, "with her sitting bolt upright and frozen to death at the reins."

...

Because of her scholastic abilities, and despite coming from a Catholic family, my mother was a teacher presiding over a rural schoolhouse by the time she was eighteen. Situated on the concession road just to the north of her family's farm, it was called the Forest School because the acre it stood on was surrounded by a thick stand of miraculously unharvested trees. The school had been built on a slight elevation between two patches of very damp land from which the lumber had never been removed.

My mother told Danny and me that as one by one those few rural children under her care opened to the miracle of knowing how to read, she realized that in some cases, their mothers, fathers, and grandparents would not have known how to do this. Still, miracle or not, reading was not available to every child who sat at a desk. Though they may have learned how to use numbers to record the sale of a calf or the cost of three bushels of oats, a handful of children, mostly boys, would spend years in her schoolroom without ever mastering the ability to mentally transform print into words.

Beyond the wonder of teaching, there was a further dimension to the schoolroom for my mother: a memory of approval-seeking and obedience. Romance. The way the imagination links a daily activity in an undistinguished room with communion, even if that communion is with the ghost of a former relationship. But this was something about her I discovered much later, long after I myself had become a teacher.

I carry the music of an old abandoned world to these new world children, in the same way my mother introduced them—through reading—to the castles and cathedrals that so often figured in the stories of their schoolbooks. The Great War would show such architectural wonders to a handful of her students before death or disfigurement shut their sight down altogether. We were horrified by this. As I've said, our family had slipped through the nets of such violence because our father was too old. But when our mother spoke about her students going to war just three or four years after they'd left her schoolroom, we, her children, counted ourselves fortunate that we were not grown enough to have been caught by it. There was grief in the countryside all around us in the Ontario we left behind, and the same grief would be there to meet us on the northern Great Plains where we settled. But so far, we had not been shaken by anything more than measles.

...

When I was too young to go to school myself, I was looked after for a time by my paternal grandmother so that my mother could return, temporarily, to that schoolhouse in the forest. There was a desperate need for teachers during the war, so the fact that my mother was by then married with two children—my younger brothers were not yet born—would not have raised the concern it otherwise might have done.

Once during this period of my mother's temporary employment, I was taken through the woods and ushered in the back door of the school by my grandmother, who then quietly withdrew on some business of her own. I must have been about four years old at the time—too young to go or to have ever gone to school. Danny would have been eight or nine, and like all other children over five, he would have been packed off each day with his lunch and a piece of firewood for the school stove. He certainly would have been present among the children, but I don't remember him being there at all. Perhaps this is because I was stunned by the new version of my mother at the front of the room. She was a woman so quietly yet fiercely entranced and driven, it was as if the information she was reading aloud was of a mystical nature, though I recall nothing about what that information was. It was a startling revelation to me that she herself had written the sums that I could see on the blackboard, and that she stood beside those sums with such conviction and authority.

We are inclined to romanticize those one-room country schools. But the fact is that this one was an ill-lit and smoky place without an ounce of cheer in it. The stove emitted a faint red glow through the three holes of its grille. The pupils were shadows bent over their desks. My mother, who had leaned her head against a pane of one of the windows, having drawn the book as close as was possible to the feeble winter light, was reading aloud to the class. I can still bring to mind my mother's face at that moment, almost mask-like in its fixed concentration, and in the combination of illumination and darkness that was visible on its surface. That focused look, and the energy glowing behind it, would have been her real self, the one that emerged when she was far away from the domestic space in which I had come to believe that she was mine. Or that was what I came to think later, when I began to consider what it was about me that made me assemble my pitch pipe, my triangle, and my six songbooks, and sometimes my little books for picture study, and brave the icy roads of Saskatchewan to bring the music and art of Europe to one small country school after another.

That moment by a dusty window in a smoky one-room schoolhouse would become the only true visual memory I have of my mother; a memory of a woman still young enough to be recalled as beautiful, standing by a winter window, caught in the act of reading aloud in a ridiculous lack of light. I have other memories of course from later, when she was thinner and quieter. And I have the stories I have been told, or the stories I have told myself often enough to believe they are true. I have her imagined house that I wander through in my mind late at night. Sometimes I can even hear the sound of my mother's voice, her serious tone. But her smile, the colour of her eyes—all that is gone. First robbed by the wind, and then stolen by it. As I have already said.

It is Monday now, and I am back from what I normally call the two Monday schools. The road to Bush's School was drifting over by the time I got to it, however, and I was forced to retreat rather than teach my afternoon class. I suspected that given the weather, most of my pupils would have been safe in their kitchens, rather than at their desks in any case. But I felt a halting moment of anger in the face of my inability to plunge through the drifts as any other woman might have done. One without a stick.

When I got back to the house, I left the car in the yard and then turned back to look at it in the fading light of a January afternoon. The last of Harp, I thought, while watching blowing snow accumulate on the windshield. Or at least the last trace for me. The world would never be finished with him. It was eating him alive before he was dead. And his discovery, well, it would go on forever.

Apart from the wind, the only sound was the squeak of snow under my overshoes. Men's overshoes—a necessity in the prairie winter, and the same ones that I wore when I stood on the morning platform, waiting for the train to take me to the palace hotel and Harp. They felt cumbersome and foolish—a variety of clown shoe— at the check-in desk so, after that humiliation, I paid for a locker at the city station and stored the offending footwear. For the duration.

This afternoon when I walked into my small kitchen with its purring refrigerator, the ghost or memory of Harp walked in with me. I recalled an odd scar on his left shoulder, and the sinews at the bend of his arms and legs. The shape of his feet. His eyebrows. But it was the ghost of his mind, not his body, that followed me into the kitchen. Or at least the echo of his mind.

And now that it is evening, even though I know I am in my house, I can see and smell the interiors of the castle hotels; their languid elegance, their furniture polish, the doors that clicked quietly and firmly behind you, two steps after you entered the room, the bleach and starch of their sheets.

And I can see Harp bursting through the perfectly calibrated door, bringing all the vitality of his world with him: the breath and hair and heat under the snow on his coat.

I allowed a half hour of picture study, this morning, in the school called Willow. The pupils looked at *The Death of Leonardo da Vinci* by

J.-A.-D. Ingres in the books from the National Gallery while I explained the famous Leonardo himself, and to a brief extent, the French painter Ingres. The male teacher smirked from the back of the room at such artsy, womanish offerings, but he still permitted the introduction of various topics. I spoke of engineering, the *Mona Lisa*, anatomy, and Leonardo's drawings for imagined flying machines, which awakened the boys in the class and led to questions. It was then that I introduced the etchings of Goya.

Harp had been to the drawing cabinets of the Prado in Madrid and had looked at Goya's etching of malicious winged humans filling a blackened sky, and had found a postcard afterwards in a gift shop. "A way of flying," he wrote on the back in his large, ungainly, almost unreadable script.

Later he had explained, laughing, that *A Way of Flying* was the title of the etching, rather than a message meant for me.

Then he looked at the ceiling and announced, "Suddenly I am quite certain I know how to fly."

"Just like that?" I had asked, opening the fingers of my right hand.

"Just like that," he had replied. His expression, casual and distanced, was bathed in the golden light of a bedside lamp.

The last image of him I vividly retain.

I tried to draw the bat's wings and cogged wheels from the postcard in chalk on the blackboard but failed miserably, so I had the children pass the card from one desk to another.

I have kept all of Harp's postcards, and the very few letters that he sent to me. My mother kept letters as well. First just one. But then, two others. They were important, and not to be read by us or by anyone. Except for her, in her quiet moments. Once, I saw her press her lips to a signature. I knew it was a signature, even from a distance. I could see the largeness of the capital letter on the first short word followed by a capitalized long word. I understood that it was someone's name, and that the tapestry of words above it contained information written by that person. I told Danny about my mother kissing the letter. But he said I was crazy, that my mother never kissed anyone. I realized he was right about this. I had never known her to kiss Danny or me, or even the little twins. Though she often said our names aloud, the first and the last, with affection and humour in her voice.

Though his own surname was English in origin, and was said to originate with a distant ancestor's resemblance to a "peculiar, gormless bird," Harp claimed to love all the nonsense connected with his mother's Scottish name. The kilts, the bagpipes. "In particular, the sentimentality," he said, laughing as he said it.

"The wee birdies sing / And the wildflowers spring
    And in sunshine the waters are sleeping."
    In all three schools today, the children sang "By yon bonnie banks and by yon bonnie braes / Where the sun shines bright on Loch Lomond" with remarkable joy.
    Immune, so far, to heartbreak, or even the loss of a loved landscape, they almost shouted the words "But the broken heart it kens nae second spring again / Though the waeful may cease frae their grieving."

And while they sang, and all the way back on the blue frozen roads of winter, grief was beating through my veins. Though what I lost when I lost Harp was difficult to measure: he never loved me. He was curious about my story, calmed by my discretion, and oddly eroticized by my awkwardness and scars. I adored him. But he never loved me. I force myself to remember this when I am filled with the echo of him.
    And he could be cruel enough to tell me about his lack of feeling. Adding that it would be unlikely we would ever meet again. But often enough he was tender, almost with a mother's tenderness, or what I imagined a mother's tenderness would be. His hands

straightening my hair, his lips on my forehead as if he were comforting me after some childhood mishap or kissing me goodnight. It was the tantalizing possibility of this tenderness that brought me back again and again to the humiliating hotels. I'm sure of this. But as soon as I write this, I know I am far from sure. Was it not perhaps the surprising incongruity of it? A man like him involved in any kind of a relationship with a woman like me; her stick, her pathetic, sentimental songbooks, her picture-study primers full of fuzzy, unreadable black-and-white reproductions of the great art of the Western world? While he paced the parquet of the world's great museums, I drove the roads and walked the floors of country schools. And waited for him. Yes, fool that I was, I always waited for him.

I climb the stairs to the bedroom, where I sit on the bed to take off my stockings, then rise to shake off my tight skirt and reach for my dressing gown on the back of the door. When I open the closet door to hang up my blouse, I see all the dresses that I wore to meet him. And standing beneath them, side by side, two high-heeled shoes.

The warm light of my father's lantern making its steady progress down the hall of our brand-new Saskatchewan farmhouse, entering the darkened rooms where we were quietly waking, then moving across the porch and out to the barn on early winter mornings, is something wonderful to recall. And if your window faced the barn, as mine did, you could see the gold seams of light appear between the perpendicular boards once he had entered the building.

As a child it would put me in mind of a line of that poem that had been read aloud to us by our poetry-loving Master back in Ontario: "'In winter I get up at night,'" he had begun, "'and dress by yellow candle-light.'" Then came the musical rhythm of poetics, with a one-syllabled final verse that began with the line "'And does it not seem hard to you?'"

But nothing about the round of school and chores and light and dark that made up the dailiness of my life seemed hard to me then. I liked to lie in bed in summer and watch the fields become dim, or to be in a half dream in winter as my father's lantern lit the morning carpet of snow. Then off on the frozen roads, the frostbite and chilblains, all for a chance of an education.

By the time I was old enough to start this education in our Ontario Forest School, the trees had finally been cut down in the surrounding swamp, and as a result, we had some light in the classroom. There were three teachers, I recall. Two of them were middle-aged women with rural third-class certificates and grown families, making a bit of cash, I imagine, during those years when their children were old enough to be independent and useful.

And then there were the comings and goings of Walter Scott Stillwell, the man who had brought his postgraduate work to us as an important temporary master. Frostily composed and stern on the one hand, he could be peculiarly sentimental on the other. Now and then, he would demonstrate an abundance of feeling, particularly concerning literature. His voice sometimes broke when he read the weekly poem that we—his pupils—were told to memorize. He could be angry with our shortcomings. I was prepared for the anger but not for the tears. For the few months that he taught me in Ontario, I remained fascinated by this unlikely show of masculine vulnerability. Nothing about my father, not even my little brothers, had suggested that men could be brought to a moment of choked speechlessness by words such as "a bunch of lace at his throat."

This was before my father discovered Henry Wadsworth Longfellow, who, to his mind, had the power to cause even him to weep.

The Master made us draw maps of remote places few of us would ever get to see, such as the faraway Rocky Mountains. We dutifully marked the upside-down *V*s required to indicate their presence on our maps. But like those cold, faraway mountains, Master Stillwell was also beautiful, with a smooth forehead and just enough curl in his dark brown hair. I was intrigued by the mystery of him. I had heard my father say that the teacher had been pauperized by his senseless graduate and postgraduate studies, and that he hadn't a penny to his name and was forced to board in a hall bedroom of one of the neighbouring farmhouses when he was in the district.

I recall my mother snapping that at least the Master had a mind. "And he has a PhD and will be a professor," she had said, after a pause but still peevishly.

"And you think he can conquer the world with that?" my father had asked, with raised eyebrows.

I had no idea what variety of weapon a PhD might be, but I knew Master Stillwell was required to live in Toronto to obtain it.

My mother, the supplemental teacher, had neither the opportunity nor the privilege of being pauperized by graduate studies. Except for the daily round of necessary domestic chores, her roles in the world were never deemed to be essential. While she stayed home, little girls would leave for school just after dawn, taking shortcuts through the woods so they could catch up with the esteemed research teacher. Never daring to say more than "Good morning" to the Master, they were able, nevertheless, to be in his company and walk beside him all the way to the school.

I was one of those little girls.

I came to believe as a child that my stern teacher carried all the possibilities of educational inquiry in the brain that crouched behind his mostly distant expression, though how I phrased this understanding in my child's mind, I do not recall. What I do remember was how desperately I sought, and never achieved, his approval. And yet, for that brief stretch of two or three months, I continued to love him. And especially during the poetry lesson.

The Master taught us about that poor girl lashed to the mast by her captain father, and the boy on the burning deck, calling out to his own father, begging to be set free. And his favourite, "The Sands of Dee," which featured Mary, who was insistently and repetitively instructed to bring a herd of cattle home across a dangerous stretch of beach. Which she dutifully did until a rogue wave swept her away. The shipwrecks and drownings and daemon lovers of the empire! Admittedly, I myself teach the equally frightening old folk songs, telling myself that the addition of melody softens them.

One day in Ontario, Master Stillwell paused near my desk and asked about my brother in a surprisingly gentle and solicitous way. "I am interested," I remember him saying, "in when he will be back at school."

It was early in the school year, and Danny, like many boys his age, was helping with the harvest and the subsequent fall harrowing. He had not yet returned to the classroom. Worried that my brother might be in some kind of trouble for his truancy, I didn't know what to say. I could feel the attention of the other children moving towards me as the Master stood by my side.

"He is working at harrowing for my father," I finally whispered, not looking up. Out of the corner of my eye I could see that the Master was fingering the third buttonhole of his jacket with alarmingly long, almost womanish fingers. "He has to do it while my father is at the market," I added, hoping that this suggestion of duty would soften Danny's absenteeism.

I had no clear sense of what the market was, just that, each year, my father was away at it for several days after the harvest.

"I see," Master Stillwell said, but not unkindly. "We can expect Danny to be back with us soon, then," he added, placing his long fingers in the pockets of his jacket. He mulled this over. "My heart's in the Highlands," he said, as if he really meant it, that his heart was far away.

Then, suddenly, his expression changed. "Emer," he announced to the class, "will recite."

"'My heart's in the Highlands, my heart is not here.'" I rose to my feet and delivered that first line to my teacher, eager for his approval. "'My heart's in the Highlands, a-chasing—'"

"Just a moment," he interrupted, and walked quickly, without taking his hands out of his pockets, to the front of the room, where he turned towards me. "Begin again," he said.

Though he was now facing me, he was not looking at me. His gaze was fixed on something to the left of where I stood. Instinctively, I twisted my head around, but I saw nothing, just a momentary shadow on the window at the top part of the back door. When I looked back towards my teacher, he regarded me with neutrality. "Begin again," he repeated.

Since then, I have come to believe it was a woman he saw, or perhaps only the memory of a woman, dim and transitory, with the light behind her. The shadow had the same shape as my mother, I now recall, though at that moment, I wouldn't have believed it was her. Neither her memory nor her shadow.

"'A-chasing the wild deer and following the roe,'" I said in that classroom. "'My heart's in the Highlands wherever I go.'" It felt to me as if the whole world were in the sound of the word "following."

Though his surname was thoroughly Anglo-Saxon, the Master had a proclivity for sentimental Scottish verse. Perhaps his mother's family name was Scottish, and that explained the Walter Scott of his given names.

He had started to walk towards me after I finished the first verse, then he turned and strode away. He pivoted when he reached the blackboard and returned with the same measured steps. It was as if he were pacing to the rhythm of the poem. Each time he walked down the aisle towards me, he came closer, swerving at the last moment and then heading back. I began to lose the thread. I could hear myself reciting random lines in the wrong sequence, and yet I could not set things to rights. "'Farewell to the straths and green vallies below,'" I whispered. "'Farewell to the mountains . . . the forests and wild-hanging woods . . . cover'd with snow . . .'" I faltered. The poem had fled from my mind.

"Who wrote this poem, Emer?" the Master asked when I could go no further.

"Robert Louis Stevenson?" It came out as a question because I knew I was wrong.

There was a terrible silence in the room. I looked at the floor with my face burning. The Master walked, step by deliberate step, to the front of the room, but he said nothing. When I glanced up for one moment, I could see that the whole class was silenced by his raising both hands in the air and adopting a grim, thin-lipped expression. Then, after an excruciatingly long period, he said, "That will do, Emer. Sit down now." He shuffled some papers on his desk. "See me after school."

I saw him only briefly after school. He was rigid and stately in his demeanour, and cold as ice. And yet at the same time, he seemed less angry than distracted, almost as if he had forgotten why I was there. I wanted attention from him—a lecture, admonitions, some sense of engagement. But I could tell that what he desired was to finish his day; he seemed to have nothing at all to say to me. He instructed me to stay in the empty schoolhouse, however, for an hour after he had gone, memorizing the poem in what he called "the correct stanzaic order."

"I am going to Saskatchewan," I said, "soon as harvest is over and my father gets paid for it." Was this my way of making him feel sorry?

"I know that," he said, shoving test papers in his leather bag and preparing to leave. "I know that very well."

Soon I would be living in a land-locked terrain, without even the faintest hint of the electric seascapes, mountains, and valleys that poems like the one I was memorizing in stanzaic order pitted themselves against. For that one hour, I studied "My Heart's in the Highlands" in the wake of my teacher's cruelty and then dismissal. But my imagination was with Mary on the sands of Dee and the boy on the burning ship's deck. They must have at least been acquainted with each other, I thought. Perhaps they had played together in some English harbour town with an ocean clawing at its seawall.

When I got home later in the afternoon, Danny was far away harrowing the north field, and my father had not yet returned from the market. The twins were playing a game with pebbles and dust just beyond the back door, and they howled when I inadvertently destroyed something they had made. They were usually not so easily cast down, even when Danny knocked over their towers of blocks while walking absent-mindedly through the parlour at dusk. I knew then that my mother had shouted at them and banished them from the house, and that they had crept back inch by inch until they were under the shadow of the kitchen, if not its roof. When they had stopped crying, I asked about this, and they nodded solemnly. "And then the teacher came," they said, "to talk to Mama."

I felt the heat of shame climbing up my neck until it reached my face, and I knew that my small brothers could see my distress. The Master had talked to her about my failings, my inability to commit the lines to memory.

The twins were back at their play. "Get out of the way or I'll beat you," one of them said to the other. "An inch of your life," the other responded, as if demanding something of the other.

"I will beat you within an inch of your life," the bully says. "Please," the hidden lover says, "please just give me an inch of your life."

My father returned from the market the following morning. And my mother was back by then. By "back," I mean she was present among us—Danny, the twins, and me—in a way that she had not been the evening before. There had been no dinner, though I had thought to give the twins milk and bread and a cut-up apple before we went to our beds. We were all full of my mother's anger and confusion, each one of us believing we had earned this change in her. But in the morning she let us stir maple syrup into the oatmeal she made. She gave us hot chocolate and a Buckingham egg, the oval of its yolk rich and warm in the centre of a piece of fried bread. When my father arrived, she laughed with joy and embraced him.

Danny asked me about school while we ate our breakfast. "Was there picture study?" he wanted to know. Yesterday was Friday, and on Fridays, if the class was well behaved all week, our handsome Master would treat us to picture study. It wasn't until Danny asked that I realized I had ruined that as well by not being able to remember the lines of poetry. Danny was keen on picture study. I was ashamed of ruining it, even though he was not there.

I shook my head and turned away from him. "I did something wrong," I said.

"What did you do?" asked my mother, as if it were the most natural question in the world.

Why, I wondered, was she pretending that she did not know precisely what had happened, didn't know about my crime of stanzaic disorder? Hadn't the Master come to the farm just to tell her?

Danny touched my arm. "It doesn't matter, Emer. Who cares? We have our own copy up on the shelf." He pointed to the row of books, mostly schoolbooks, my mother kept at the other end of the room. "We don't need him to show us pictures."

He was disdainful now, and shockingly untouched—to my mind—by the spell this important teacher cast. My brother was seeing things differently than I saw them. As I write this, I remember the stars out the train window on our way west, my fear that they weren't the same as Danny's stars, and the kindness of Mister Porter Abel as he spoke about the importance of faraway hills.

The first two years of our lives in Saskatchewan were ones of cheerful industry, if not prosperity. Our father was the happiest among us, always making something appear where he claimed there had been "nothing before." A house, several fields, a barn for the cattle, a well with a pump, and even some rough furniture sprang into being under his hands, and so speedily, it was almost as if he were sketching such phenomena, not physically hammering them into place. We stayed in the large canvas tent, which composed one of the bundles we had brought with us from Ontario, until the lumber for the dwelling house and barn was hauled to our acreage by a long wagon drawn by two large horses. I kept a wildflower diary in an old used-up scribbler I had brought with me from Ontario. It was full of sentences I had copied from the board during my last month in the east. When I pierced its pages with the stems of scarlet mallows or wild bergamot, I could see the Master's cursive writing on the blackboard of my mind's eye.

Danny told me the timber was floated down the South Saskatchewan—"from the frozen north," was how he put it—until the river came near a road where the lumber could be loaded onto a wagon. The same went for the firewood that Danny and I were required to stack in a series of conical structures so the snow would slide off the stove-lengths come winter. And miraculously, by the time that winter arrived, Danny and I were both seated most days inside a school called Pine Grove, one that was identical to the schoolroom we had left behind in Ontario, with two important differences. The light in this school was dazzling and dependable, regardless of the season. Even on days when there was no sun, light raked the tops of our desks and touched my own small hands, the smooth oval shape of which I can recall holding a pencil or a piece of chalk. I remember the dust on the floor, and the imperfections of the pine boards where my shoes rested. I remember the cracks in the leather of my shoes, their scuffed toes. That was the kind of light it was.

The second difference was that the important, handsome Master was not in the schoolroom.

As an adult I have returned to that school on many occasions, and I am always pleased that I can bring music inside its stark walls. "'White coral bells upon a slender stalk,'" the children sing. "'Lily of the valley deck my garden walk.'" The smaller children sing with enthusiasm, the older with discretion; the big boys at the back of the room look bored, though some of them sing as well. There is always the sense of some new, barely supressed agitation around boys like this, an impatient vitality. They want to be elsewhere beginning their adult lives. They want to tear the earth open. Then they want to harvest whatever it is they have forced that broken ground to grow.

One autumn day at Pine Grove School, our teacher, the plain but worthy Mrs. Robinson, said, "We will have an important person in our classroom soon, boys and girls."

I half believed the Prince of Wales might visit, or Lucy Maud Montgomery, whose long chapter books I had recently come to admire. But Mrs. Robinson said the inspector was coming. He, apparently, was to be much feared: at least it looked as if Mrs. Robinson was afraid of him. We were all put on cleaning duty, scrubbing the ink stains from the tops of our desks, wiping the soot from the windows. The older children, Danny included, were to empty the ashes from the Quebec heater then rejuvenate it with stove polish. Books had to be set straight in our small library, which consisted of only one modest bookcase of three open shelves. Even Mrs. Robinson felt she had to improve her territory and reorganized her own desk. At recess there was some debate about whether she swore aloud while she was doing this.

Three days later I was told to take all the blackboard brushes outside and bang them together to remove the chalk dust. It was a coveted job, and I knew I must have pleased Mrs. Robinson—in some mysterious way known only to adults—in order to be the chosen one. I liked being the only pupil on the other side of the door in the playground: it had an air of truancy about it, but without truancy's tension of being caught. I loved the brushes, which were red, white, and blue like the Union Jack. And the faraway horizon was something I could look at and think about. Everything in the autumn season in the prairies is pale shades of brown and yellow under the sharp scrutiny of the immense blue sky. The prairie was huge and oddly still. No wind at all, as I recall it. And so I heard the car before I saw it. I might have picked out the sound of the engine earlier if I hadn't been so furiously beating the brushes. By the same token, I might have seen the car sooner if my vision hadn't been obscured by a cloud of chalk dust.

First there was a black dot on the horizon. Then an ovoid shape with a plume of dust in its wake. When I realized it was a car, I burst in the door to tell the teacher and the class. "Excuse me," I announced, "but I think the inspector is just now coming up the road." When I said this, Mrs. Robinson put down the chalk she was using to complete an arithmetic problem on the painted cardboard blackboard. And the big boys—Danny included—sat up taller in their seats. Then Mrs. Robinson made her own announcement. "Master Stillwell will be in this room shortly," she said. "Pay attention."

From where I stood in the doorway I locked eyes with Danny, who brought his shoulders up to his ears and opened his hands. This was a familiar gesture from our games of charades and our teasing with riddles and jokes. It meant that he gave up. It meant he wasn't going to search any harder for the answer.

These days, each time I walk through the door of Pine Grove School, I instinctively look for Danny at the back of the room. Then I remember he is grown-up and safe in his monastery. The restlessness of boys his age was in him as well in the old days. But, I know now, he always saw things differently. My mother must have sensed this because often she would pause in the middle of a chore to study him. When he was home after school, for instance, sitting at the long kitchen table and intent on spreading as much butter as he could on the back of an oatcake before devouring it. Or when he was hunched over a scribbler with a pencil in his teeth. She looked at him as though she wanted to make a memory of him, I thought.

Sometimes, especially after the important Master came to the prairies, she asked about homework, whether it was harder now with the more educated man occasionally at the front of the class. I can't remember the homework. But I do remember Danny's reply to my mother. "Not harder," he said, "but more difficult."

The morning in June that changed everything, I had taken my pony, whom I called Bruno Saskatchewan, out for a ride in order to return a book to the Muenster Public Library. I had received Bruno as a twelfth-birthday gift in April, and he came with dire warnings about what would happen were I not to take adequate care of him, as, according to my father, no adult or sibling was going to make up for any oversights on my behalf. I wanted my pony, therefore, to have a robust name, and Bruno Saskatchewan—two strong syllables followed by the tumbleweed of bristling sounds composing the name of the place where we lived— seemed to me to fit the bill.

Added to this was the fact that the town of Bruno, near where Bruno was born, was named for Abbot Bruno Doerfler, who had come to Saskatchewan a handful of decades earlier to begin a German Catholic community. He founded a prairie Benedictine monastery and, in 1903, built the abbey church (almost a cathedral), an idea so improbable and delightful in the place it was situated that normally incalcitrant donors stepped forward with money to fund it. A liturgical artist painted its interior as a gift—not to God but to the abbot himself. The abbot in the murals was pointed out to me when my family attended the church, which we did only now and then in order to satisfy my mother. There he was, beaming down at us from his gold-leafed surroundings, a hint of pomposity in his expression, or at the very least, self-satisfaction. And certainly looking as if he could survive all adversity, even if, I reminded myself, he had died a couple of years before we came to the northern Great Plains.

Any pony named after one who was celebrated for both strength and holiness would be able to live through a day or two of neglect, I reasoned, should I be snow-bound at school or captured by Indians. It didn't occur to me then, as it does now, that there were no Indians in our immediate vicinity, that the few who remained on the land had moved farther north to accommodate the white homesteaders who were washing like waves over the prairie. White homesteaders like us.

Peter Pan and Wendy by J.M. Barrie was the book I returned to the library. I had already read it in Ontario two years before. Famous there, it had only recently made itself known in the Muenster Public Library, and many of the children at school were talking about it and pretending at recess to be Captain Hook or one of the beautiful mermaids. Over the period of those two eventful years, Peter Pan had become fuzzy and remote, but now that I had reread the book, and in spite of the fact that I had, in effect, graduated to the much longer and more realistic novels of Lucy Maud Montgomery, the narrative was reawakened in me. It was Wendy, however, rather than Peter about whom I was thinking, and I wondered how I could have forgotten about her. Had I been too young for her in Ontario? All that I knew about Wendy's London—its steeples and chimneys, its nurseries and politely detached parents eternally clothed in evening wear—came to me through the rereading of the book. Beyond the faux palace hotel in the mountains on the postcard my mother showed me and the Union Jack that decorated our schoolroom, the London of the book was as improbable and magical as the Never Never Land the children escaped to. I believed in the flying children and the dog, Nana, because they were so far away.

My reality, in an ordinary, daily way, often consisted of a view of Bruno's neck and ears set against the gravel road or path we were following, and prairie grasses bending to the breeze to my left and right. That morning, after we came home and I dismounted, Bruno had tossed his head and delivered an angry look. And then, as I was leading him into the barn, he had bitten me on the back of my arm. A backbiter at heart, he was nevertheless usually gentle. But this time I felt he might have broken the skin. My skin.

I waited until after I had closed the barn doors to look at my wound. As a result, I was caught in the awkward gesture of trying to examine the underside of my upper arm when I glanced towards the horizon. And as I did, I saw our neighbour's farmhouse, no larger than my thumb in the distance, tremble and then explode.

There was no precedent in my then short life for what I had just witnessed: I was not even sure if what I had seen was real. Rather than theorize, however, I rushed to a conclusion. Buildings can blow up, was what I suddenly thought, and that would be a bad thing for anyone caught inside. I flung open the barn doors and ran towards the stalls, where I pushed Bruno's gate to one side. He bit me on the hand as I did this. Then both of us escaped into the yard.

Bruno was found a week later. He was nine fields away, with no gates open between them. His story became legendary among the relatives in faraway Ontario, though it was a tale that altered completely with each telling. In one version he was a kitten, in another a piano—parts of this version were accurate, because the keyboard was found intact in the place where the barn once stood—in still another version Bruno became a great-grandmother in a rocking chair. My own favourite was the version where he became a whole gang of bandits on horseback, a gang whose members were so stunned by their encounter with the wind that when they landed, they just stayed quietly in that ninth field for several days with their horses grazing beneath them.

I wasn't very fond of the version that turned Bruno into my mother.

I do not remember being found. My father said they had looked all over the torn farmstead, all over the fields. Eventually he and my brother were alerted to my whereabouts by one of several runners from the village who had glimpsed what he took to be my dead body as he passed by the remnants of my family's farm. My father would tell me later that after the big wind, everyone ran everywhere. "As if they were hell-bent on escape," he said. It seems to me, looking back, that they were running to save their lives, or perhaps to fully flee from a life that had proved, in its painful unreliability, to be too much of a burden.

It was Danny who found me. I was completely broken, with the lower part of my body immersed in one of those prairie ponds called a slough. I was barely conscious, he said much later, and yet I was asking about the pony and talking about the coldness of the water. It was that slough, the same source that fed the fields, that likely saved my life by keeping me alert, or at least conscious. What I remember was the withered stem and leaf and flower of a particular plant that must have been dried by autumn, preserved in its dried state by winter, and unwilling to come back to life in spring. It was just inches from my eyes when I opened them. I remember the stiff, lifeless stamens of that former flower. And the fact that I knew the word "stamen" because of a labelled diagram that I had copied into my notebook from the blackboard in my school. From that perspective, the orderliness—the dailiness—of school seemed like a miracle to me, even though, in the past half-year, its orderliness had been disrupted now and then by the new inspector of Saskatchewan schools, Master Stillwell, teaching a weekly class.

The front door, which had been so hard-won, was the only feature of our house left intact. My father was an unreliable farmer, but a decent carpenter. He had finished framing that house in short order, but he knew he would have to go into the town to find a bench joiner for the kind of door he wanted. There followed much dinner table talk of diamond-paned sidelights and sunburst transoms, but in the end, my father settled for a door with two small rectangular windows sur-mounting three cross rails and eight raised panels, all of it solid oak, and hung on what my father called "dignified hinges," then painted white. That bench joiner, whoever he may have been, was involved not only in dignifying our simple prairie house but also in saving my life. After the storm, my father and brother brought the beautifully made door to the slough and gently lifted the brokenness of me onto it. I recall Danny saying, It will be all right, Emer, just hold on. I loved Danny. I held on.

So they made a stretcher of what had been the formal entrance to our home. But there was no home. The formal and informal structure of it was all undone. And our mother, the very centre of it, had been tossed aside as if something, someone, of no importance. My beautiful, distant mother, whose pain I sensed and whom I loved. That woman who whispered words of quiet anger when she thought no one was looking, and who had important letters locked in a drawer that no one except for her knew about. Where were those letters now? I wanted my mother. But soon I could think about nothing but the bright blades of pain in my legs and back, so I did not ask for her. Not then.

I did not know where I was being taken. I didn't understand that my smaller brothers had been left behind to temporarily fend for themselves on the ruined farmstead. Danny talked quietly to me as we moved through the whispering leaves of the birches and willows, and across pale yellow-grey prairies where grasses brushed my face and feathered along my destroyed legs.

My father said nothing to me. But I could hear fragments of a conversation between my brother and him. I could hear the word "train."

I now know that it was five miles from that farmstead to a train track, and that only two trains moved down that track on a regular day. The image of my father and my brother, carrying me such a distance through a thinly populated, almost empty terrain, on a much-prized, beautifully constructed door, then waiting for a train whose schedule they could not possibly have known, with the worry of the smaller and now motherless children left behind, brings me to tears each time I think of it, even all these years later.

...

Danny has told me that until he and our father heard the train, they had both been on their knees praying by the side of the track. I was not praying. Once I was no longer being carried, my face was on the level of the dusty, ground-crawling prairie grasses, and I thought, These are what will cover me when I am dead. I knew I was still alive, however, because no one experiencing the sensations I was experiencing, the now sensory, sonic, and visual pain—the pure strength of it—could be anything other than alive.

My father and Danny leapt to their feet at the sound of the whistle, and then, without consulting each other, they took off their shirts and waved them against the sky.

When Danny speaks of this, now that we are older adults, he always laughs at this part, and claims that he and my father must have believed the sight of their naked bodies would catch the attention of the engineer if the clothes they were waving in their hands did not. The train, he told me, seemed to take hours to come to a halt.

Then, each time, he speaks of something extraordinary. He always says that lifting me on the white door into the hands of the railway employees was like a miraculous ascension, and that he had never recovered from the effects of that miracle, or his own conversion that was a result of it.

So it was Danny who put the notion of conversion into my mind. I once asked him if there was such a thing as a recovery from conversion. This was shortly after I had been mentally and sensually carried away by the man I loved. I would later come to know he was my road to Damascus, from which there is no turning back. But at the time I was still hoping to recover my previous self. That woman I used to be? I wanted her back.

Danny had considered this and answered quietly. "No one recovers from a true conversion," he said. "But his honour?" he continued. "Who is he beyond what you have made of him in your imagination? Not a religion, that's one thing certain." There was a wistful tone in his voice as he said this. He disapproved, and because he loved me, he was eager to blame this individual who slid into and out of the neighbouring city and saw me only at his convenience. But Danny was compassionate. He had been in love as well, before he turned to the monastery. He chewed his lip and looked away from me, thinking. Then, after a few moments, he brought his hands together near the cross that hung from his neck. "Perhaps he is just life, Emer," he said, maybe speaking about our separate passions. "And that is what is compelling about this—" He stopped, then spoke the word "liaison." He looked me fully in the face, opened his hands, and pulled his shoulders up in that gesture I remembered from the morning schoolroom when we both knew that our Ontario Master was driving up the road to inspect our class. Danny was no longer looking at me, had turned inward, when he repeated the word "life."

The images I retain from those hours in my childhood when I was carried to the train are fractured, split apart by pain. The silver trunks of birch trees, a torn white cloud in a blade blue sky, the hip pocket of my father's pants, dreams of varying vividness. Nothing inside my body felt known or reliable. My bones were an agonizing, unfinished, and now broken work of architecture that my skin was forced to bandage and contain. When I closed my eyes, I saw the neighbour's farmhouse explode on the horizon, over and over. When I opened my eyes, the yellow prairie grasses radiated brass-coloured and sharp yet ghostly waves of pain. I was arguing with the pain, which was a fiery, pulsing orb in my mind. I was trying to convince the pain that I wasn't available, or if I was available, I wasn't valuable enough for it to bother with.

At one point I heard my father remark to my brother that he was in despair about the neighbour's new-born baby being ripped from its mother's arms by the wind.

The mother was her family's only survivor. I would be told much later that she had burst into our ruined farmyard, wild with grief. "It took my new-born baby," she had cried. She was beside herself. But even so, she had agreed to stay near the twins. Clawing at my father's sleeve and jerking her head in the direction of the terrified toddlers, she had said, "Otherwise, it will take them too! You can depend on that!"

I understood that whatever "it" was had already taken me. A furious pied piper, it had tried to round up all the children in the vicinity.

"You were like an adolescent martyr," Danny later told me. "Like Sainte Reine or Maria Goretti."

Danny spent his study hours in the monastery's liturgical library, reading about saints. Almost every sentence he spoke contained a reference to his research.

"Remember," he said to me, "there is no going back afterwards. No recovery. Santa Chiara, after she came to spiritual consciousness, departed from her childhood home using the door of the dead on the second level of the house. Not the front door that the family members used when stepping into their carriages, or the back door that the servants opened to go to the market. She departed from the coffin door instead. She knew she was never coming back."

Did I ever truly come back? I wondered.

Carrying my broken self on the white door was like a translation of relics, he explained, like the moment when the bishop decides that a collection of some poor martyr's broken bones is worthy of greater veneration, and that these bones must be carried to a more important part of the church. Or perhaps to another church altogether. Bits and pieces of the saints and martyrs were scattered all over Europe. Just as my bones were smashed up and scattered around inside the envelope of my skin.

"It was the first time I really prayed," Danny would say afterwards, "with any kind of fervour. That wind blew me right out of ordinary life, towards all this," he would say, with a rotating gesture of one hand that took in the whole monastery. "There was no point of entry for an ordinary life," he said, "after that."

...

In the early morning before the storm, just before I took Bruno out, my mother had hung a silver chain and cross around my neck. Put your hand on this when you pray, she had told me, lifting my arm and moving my wrist towards the crucifix, her face tender and, for once, absorbed by me, her daughter. As I have said we had been once or twice to mass in the abbey church, but mostly we went each week to the Protestant Methodist church service in our village. I often prayed during the year that was about to unfold, and when I did, my hand drifted towards the silver cross my mother had given me that morning. But I did not become intimate with desperate prayer, with bargaining, until much later. Not until after I came to fully know the man I loved.

Danny and my father stood half-naked on the prairie and lifted me on a pure white door towards the dark of the waiting boxcar. The landscape would have been lit by the gold of an early evening sky, and the men, their upper bodies pale in the light, would have been athletic in their desire to bargain with all things industrial, now approaching them in the form of a black engine, white steam, and terrific noise. And there they were, with their grey shirts waving like banderoles above their heads. You would expect that the surrounding air had stilled to a quiet hush. (A panel painting from the Sienese School, Harp commented later.) But in fact, what I most recall about that moment of ascension was not the golden light of an early summer evening, but rather the operatic, cacophonic noise of the train itself. The engine seemed to be panting—deeply and impatiently—as if it had been rampaging down a path of its own choice and had just been brought to a halt against its own will and better judgement. As if it were alive.

The very same Mister Porter Abel who had told me about the faraway hills received me in my ruined state. Pain was moving in a frantic way inside my body: perhaps the child I was then believed there was only one person in the world in whom the professionalism and self-assurance that emanated from a porter would be manifest. My father evidently believed this as well. "Please," I had heard him shout to Mister Porter Abel, who was running from his sleeping car to the boxcar to open the doors. "Please take this child to a hospital."

Even though they both wore railway employee uniforms, Mister Porter Abel was completely unlike the Conductor who was waiting inside the boxcar into which Mister Porter had climbed so that he could lift me up on the white door and receive me. The conductor, who made no offer of help, was a man with a pained look, a neatly trimmed ginger beard, and skin tinted an odd shade of powder blue. Mister Porter Abel always paid attention to children, laughed with them, and gave them advice and peppermints. The conductor was a man unlikely to pay any attention to children at all, except in casual, malicious ways, as I was discovering.

In an alarmingly intimate manner, he ran his eyes all over my body, sniffing the air as he did so. "Doesn't look good," he said to Mister Porter Abel. "Not long for this world," he added.

A disturbing amount of saliva covered his lips, making them a deeper shade of blue. He wasn't quite drooling, but an unwholesome appetite was suggested by all the slick moisture around his mouth. He grinned, and I could see a string of saliva between his upper and lower lip. The smile snapped shut rather than faded. Then he spun around and withdrew into the shadows on the opposite side of the boxcar, only to whirl back a few minutes later. "Tickets, please!" he said, brandishing a metal punch.

I knew I had no ticket but was unable to say so.

Mister Porter Abel, however, lowered himself to sit on the floor beside me. "Now, don't you worry about a thing," he said, softly. "Just forget about it."

I did so. I could forget about anything, everything except the pain that was stamping its feet and demanding to be heard.

One of Mister Porter's brass buttons was ablaze in a thin shaft of late afternoon light that had come through the gap in the sliding doors. "Button," I said.

"I think I'll call you Buttons," he said. "Might just as well."

The train began to move.

"Hold on there, Buttons," he said.

"Buttons," I repeated. Then the train jerked and swayed, and I cried out in pain.

The conductor reappeared, leaning over the porter's shoulder. Very sarcastically and menacingly, he sang the words "All aboard!" There were grey teeth, now, behind his slick lips, and beyond that nothing but the yawning darkness of his mouth.

Mister Porter Abel paid the conductor no mind. He talked and talked and wouldn't let me go to sleep, which I longed to do to be free of the pain. He talked about his children, who lived far away beside the sea, about how there was a girl about my age who was giving her mother "the dickens of a time."

"Wants to get her hair cut off," he confided, "but her mother says no, she is too young. Wants some kind of sleeves on her clothing that her mother doesn't approve of, or no sleeves at all, which her mother approves of even less. Furthermore, she has been seen laughing to beat the band with her older brother's friends."

He took off his cap and ran his hand over his hair. Then he put his cap back on. "I myself stay out of these discussions," he added.

This was not difficult for him to do, he confessed, in that, being a porter, he spent most of his life "rattling back and forth across the country on this train." Did I give my mother the dickens of a time? he wanted to know. I couldn't answer, so he talked some more. I lost consciousness at times while the whole world lurched under me, and long, thin bars of piercing light slipped in around the shape of the boxcar's door jamb, appearing and disappearing with startling frequency.

Once, I opened my eyes to find Mister Porter Abel's anxious face close to mine. "Here, now," he said. "You stay with me, understand? You pay attention to the long view. I am imparting some very important information to you, and I won't have you drifting off. Understand?"

I nodded my agreement, though not really intimidated by his stern tone.

He was quiet for a bit, then he touched my left shoulder gently. "My name is Abel Jackson," he said. "Will you remember that for me? We porters are called George, the same way as we used to be called boy, and sometimes we still are called boy when we take off these uniforms. Or sometimes even when we have the uniforms on. Don't drift off now. Stay here with me."

Suddenly this lovely man, who was now called Mister Porter Abel in my mind, and the man who shall forever be recalled by me as the Conductor were both talking at once to two white-coated men.

Mister Porter Abel was saying that as far as he could tell, there were lots of broken bones in my body.

The two doctors were ignoring the train employees, speaking only to each other without taking their eyes off me. I could not hear, or at least I could not understand what they were saying. It was as if my brain had reset on the train to only receive information given to me by employees of the railway company.

The cold blue Conductor with the ginger-coloured beard pushed in between the two doctors. He looked sombrely into my eyes for what seemed like a long time, then announced, "She is thoroughly dead."

Mister Porter Abel said I was most certainly not dead, but that most of my bones were broken.

I recall two nuns who were carefully cutting off my clothes with large steel scissors.

"About as dead as a person can be," the Conductor said, craning his neck above them and delivering this line while shaking his head with sarcastic sadness. "Oh dear," he said. "Oh dear, dear, dear. What a tragedy, and her so young!"

The two doctors used the word "fracture" quite often, and the phrase "internal injuries." One of them said he would write a poem with the title "Internal Injuries."

I wonder now if this is a true memory or something I have invented based on what I later learned.

"Take her to the morgue. Plan the funeral," the Conductor advised. "Dead as a doornail!" he added, laughing softly.

Mister Porter Abel bent to look down at me with that sad and angry expression.

He thought the doctors should leave me on the white door and said so. "I can't bear any more of her pain," he explained.

"Better get her off the white door and into a coffin," the Conductor said.

One doctor said yes and the other said no, and the nursing nuns glided closer and put their hands under me. One of them said, "Now!" I could feel the skin of their arms on my skin. And then I was gone again. With two last words. As Mister Porter Abel told me later.

Those two last words were "Bruno" and "Buttons."

During the early days of my brokenness, I sometimes believed that everything in the world, and everyone who lived on it, was doubled, and that there were stubborn arguments going on between each entity and its twin. These debates were going on inside my own body as well. Between my left and right arm, for example, or my left hip, my right knee. The memory of the boxcar—with all its jerking and shuddering, and its noise—was particularly vivid and contentious. The wall that contained the sliding door and bars of sunlight was in direct opposition to the darker regions that the sun didn't even attempt to enter. Those were the kind of places the Conductor called home; he had emerged from those shadows only long enough to blow whistles, to invite more and more people to board the train, and to now and then examine me. Sometimes in dreams or memories, he strode into and across the bars of sunlight on the boxcar floor, only to glance down at me and shake his head in a pessimistic way. "She's finished," he would say.

The sounds on one side of the car were different from those of the other as well, and all the noises were argumentative. A slower choreography and a deeper, more musical sound resided in the darker parts. I was aware of the pale bluish Conductor pacing quietly back and forth in those murky regions, almost as if he were slowly dancing in time to the swaying of the boxcar. Sometimes he hummed a little tune as if—impatient though he may have been—he was endeavouring to give the impression of patience.

At one point, I thought there were two trains, both carrying my broken body in a boxcar but travelling in different directions. That thought took the Conductor away from the company of Mister Porter

Abel. The Conductor was attending to me on a train travelling east, a train that was densely freighted with darkness, the only exception being a cold blue glow that followed him as he moved back and forth. Mister Porter Abel was attending to me on a train travelling west, one where the car in which I travelled was filled with swords of prismatic illumination, the kind of light that pierced right through your eyelids when you closed your eyes against it. The Conductor was efficient and humourless, and oddly and terrifyingly graceful. Porter Abel was anxious and alert to my needs, always worried but sometimes rollicking with warm laughter. The Conductor was obdurate, grim. "No future for you," he said. "You've eaten the never-wake-up berries."

The two doctors were on similar opposing teams once they took me into their care. Though one of them was more like Porter Abel, neither had fully aligned himself with the Conductor. I instinctively understood, however, that they both knew him well. I named the one who seemed to be Porter Abel's friend Doctor Angel. The other, who was rougher with me, was Doctor Carpenter. Everybody claimed they had my best interests at heart. But one was carrying me east, and the other was carrying me west. And each one had a quarrel with the others.

There were train tracks all over the new province at the time I am speaking of, sometimes emerging overnight, almost as if the railroads themselves, with all their steam and steel and noise, were natural phenomena, or an invasive species of strangling vine running roughshod over everything that was there before. In town, if you were a child who couldn't sleep, you could listen to the locomotives calling to each other far off in the velvet black of the prairie night, the way that mother buffalo might have called to their calves if the buffalo had been spared to graze and roam on the hijacked land. For my first days and nights in the hospital, I could not free myself of the motion of the train. The ward itself rocked and shunted under my bed, and the noise of cars coupling, and brakes screaming, and steam hissing was always inside my mind.

Today I drove out into one of the "foreign-speaking districts," as they were called at the time of the Master's research. The generation of children he was studying have, of course, now entered adulthood, married, and brought forth a new generation of pupils who haven't even the trace of an accent.

I know a good deal more about Walter Scott Stillwell now than I did at the time. But I was gradually beginning to understand that our lives were such that he might suddenly appear in our classroom, and that no amount of moving away would prevent this. He might stay away, but nothing we did could make him not appear. He could get on a train anywhere and days later be within shouting distance. He never shouted. But we were afraid of him anyway.

Elmdale School was relatively new as these simple structures went. It had replaced a schoolhouse built—and burned down—in the 1920s, shortly after my family migrated to the prairies. At that time, some families of the foreign-speaking districts were not eager to have their children educated, such vanities being in opposition to their religion and the way they felt their lives should be lived. It was said that these families burned the school themselves in protest against what they saw as an attempt at government control.

The new school provided a classroom for the third generation. These children might have been able to speak a few words of the "old" language in the company of their grandparents, but in all other ways, they were British subjects. As such, they were required to sing "God Save the King" each morning.

Some of the boys still automatically sing "God Save the King," King George VI having died so recently, and the young Queen crowned just last June.

Today, I brought my pitch pipe with me to divide the class into altos and sopranos for a harmonized version of that anthem, which will be sung by them when the new minister of finance passes through the nearby Humboldt railway station, to which they will have been bused for the occasion.

When I suggested—how could I not?—a life together, Harp responded with feigned bewilderment. "Why would I want you to be other than you are?" he asked.

I looked at his profile while he gazed into the distance of the rented room. Then he turned his head towards me, his eyes warm and lit with laughter. "I couldn't bear to think that it was I who came between you and your pitch pipe."

In another man, this remark would have been cruel. In Harp, it was merely playful. Cruelty, when it surfaced, was more direct. No metaphors were used.

I found myself, often enough, trying to read his face without him turning to me at all, playfully or otherwise. There was something of the hero in him, and a stalwart avoidance of eye contact stubborn enough for a Napoleon or a Roman emperor on a coin. I came to know his profile, the curve of his brow and the line of his nose, much better than I knew his full face.

This time he continued to let me see his eyes while he said, "You've never heard me sing."

I agreed that this was true.

"Well, you should thank your stars for that," he said. Then, "Trust me, love—I am not an instrument of music."

A year after the beautiful white door was installed, a musical instrument entered my life in the form of a second-hand player piano that my father got from a more prosperous farmer in exchange for a Guernsey calf. The piano had a long history and had often been badly treated. Once, for example, it had been borrowed from the neighbour who owned it by the wild Quinn boys, who lived on the next section down. They had carried it over the fields to a barn dance, then they had dropped it two or three times on their drunken way back. When we got it, four of its strings were missing and others were damaged. But all in all, the mechanism was still operating well enough that Danny could pump the pedals and the two of us could hear "In the Shade of the Old Apple Tree" or the thrilling *William Tell Overture*.

My father had brought it home as a birthday gift for my mother, knowing she had had a piano in the house where she grew up, and as he told us, she was even given lessons. Though she smiled with surprise when it was presented to her, she rarely played it—put off, I imagine, by the broken strings, the tinny sound, and its overall suggestion of honky-tonk vulgarity. But when I began to lose interest in the player rolls, and to show proclivity for picking out tunes by myself, she got the same person who had replaced the four strings to give me a lesson now and then. Danny wanted lessons as well, but it was suggested to him that pianos were a variety of women's work. He was hurt by this and walked sulkily out of the house whenever I played.

My teacher's name was Mister Lysenko. He came from one of the foreign-speaking districts and worked as a harvester in the late summer and fall. The rest of the time he travelled from farm to farm in an old trap, drawn by his even older horse, Mussorgsky, tuning pianos and teaching lessons. He had his own piano, he said, in the kitchen of his little house in the town. "I sleep in one room. The piano and the stove sleep in the other," he told me with apparent delight. "We are both very warm and safe from humidity."

I was not particularly gifted or driven, but I could carry a tune and enjoyed the songs I was able to play without the player's help. Mister Lysenko once told me I had perfect pitch, though no real ability when it came to tone and expression. I must have looked crestfallen at the news because he quickly added, "Don't be so dismissive about pitch! My own teacher in Kiev had to flee the city—in fact, he had to cross the Black Sea, and eventually other larger seas—because of killing a fellow piano tuner in a duel. He was defending philharmonic pitch, you understand, and his opponent was defending the adoption of diapason normal."

Full of energy and eager to get to his duties at the next farmhouse, then back home to his private piano in his warm kitchen, Mister Lysenko was packing up his satchel of music as he spoke about this. "I had to flee myself," he said, "which is why I am here teaching you."

What he meant by this ambiguous statement I have never completely known, any more than I grasped whether my teacher favoured diapason normal or philharmonic pitch. I wanted to believe, however, that this effusive, musical middle-aged man from Kiev was, like his teacher, someone who would challenge another to a duel. The romance of the story, and the old tinny keys of the player piano, whose strings could never hold their tune and often made me wince: all this was the beginning of something that would be with me for life. Each time I strike the tuning fork and hold it in the air at the front of the classroom, I think of him, though I never saw him again after the big wind. I think of the piano tuners' duel.

The last time I saw Mister Lysenko, he gave me the gift of the triangle that now announces my arrivals and departures to the classrooms of my small portion of the northern Great Plains.

The man I loved may not have been musical, but he was alert to intensity in others the way that a musician senses a colleague's tone and rhythm and tries to either follow or compete. That alertness might, indeed, have led him to challenge another to a duel if we had lived in a duelling sort of country. It was as if, long before we met, he had thrown himself headlong into the task of becoming dynamic and had never been satisfied with the results—as if something more terrific, or possibly even more terrifying, was needed, but he hadn't yet discovered what that was. I am not suggesting Harp was self-regarding or envious. He was far too curious about the world for that. But intensity in another drew him in. Even my intensity—my pitch pipe, as he called it.

But he had little patience with intensity in love. As Danny pointed out, he saw me at his convenience, and neither of us harboured any doubt as to whose timetable was the most important. I suppose his sense of entitlement was enlarged by his celebrity, but in those days, and in the grander scheme of things, it was the irrefutable fact of his manhood that drew up the conditions between us, as it did between so many men and women, married or otherwise. It was a man's world then. Up until the war, men owned the forward momentum that was essential to a vital life.

Like one move after another in a glacially slow board game, this began to change after the war. There would be an incremental shift forward on the part of women, a setback, usually triggered by men, and then another slight move forward. The man I loved did not live to see a noticeable change in gender relations. But I continue to believe that, had he done so, his charisma would have kept him safe from the wrath of women.

I eventually came to know that the intriguing variation in our unwritten contract was that as a woman, I was surprisingly not, for all practical purposes, required to do anything *for* him. I did not raise money for his research; I did not foster his ambition by introducing him to rich, influential people. I neither cooked nor cleaned for him. I had no knowledge of shorthand, and few public relations skills. I wasn't even one of those women who could elevate a man's status, and his sense of self, simply by her raw good looks.

Early on Harp explained, or tried to explain, the fascination of science to me. But the only aspect of all this I recall is what he told me about his fondness for the atmosphere in the lab, the warmth and the camaraderie. And then how much he hated the competing ambitions and jealousies that inevitably came about in the months following the magnificent discovery. Everyone wanted to own both the theory and the man who had invented the theory; so much so that the discovery itself, he told me, became like a country under siege. There were those who wanted to steal it, and those who wanted to disprove and discredit it. Long friendships were broken. Academic associates became vicious, and the few who remained loyal were felled under the weight of Harp's own quickly developing paranoia.

"Reporters were everywhere," he told me. "And drug companies. Both were hell-bent on destroying me, whether they knew it or not." He was pacing in the room and stopped to look fiercely in my direction. "*I* knew it," he said pointedly.

It was afternoon in a palace hotel when he said this, perhaps in early spring. The room was west-facing, I think, because there was an unusual amount of light coming through the thin curtains. This made a large ochre square on the floor and on the wall behind Harp, and his pacing shadow was bent at the hip because of it.

He claimed that, truly, he had merely stumbled upon his discovery, and did not, at first, experience pride of ownership. But then, he admitted, the attention and the pressure made his mind slip into another gear. "I became covetous, and in the same breath, utterly furious."

He looked furious, with his broken shadow behind him.

"Who were you furious with?" I wanted to know.

"With my fellow scientists, with journalists, with academics, and finally with all institutions—particularly the institution of marriage."

I recall that he glanced away from the centre of the room as he said this, his face flushed. I had stopped looking at the shadow because I wanted to see his expression. But beyond the flaring up of colour I could not read his thoughts. Then he walked quickly over the roses of the carpet and faced the window, as if in embarrassment, revisiting his anger and not wanting me to see that. With his back to me, he put both fists on the sill and kept his head low, his body still. The curtains were partly pulled. He was not gazing down into the street.

"Well," I said, "you weren't married to an academic faction."

"My wife," he said quickly, almost in a whisper, as if he didn't quite believe it was true, "was out and about being Mrs. Discovery." He had removed one hand from the sill and was moving it around in his jacket pocket. "And I was enraged by this," he added, with that cold, quick softness in his voice. He turned back towards the room and stood very still, both hands in his pockets, so that now the shadow had ridiculously long legs beneath the triangles made by his elbows. "To be fair," he admitted, in a more ordinary voice, "it wasn't really her I was angry with—though no one could tell me that at the time."

They had divorced, and he had remarried, someone closer to his own interests, someone who understood science and the lab. "But I remained furious," he said. "No amount of remarrying could get that anger out of my system." There was a light switch near the door. He walked over to it and flipped it down. The faux chandelier overhead became dark. Now the sun, filtered by the yellow curtains, filled the room with a different, less glamorous, and almost jaundiced atmosphere. We were like a couple in one of the rooms that an American social realist of the time might have painted. Lost, vaguely sordid, simply a man and a woman in a hotel room.

Harp started to look for his cigarettes, patting himself down in the process as if he were his own arresting officer. He made a sound of impatience and crossed the room to the closet, where he eventually discovered a half-empty pack of Lucky Strikes in a pocket of his overcoat.

"No one ever tells you how brutal success is, how it causes you to doubt and hate yourself while blaming everyone else. I never wanted to be a science saint, but once I was canonized, I quickly learned my role. It was such an extreme alteration, with no going back and little hope for character-building in its aftermath," he said, igniting a slim silver lighter. "I was a better person before all this happened." His expression abruptly became that of a carefree raconteur, and he grinned at me with, I thought, a hint of sheepishness. "A witless farm boy, really. But honest, at least."

I asked about that boy. I had been a child of agriculture; we could talk about fields, tractors, the lantern, and early mornings in the company of livestock. "Just tell me one thing about the farm," I said. "One thing. The name of your school. Or your dog. You must have had a dog."

But that part of the past had rolled up behind him, he explained, like an ancient Chinese scroll. It would crack and disintegrate were he to try to unfurl it. He insisted on this. He absolutely refused to look at it. And he was skilled at refusal. "Stop, stop," he said. And though there was laughter in his voice, he was no longer looking at me.

I was not skilled at refusal. Particularly when it came to Harp. I stopped.

But what he didn't know was, compliant though I appeared to be, I wanted everything he had. Every stray thought, each gesture, the length and breadth of him. It wasn't enough for me to accept the wonder and mystery that the love of him brought out in me. I wanted pledges and allegiances. I wanted complete surrender and treaties with firmly emplaced measures and reparations. In truth, I wanted to clear his wildernesses and plant his fields and colonize him. As he had colonized me. Because I could never recover from the advance of his armies, from the catastrophic stillness he caused in me each time we met.

Outside the window was an urban landscape where no urban landscape—even one as modest as a small prairie city—was ever meant to be, and the view included brick walls, ventilator shafts, fire escapes, and the broken windows of sunless alleys, not the swaying elms that lined the hotel's facade. When I had pulled up the sash earlier that morning, I was confronted by the warm, faintly sweet smell of kitchen grease. Pig slops and the summer odour in the outhouses of my childhood came to mind.

Harp was familiar with the caprices of human disease cycles. The condition he studied played havoc with the immune system, and he had made his never-to-be-repeated, miraculous breakthrough discovery in that field of investigation.

"Don't look back," he once said. Our uneasy alliance had already gone on for a long time when he gave me this advice, and I was looking back and speaking about the thick, lengthy calendar of it.

I now know that the pain I experienced, the pain that our union caused and that I had thought ennobled me, was in fact just as fierce and ordinary as any other kind of pain, and as exhausting. Perhaps my need to look back was simply an attempt to tolerate the blinding intoxication of him. Intentionally or otherwise, he had never stayed in my arms long enough for me to develop any variety of immunity. Each encounter was as moving, and vital—and ordinary, visceral, and brief—as the one that preceded it. And the recovery was just as lengthy.

On that afternoon when he and his shadow met at the edge of the bed where I was waiting, his face had changed. And the anger seemed to be gone. "Trust this dishonest man," he said, grinning. "Don't ever look back."

The wall near my hospital bed was painted powder green. There was a crack that forked like dark lightning down from the ceiling. Like lightning, yes, or more accurately like rivers, streams, and tributaries. But it was neither lightning nor rivers that came into my mind when I opened my eyes. I believed that the doctors and nursing nuns had positioned me facing that wall because drawn on it was a map of the mainlines, branches, and spurs of the railways of Saskatchewan. This was, in fact, what I had been studying in school the week before the big wind came. That and the parliamentary system, which the Master insisted we all learn. I suppose the railways stayed with me in an exaggerated way, being one of the most recent things I had learned, and more interesting than the ship of statehood and the unintelligible politics that attached themselves to it like carbuncles. And then, after I had memorized definitions such as "The Senate is the watchdog of Parliament," came the big wind, pain, and the grinding, screaming noise of the railroad. All this was still alive and panting in my brain.

During geography, before the Master came to be among us, our ordinary teacher, Mrs. Robinson, had written words such as "grain" and "cattle" on the board. She then told us these essentials would have been "thin on the ground" in the rest of our country without the railways fetching and carrying them. As if the words "grain" and "cattle" could never have come into being without the railways shipping them into the human brain. I don't recall the word "buffalo" being written on the board. But the buffalo themselves were almost gone by the time the railway arrived. Killed by men with iron weapons, men who increased tenfold once their iron vehicles, with their colonist cars fully occupied, brought white settlers to the northern Great Plains. Some from far away across the ocean where the ghost of Mary still haunted "the sands of Dee." Some, like ourselves, English- and French-speaking second- and third-generation British North Americans, from relatively nearby Ontario and Quebec.

When he arrived in the prairies all the way from Ontario, the Master wrote the words "Crown, Governor General, Senate, House of Commons" in descending order on the blackboard, which was made not of slate but of painted cardboard. (It would be years before these schools could afford slate.) He explained the notion of political parties and wrote the words "Conservatives" and "Liberals" with his white chalk. He said that he himself was a Conservative, but that we, when we grew up, would be free to join or vote for any party that we liked. Then he added that the railway would not have been possible without the businessmen and "entrepreneurs" (a word we did not understand, so he wrote it on the board) who funded it and were Conservatives.

The almost-dying child I was in that hospital ward believed utterly that her changed reality was connected to the greater ongoing world brought into being by iron rails. I knew that what was left of my life after the chaos of that extraordinary wind depended upon the existence of a railway, and I concluded, therefore, that all life must be contingent on the availability of the steel rails that led from where you thought you had settled to somewhere else altogether. I understood that the crack in the wall was a reminder that the railways of Saskatchewan would be forever in my purview, and that I never could have survived—and would not continue to survive—without them. A map of cracks on a green wall and the similar diagram of the railways of Saskatchewan that the teacher had shown us in school were, in my child's mind, also married to the map of my ligaments, tendons, and cartilage, and the map of my circulatory system. And when I closed my eyes, I could visualize the bifurcating, branching paths of my own lungs—lungs that, until that excoriating wind, had innocently and dependably inhaled the prairie air without my taking the slightest notice of them.

It was the pain, of course, that made me attentive to the geography inside my body, the same pain that had delivered me into the hands of the cartography of the railroad. I had never seen a hospital, though I had heard that they existed in places such as Saskatoon and Toronto. Because I was not familiar with such cities, and because I had not even seen a photograph of a hospital, I was not quite certain where I was. I wondered (or perhaps I secretly hoped) if the doctors were not themselves connected to the railroad, or if they might be the white-coated employees of the fancy dining cars or of one of the famous railway hotels. When my mother spoke about the hotels, she said they were like palaces, with lights burning at all times of the night and day, and with pools inside where you could swim, and with hot and cold running water in all their hundreds and hundreds of bathrooms. She had shown me a postcard of what looked like a thousand-windowed castle in the mountains, and had told me that once, only once, she had stayed there. And once, only once, she had stayed in Toronto, in another castle that looked like the one she was showing me. But it was in the city instead, not in the mountains.

Friedrich, my roommate in this ward, had been in the hospital for some time before I arrived. He was eager to explain the vagaries of both his condition and the hospital as soon as I was brought into what he called *his* quarters, but because there were two cracked vertebrae in my neck and broken bones all over the rest of me, I was unable to roll over and look at him. And therefore, for the first week or so, I half believed his voice was inside my own head. It wasn't until—with great difficulty—I blurted out the word "railroad," and in response, he earnestly described the model railway he had left behind at home (when he had a home, he qualified), that I began to believe in his corporeality. His railroad, even if it was nothing but a toy, was something no child I had ever known could even imagine, never mind lay claim to with such assurance. It absolutely defined him and made him real to me. I longed to see his face, but as I said, I could not move my head, and he, because of his legs, could not rise from his bed and stroll over to present himself to me.

"Legs are in ruins," he told me. Not that I had asked. "Dance career in doubt," he added, making me wonder about his life, though I could not ask about it. "Still," he confided, "as a result of my tragic decline, I intend to compose a beautiful piece of music in the heart-breaking key of E minor."

At that point I could say only the word "railroad," and even that very infrequently. I knew about the key of E minor on the piano because of Mister Lysenko, though not about its tragic nature, but I could not think long about it because the map of the railways of Saskatchewan had swallowed me up for what seemed to me to be hours and hours. But time and its measurement had been blown right out of my life, so how could I know for sure?

"My mother was a bossy stage mother," my roommate was saying, "and for that I am very grateful. She had high hopes for me being a star of stage, screen, and radio." I could hear the tinny sound of his bedsprings as he shifted his position. "A child star," he explained.

There were a few moments when he was silent, and I felt the tug of his thinking pulling me away from the railways of Saskatchewan. It was likely the word "child" that did that. And the word "mother."

"I have met all but one of those hopes," he eventually said. "Sadly, I have not performed on the silver screen." He paused here, as if making a mental note to correct this oversight. "Nevertheless, by the time God came to take my mother, I had been trained for a career," he continued, "which is more than can be said about most nine-year-old orphans. I could dance, orate, sing, and whistle."

I wanted to know if he had cried when God came to take his mother. But I couldn't find my voice to ask, and he didn't seem inclined to voluntarily tell me. Instead, he began to whistle a lilting yet sad tune, presumably in the key of E minor, which made me feel that his bed was turning in a slow spin and that my bed was turning alongside his. Then I felt as if our beds were slowly somersaulting, end over end, and I was afraid I was going to throw up.

To stop this, I forced myself to open my eyes and look at the wall. There was an unusual stain beneath the railways of the northern Great Plains. Maybe it was a picture of the dimensions of the new province of Saskatchewan. But more and more, because of Friedrich's speaking about his mother and my thinking about whether he had cried when he lost her, the stain put me in mind of the shape of my mother's one good dress.

My mother's one good dress was a constantly evolving garment, so it was difficult at first to decide if the stain purporting to be its portrait was accurate. It was a dress that had been altered many times, my mother had told me, most recently by her high-spirited cousin Fiona, who was an itinerant dressmaker back in Ontario. (Just as I am an itinerant teacher here in Saskatchewan.) Depending on the fashions of the period, and who was going to wear it, the dress would be trussed up or stripped down, my mother said, flounced out or gathered in. It was always being updated, so accuracy in terms of this stain on the hospital wall, I decided, was incidental. And it was even possible, my mother had said to me, that the dress might be passed on to me, as it had been to her from her own mother, my grandmother. She, my mother, would sometimes open the cardboard box that contained the dress so I could see it. The image that it presented—black shiny material swaddled in white tissue paper—has never left my memory. The dress moved with us to the prairies, but once we settled there, my mother did not open the box again, or at least not in my presence. Because of this, I believed that here in this flat land, far away from the likes of lively cousin Fiona, there would not ever again be a new version under construction. The dress, I concluded—as it turned out, correctly—would not be passed down to me after all.

My mother had been born on what was referred to as her family's, the Kearneys', "original" farm. It wasn't original at all, of course, as there had been a flax farm in Ireland that was sold or abandoned when trouble and famine had made themselves known in that country. As legend had it, when my mother's grandfather gave up in despair, rounded up his family, and departed for the "new" world, he was hoping to import flax farming to the Upper Canadian wilderness, which he claimed was known to suffer from a want of the good linen for which flax was grown. It soon became clear, however, that it would be impossible to grow a crop of any kind on the rocky, sloping Upper Canadian acreage he had been persuaded to purchase, and he was therefore required to invest his last five pounds in a few animals. The few (heifers and one bull) became a couple of dozen, then more, under the stewardship of three or four of my mother's grandfather's many sons, her father among them—the same sons who had cleared the land. Eventually, sheep were added to the pastures in hopes that the sight of them might bring some comfort to the old man, who had been rambling on about the beautiful green fields and peaceful flocks of his native land. He died nevertheless in great anger and sorrow, cursing the British in England, Ireland, and North America, and insisting that only the word "Ireland" be carved on his gravestone, along with his name and the date of his death.

The ranch, as the original farm was called because of the animals, remained a thorny, shadowy place, even after it was fully cleared. Swampy in its damp declivities and consistently attempting to go back to bush, it would never achieve the velvet green of the fields of Ireland, sheep or no sheep. The huge stumps, winched out of the earth by my mother's uncles after the trees were felled, still stood as fencerows, taller than the tallest man and ridiculous and sometimes downright frightening in their gestures. It was not uncommon for a lamb to become entangled in a stump fence, and the subsequent bawling by lamb and ewe would finally irritate one of the men enough that he would curse, storm outside, and help the poor captive escape. And beyond these menacing fencerows, as far as the eye could see, curved mile after mile of pine-covered hills; darkly dressed, impenetrable.

My mother was a clever woman, and the combination of this fact and her third-class certificate qualified her to be a teacher. In the early days, this would have freed her from the tyranny of that ranch and the men who ran it. She loved her brothers, but the household reeked of the sweat and the mud the boys brought into it, mixed with the greasy smell of the beef and barley soup eternally simmering on the stove. With a nod to refinement, her own mother had taught her to work the treadle sewing machine, a decorative contraption much scoffed at by the men. But she never fully took to it. The machine confounded and often infuriated her.

Here is what a good dress was like in those days in the backwoods, or at least the kind of dress an itinerant dressmaker would want to create, and later want to revise or update. Not ever to be confused with a housedress, it would be made from a fabric so exotic that no one was certain where that fabric had come from, though the Holy Land was often alluded to, it being in the mysterious and silk-laden East. Adorned with cushioned buttons and silken braid, which could be altered for various occasions, the good dress was almost always black, brown, mauve, or in rare cases, dark green. All other colours were deemed to be immoral on the one hand and impractical on the other, given the number of funerals one attended.

My mother considered it fortunate that she had inherited it. It might have been buried with her own mother, except that, on account of its frills, it was declared by the men to be unsuitable as a coffin garment. Even Ewan, the youngest, had said in an offhand seven-year-old way that the dress was not right for a dead lady. To his credit, he then burst into tears when he remembered that the dead lady under discussion was his own dear mother.

Her dressmaker cousin, Fiona, had come "sailing down the drive" six months after the burial, in a much-envied horse and trap that belonged to Fiona and to Fiona alone.

It was common in those days for an itinerant dressmaker like Fiona to spend close to a week revising a "good" dress. The work was long and hard, and the farms were scattered. Members of the Kearney family were kin to her and were therefore forced to be welcoming for as long as she needed or wished to stay.

Shortly after her arrival, Fiona and my mother, Laura, laid the dress out on the pristine matrimonial double bed. (My grandfather, now a widower, had decided to sleep for the rest of his life on the daybed in the kitchen.) There it lay, looking like a dead woman itself, were it not for the fact that the bustle had caused the waist and upper skirt to jut out in a lively and unseemly fashion quite unknown to the woman who had worn it. "One of her aprons smoothed out on the coverlet would have caused more sentiment," my mother assured me, "as that was the costume she most commonly wore."

Fiona had announced that the things that needed altering on the dress were "many and various," my mother said. The waist needed cinching, the bodice would have to be pleated, the sleeves needed to be taken off and replaced with pagoda sleeves. The hoop skirt should be narrowed, and the hoop itself should be thrown out behind the barn or burned. Both the bodice and the skirt needed shortening, and it was essential that a series of extremely small and delicate satin bows be sewn up the centre of the back. As for buttons, the decorative and some of the practical ones must be replaced with pearl buttons, or in the case of fabric buttons, with ones that were neither soiled nor frayed. There should be much more satin braid and much less lace. But most of all, the bustle had to be reconstructed. Times being what they were, this revised dress would need much more than just the suggestion of a bustle.

Those girls, I realized, would have paid absolutely no attention to the landscape, which with its muddy roads and murky vegetation wasn't much to look at anyway. Much more interesting to them was the dark dress flung on the white bedspread. It would have seemed surprisingly alive. But not with anything resembling the life that its previous owner, my grandmother, might have lived.

I could see my mother's bustle in the stain on the wall. "It is just like those traps you set in the attic to catch squirrels," she had remarked to me when she was showing me the dress. She had been laughing then.

...

The high-spirited Fiona was pregnant by the time she married one of my mother's brothers. A few months after that, in the dark of winter, she died giving birth to stillborn twins. Her own mother, whose husband owned the better farm in the south of the county, saddled up a horse late at night and attached it to a wagon. Then she drove out to the ranch—that original farm—and without a word to Fiona's husband, she put her daughter's body and the bodies of the dead twin babies on that vehicle, along with her daughter's beautifully sewn trousseau, and drove angrily, sorrowfully away into darkness and snow.

I, like my beautiful and destroyed mother, became a teacher of children. Sometimes there are silences even in a class devoted to music, while pupils copy the shape of a treble clef on the five lines they have drawn with a ruler in a scribbler. I look out the window at such times, and often it seems as if all sound has transformed itself into light and atmosphere. Then almost before I know it, there is the sound of children's voices again, singing the songs of a country they will likely never see, unless they are called to see it in battle.

How strange we all are! Most of us come from Irish and Scottish tribes cast out by the mother country. But we are still reading her poems and singing her songs. How odd that we define foreignness as those whose speech holds the trace of another language, and then we ignore altogether our own foreignness on land that was never our own.

Almost nothing we learned as children, and eventually taught to other children, was known or felt by us on a personal daily level, or increasingly, as the decades passed, even on an ancestral level. Nothing in our own surroundings was permitted to define us. Instead, we pledged allegiance to an island thousands of miles away where they had queens and castles and princes, an island we were required to build in our imaginations. Never Never Land.

My mother taught for a term or two, then married my father and taught another term after surviving the births of Danny and me, and becoming pregnant one more time. Her inner life remained unknown to us. Then something wild and ridiculous snatched her from us. That angry wind was after me as well, but in the end, it had to content itself with only her.

"'Rule, Britannia! Brittania, rule the waves,'" we sang, in that province without ships, without coasts or waves.

Harp once told me that the German literary man Johann Wolfgang von Goethe had become immersed in science—in botanical studies, to be precise—later in life. In no way a modest person, and after a prodigious amount of creative achievement, Goethe fell upon the idea that the story of his own life symbolically mirrored—and was therefore responsible for many scientific breakthroughs that had occurred in—the study of plants. When questioned about this, Goethe maintained that the public simply had not been attentive to some of his earliest publications; his 1790 *The Metamorphosis of Plants*, for example, was to his mind pivotal. Later, he would list, with great suspicion, every scientist who had ever quoted a sentence from *The Sorrows of Young Werther*.

"You see? You see?" Harp stabbed the air above the bed with his cigarette. "Science can outrun even literature for breeding egomaniacs and paranoiacs."

Goethe's own variety of scientific paranoia had deepened, Harp maintained, when a much later collection of his writings about nature was described by a French critic as "*botanique pour les dames, les artistes, et les amateurs des plantes*." Harp suspected, and I didn't disagree, that it was likely the reference to "*les dames*" that really put him off. Angrily refuting the critique, Goethe cited a journey he had taken half a century before— one during which a peasant boy ran up to and away from his carriage, joyfully employed in finding and then delivering specimens of the plants growing along the roadside. Young Friedrich, as Goethe called him, was one of several rural children from farming families who had learned Linnaean nomenclature in order to gather seasonal plants for urban pharmacies. But to Goethe, Friedrich was Pan himself, sent to him for the purpose of authenticating the poet's entitlement to scientific authority.

Was Goethe's young herbal messenger really called Friedrich? Or is it just my own memory, trying to connect the name of a youngster who long ago caught the attention of a great poet with all I came to know about a boy with the same name? Do I—like the old poet himself—want my time with Friedrich in that hospital to be larger, more significant than it was? Goethe was able to change the life of his Friedrich, if that was his name, arranging for an apprenticeship in the extensive gardens of a literature-loving duke. Harp claimed that this aristocrat often released brightly coloured hot-air balloons from the terraces of his house into the varying blues and whites, greens and yellows of the surrounding landscapes.

All this was told to me by the man I loved.

I have not travelled. Nor was I alive when all this happened. I will never know how the greens and yellows of a previous century darkened under the shadow of a great balloon. But somehow, I was able to visualize all this while the man I loved was speaking. It was his great gift to me that when we talked, he caused fully realized scenes to appear in my mind, so that years later I could recall a bend in a European river or a carving of a lamb from the tympanum of a cathedral, though I have never left these plains.

All this because of the way we spoke, and what we spoke about, when we lay together after love.

My roommate, Friedrich, was both the most abandoned and the most loved child I was ever to meet. He had the gift of utterance, and everyone around him loved him for that: the intonation and the poise of his speech. But there were other intriguing sides to his personality as well. He could charm animals, he explained, particularly dogs, because part of his job with the Company was to rapidly train the "daily dog." Even the most reluctant farm dog in Manitoba or Nova Scotia could be coaxed by him to hop on stage and play its part, according to him. What stage? What part? I had no way of knowing, then, what the Company was, but I would find out. Very soon.

Because he was so adored, he was much visited by the members of this Company. "They are all crazy about me." he said. But as I was to learn, because he outshone everyone else in the room, he was also much visited by visitors meant for others. Taciturn Doctor Carpenter paid an unusual amount of attention to him right in the middle of the day, and often when I felt he should have been talking to me, in that gruff and offhand way the doctor had. The nursing nuns also attended to Friedrich and apparently loved the lies he told. Or at the very least, they didn't object, even when he was obviously lying. He joked with them but listened seriously when they gave him advice. Then *they* listened seriously when *he* gave *them* advice. Like me, he could not move his legs. But unlike me, he had a variety of stories that he could say aloud, about the times when he *had* been able to move his legs. He had been a tap dancer, he had been a runner, a pole-vaulter, he had been the one taking home all the red ribbons at his school's field day— when he still went to school. And when he joined the Company and there was no more school for him, his achievements became legendary. But before that, he had been a celebrated hopper, skipper, and jumper, as well as a climber, a skier, a skater. He had been a mountain walker. "Val-deri, val-dera," he sang. Even motionless, he was filled with energy. I loved him long before I could speak to him.

He had taken the saint's name Ursula on the occasion of his First Communion, with everyone in the Company, he claimed—including the dogs—in attendance. Because my speech had not yet come back, I couldn't ask what drew him to Saint Ursula, but he told me anyway.

"It was because of the nuns," he said, "and all those girls in the story." He couldn't quite explain it, but those girls standing so still on their ship in their pastel robes, those girls clearly loved Ursula. "I loved my mother," he confessed, "and sometimes, before God came to get her, I would just stand as still as possible in the closet with all her skirts." He had never seen a ship, he admitted, but he had seen the mountains. The ship in the coloured engraving the teaching sister showed him, that ship was one of the great mysteries, a true wonder. It held eleven thousand virgins.

"That means," Friedrich told me, "the ship was filled with very young girls. Not baby girls, but girls about your age."

I had not considered the more prosaic side of virginity at the time, and at first, I assumed he meant there were eleven thousand Virgin

Marys standing on the deck, looking out to sea. Because of miracles, I decided, this multiplication of the Virgin would be possible.

But a gathering of this many girls about my age was impossible for me to conjure.

Though I didn't have a voice to ask the question, Friedrich intuited my doubt. "Some of them were maybe two or three years older than you, but the rest were your age, more or less," he assured me.

I thought about the girls later in the evening, when I couldn't sleep because of the pain, and I decided that if I had been one of them, I would have wanted to go home because of the crowding and milling about on board that ship. Then I remembered the shipwrecks in the poems the Master had taught us.

"I would have liked to be one of those girls," Friedrich had said earlier, confusing me further.

I should say more about the doctors who cared for Friedrich and for me. They were still vague—almost transparent—at this point, and at the same time very startling when they appeared near my bedside. In that way they were more like religious visions; often they dissolved before my eyes. They were miracles, in that they took the edge off the pain with their needles. And then, at other times, they were a catastrophe when, dressed in green, they wheeled me away to perform surgery on my bones. The one whom I called Doctor Angel would say things like "Not too often; they are only children after all, and we wouldn't want to make any mistakes." The other, whom I called Doctor Carpenter, would remain silent as he removed me from the room. Then he would say, "It's all for the best. Believe me."

When he said that, I knew that either Friedrich or I was going to have the edge taken off our pain with a particularly vicious and long needle. Or one of us was going to be eviscerated with a sharp knife.

Sometimes, when I heard Friedrich whimpering, I believed that he was experiencing my pain, and sometimes, when he was quiet and I was whimpering, I believed that it was I who was suffering *his* pain.

We lived inside each other that way. Though I had yet to really look at his face, I came to believe that I thoroughly knew the expressions that face would assume. This was because of everything he was telling me, in such a cheerful voice. I imagined a look of innocence combined with gleefully raised eyebrows, suggesting trickery was behind almost everything he said. The doctors, always so business-like, groaned when he told them things, but they never asked him to be quiet.

The first time that either doctor spoke to me at length was late at night. I was awake and in pain when Doctor Angel came in the door, walked over to my side of the room, and sat sideways on my bed with his back leaning against the wall so he was able to see me. Because it was night and because of his white coat, I truly believed he was a ghost or a seraph. By now I knew the two doctors were not necessarily working against each other. Still, I suspected that there might be two versions of each man, with a little bit of Doctor Angel in Doctor Carpenter and a little bit of Doctor Carpenter in Doctor Angel. I knew this because, young though I was, I was well enough acquainted with my brothers and my father to understand that this division was an unconfessed part of being a man. During the period when I couldn't talk, Doctor Angel often came at night and sat on my bed. Sometimes he slept a bit sitting there. Sometimes he said things I didn't understand. His words were like singing but without the music.

Maybe a week later, as if he had sensed what I thought, Doctor Angel said that in his own mind, there had been—over the years—several versions of him, and that some of those versions gave him a "spot of trouble."

"Trouble," I repeated. "Version." Each word I was able to speak felt as if it were new in my mouth. For the past few days, although I could not think of a word in my brain and then say it aloud, I had been able to repeat the odd word that came out of the mouths of others.

I had been crying on and off all evening. Doctor Angel wanted to know why. "Is it the pain?" he asked.

But no, it was not the pain. The pain caused me to whimper. This was an acute sadness. "Mother," I sobbed. This was the first time I had spoken a word not already spoken by someone else.

It was also, of course, the first time I had mentioned my mother. All day my mother's one good dress had been near me, its empty arms open in my mind. So "mother" was the first word I was able to say. If I had been younger and less self-conscious, I would have said "Mama," as that was really what I called her.

Doctor Angel began to tell a story about his own mother. "I called her Mama," he said. She had died, he told me, when she was still young enough to be beautiful.

"Dress?" I asked. The second original word.

"She had a wonderful rose-coloured dress," he said. "It was lovely in the extreme. Everyone who saw her in it fell in love with her," he said. "She died of tuberculosis, and she died in her prime. She wanted me to be a doctor, and that death of hers, well, it hammered the idea home. I became a doctor."

"Mother beautiful," I said. "Dress dark." Will my mother wear her one good dress when she comes to visit? I wondered. The concept of being visited had just entered my mind, along with my slowly reviving vocabulary.

"Our mothers!" Doctor Angel said, in a tone that suggested both exasperation and love.

"Dress was from her own mother." I knew she had inherited it, but "inherited" was too big a word for me just then.

"People often do that," he said. "Hand-me-downs."

"She hasn't worn it lately." My most complete sentence so far.

"That can happen," Doctor Angel said.

I said the word "Friedrich." He was breathing evenly in his bed not five feet from mine. Doctor Angel said he would explain Friedrich, but first, he said, he had to make something clear. "Do you know why I am here in the middle of the night?" he asked.

"Crying?" I asked, knowing that I had been doing so quite loudly.

"Yes," he said. "Partly. But I wouldn't have heard you crying unless I was here in the hospital."

Faintly hurt that Doctor Angel had heard my sobs not somewhere in his inner being, but only as ordinary people hear things, because he happened to be out in the hall, I remained very still and said nothing.

"I was here because of a difficult birth. A mother was having a baby that was reluctant to enter the world." He leaned sideways and turned his head so he could see me better. I could tell he wanted to know if I was listening. "Well," he said, having assured himself that I was awake, "that baby finally came, but that baby . . . that baby lived for only ten minutes and then she died."

"Emer is my name," I said, though even I knew this didn't apply to the baby and was only me trying out my voice and short sentences.

"Well, I'll be damned," he said, shocking me somewhat. "So it is!" He reached over and put his hand on my shoulder for a moment. "The important thing," he said, "the most important thing I want to tell you is how distressed this mother was by her baby's death. She was filled with a terrible grief. Mothers should never outlive their babies." He shook his head sadly. "Friedrich's mother did not outlive him."

After saying this and gesturing in the direction of Friedrich's bed, Doctor Angel started to nod. Now he was falling asleep. At that moment I realized that even Doctor Angel was mortal and needed rest. Then, startled, he sat upright. "But that doesn't mean Friedrich doesn't have a family. He has a family all right. Does he ever!"

And with that, the doctor was again suddenly asleep, quite profoundly this time, snoring softly and propped up against the wall that contained the map of the railways of Saskatchewan and the portrait of my mother's one good dress. I could hear Friedrich's regular breathing, five feet away. And then this doctor-angel's soft snoring. There was a rhythm being set up by it all that indicated life was tender, and plausible. I also fell asleep, descending to a depth that was more absorbing than the surface level of the wall and the bed where the pain strolled.

The man I loved caused me pain. But like Doctor Carpenter, he was also able to bring about the cessation of pain, able to make me happy. After years of trying to solve the mysterious and maddening puzzle of this, I now finally understand that if I hadn't loved him, I wouldn't have felt either the pain or the happiness. There was nothing he could have done to make things any different. What he unknowingly contributed to this ordinary mix was intensity.

The doctor was gone when I awoke the next morning, as if he had never come at night and snored with his back resting against the wall. Friedrich was singing again, but this time something sadder and more sinister. I could tell he was singing to himself thoughtfully but also angrily, as if the song demanded both contemplation and rage. He was not performing, but singing, instead, as if he were all alone and his heart was both angry and broken. I knew by now that when he sang to himself like this, with words I could not understand, it would be a quiet day. You in your small corner, I thought, and I in mine.

As the song Friedrich was singing moved through its stanzas, it became angrier and less contemplative. Much later I would discover that the ominous music was Franz Schubert's "Erlkönig." The only words I understood were *"Mein Vater, mein Vater,"* because they sounded like the English I was used to. They sounded like me, calling my father.

I closed my eyes and saw sheet music with a panic-stricken sadness tangled up around its delicate straight lines, heavy black bars, and wasp-like notes with stinging tails.

When the doctor came in that morning on his daily rounds, Friedrich was still singing the angry, sad song. The doctor's footsteps passed my bed and stopped near Friedrich's melody. It was Doctor Carpenter again, not Doctor Angel.

"Tell me what's troubling you, son," he said to Friedrich.

Friedrich stuck to his music. "*Mein Vater, mein Vater,*" he sang angrily.

"I have ordered some special braces for you," the doctor said. "And a prosthesis. Something to get you up and walking."

I was interested in this. Were there not going to be any special braces for me? I asked myself. But then I remembered that I wasn't entirely sure how to find my legs.

"Dance career in doubt," said Friedrich. He had abruptly stopped singing.

There was a tense silence in the room. Doctor Carpenter said nothing, but I could tell that he didn't exactly disagree with Friedrich on this point.

Finally, the doctor said, in an offhand way, "The Company is in town, you know." Because of the emphasis everyone put on the word "Company" when they said it, I knew it had to be spelled with a capital *C*. Everybody but me seemed to know what this Company was.

The doctor crossed to my side of the room. "Emer," he said to my back, "we are going to turn you now." I opened my eyes and there was nothing but plaster and cracks on the wall. No pictures at all.

I could hear footsteps approaching. I whimpered, knowing what the pain would be like once there were two people handling me. The doctor put a rubber mask over my face. "Ether," he said, as if he believed I knew what that word meant. I wondered if he was trying to use my name and had made a mistake with it. "We will do this starting now," I heard him say to the other handler. "Twice a day because of bedsores." Then suddenly I was far away.

I awoke hours later to complete pandemonium in the room. And a feeling of alarm in my soul. Now, because of being turned, there was the shock of seeing the room for the first time. Until this moment, there had been only the wall with the railways of Saskatchewan and my mother's one good dress. And all that I could think about regarding these two things, which turned out to be quite a lot.

Facing the room there was a whole new zone of possibilities: sun outside the window and a piercing blue sky. And there was Friedrich, whom I had not yet seen. He was sitting up—alert and happy in what appeared to be an anticipatory sort of way—against his pillows. His blond hair shone in the sunlight that came in through the window. Even his eyelashes shone. There was something so graceful about him, even though he wasn't moving at all, that I was scared to death and tired right out by his beauty, and abruptly fell asleep again.

I awoke the second time to the anxious yelping of dogs, combined with the sound of the clicking and scraping of dogs' nails on the hall flooring. Then, before my eyes, barking to beat the band, four very dissimilar tail-wagging dogs hurled themselves into the room. They had their front paws up on Friedrich's bed before you could say Jack Robinson (one of my father's expressions). The smallest one jumped right up beside Friedrich's pillow, then turned and barked at me in a protective kind of way. He or she looked like the kind of dog that should be pictured in a magazine. Short legs, rectangular body, covered with straight white hair, but with a sweet expression despite the barking.

"Don't worry about her, Scottie," Friedrich said to the dog, jerking his thumb in my direction. "She can't even talk."

"Yes, I can," I said, startling myself because, having forgotten about my conversation with Doctor Angel, I believed this was really the first statement I had uttered in what seemed like a very long time. "Whose are these dogs?" I asked.

Friedrich looked at me in surprise. But before he could answer, a small crowd of noisy adults galloped, laughed, and chattered their way into the ward. Each member of this group was wearing a different faintly ridiculous hat, and each was carrying at least two gifts. One, who was wearing a tutu, pirouetted through the door and across the room, then stopped and turned round and round in one spot. The rest busily hurried to Friedrich's bedside and poured the gifts onto his lap.

In this way Friedrich received modelling clay and cakes of poster paint, different-coloured pieces of paper, a package of brightly coloured jacks complete with a tiny rubber ball, and several books with colour dust jackets featuring cowboys and Arctic explorers. He also received pea-shooters, slingshots, and at least one cap gun. (These hazards were later removed from the premises by the nuns, who found them hidden in his bed.)

A beautiful woman in the group was wearing my mother's one good dress. But it was fashioned as it had been in my grandmother's time, and still included the hoop that had been thrown out behind the barn. Something else about the dress was different. The beautiful woman's shoulders were bare, left and right, and the crease where her bosoms began was visible, front and centre.

"What do you think of my costume, Dogcatcher?" she asked Friedrich while performing a series of grand jetés, during which the vast circumference of her hoop skirt swept the room. "Simmer down, Moosejaw!" she said to a long-eared, and long-legged, hound who in some odd way appeared to be also part collie, and who was running in circles, wanting to join in the dance.

The two other dogs had begun to take an interest in me. "Prince Albert! Yorkton! Get back here!" a young man in a bowler hat commanded. "Leave that poor girl alone!" And then, turning to Friedrich, "She is a girl, isn't she? Difficult to tell the way she's all trussed up."

It was the first time since the big wind that I had considered what I must look like.

"Yes," said Friedrich. "That is Emer. But she can't talk."

"I can so!" I objected.

The largest dog, whom I assumed was called Prince Albert, had paid no attention to the man in the bowler hat and was licking my undamaged and therefore available hand.

"Why does she call you Dogcatcher?" I asked Friedrich.

Before he could answer, the beautiful lady, making a modest curtsy, lifted her skirt almost to knee level, and a quantity of red, white, and blue rubber balls bounced out from underneath her hoop and petticoats, causing chaos among the dogs. The beautiful lady then produced a galvanized pail from beneath the skirt and banged it on the floor three times. This quieted the dogs, and they all sat down and looked at her attentively. "Fetch," she called out operatically.

The dogs nosed around the room collecting balls. Then they dropped them, one by one, into the pail. When it was full and there were no more balls in the corners of the room, the beautiful lady hitched up her skirt, lifted the pail by its handle, and attached it to what I presumed was a hook somewhere beneath.

None of the men in the room—nor any of the other women, for that matter—paid the slightest attention. One or two were in chairs reading magazines; another was lounging near the foot of Friedrich's bed, vaguely attempting to feed a paper ribbon of caps into one of Friedrich's new cap guns. Several more had bundles of papers in their hands from which they took turns reading aloud while gesturing in an exaggerated way. The dogs swarmed and panted and wagged their way between the beds.

I was completely exhausted by all of it.

"These dogs are named after the prairie towns they come from," said Friedrich. "They have all played the role of the daily dog on stage. Some daily dogs go home. But most daily dogs prefer to remain with the Company when it leaves the vicinity."

Sister Hildegard entered the room, glanced at the beautiful lady in a disapproving way, and said that visiting hours were over. It was one of Sister Hildegard's duties to say that visiting hours were over. She was short and round and carried herself with magnificent authority and dignity. A pocket watch, which she consulted often, was safety-pinned to her habit.

"They are not!" said the beautiful lady. "They aren't over until the fat lady sings." Unlike the balls and dogs, this caused hilarity among her companions; they laughed and laughed. Then they rose from their chairs, stopped reading out loud to one another or loading cap guns, and began saying their goodbyes to Friedrich while the dogs nosed around his bedside for a farewell pat. "There'll be more of us tomorrow," one of them said. "Jackie, Dyno, and Elzivir are sewing curtains."

Despite Sister Hildegard's strict stance, and her attempt to enforce rules, the truth was that because Friedrich had been in the hospital for over a year, all the nuns knew and were fond of the members of the Company. They had provided a liturgical chair or two for the set of the current play. Now and then they could be persuaded to remove the velvet drapes and brass rods from the priest's house so that the set's painted windows could witness a moment when the curtains were drawn back to glimpse a significant arrival. And there were other acts of mercy; they loaned the actors one of their habits, for instance, if the play they were performing had need of such a costume, and they furnished holy candles if the usual lighting was felt to be inadequate. Sister Philomena, who was more statuesque than Sister Hildegard, even had a walk-on part in *Masked Revenge*, during which she had to scurry onto the stage, shout the word "sinners" in the direction of a gang of departing robbers, and be jostled by three policemen and three dogs bent on pursuit before the curtain fell on her performance.

One night the holy candles set the priest's curtains on fire, and there was much discussion about what that meant. Suspicions arose when it was discovered that Malachiah, a member of the Company who, in Sister Hildegard's opinion, tap-danced with such rapidity his gift could only have been given to him by the Devil himself, had the second name of Sammy, which, again according to Sister Hildegard, could have been a contraction of either Samuel or Samyaza, the fallen angel who had brought the sin of pride with him when he fell to earth. But mostly the nuns loved the Company, and if they could, they attended each of the four plays that trekked through town in the summer. All of them confessed to envying Sister Philomena's moment in the lights. They agreed among themselves, however, that it would take someone with Sister Philomena's spunk to respond to the request, and that they, gentle flowers that they were, would never have found the courage to call that sort of attention to themselves.

"Did the curtains catch on fire again?" Friedrich asked.

"Always the way," said the man in the bowler hat. And then, just as my own dark curtain of sleep was once again falling, they were gone.

I think I may have heard Friedrich say, "She calls me Rabbit Hunter as well," but I am not quite sure. As I said, I was confused and tired by all that had been going on in the room. The sunlight, the sky, Friedrich's beauty, and this madcap collection of adults and dogs who were somehow connected to him, and who seemed to me to cluster and play like children. After I had been turned to face Friedrich and had seen these extraordinary visitors, the wall and its intimate maps and private portraits ceased, for the moment, to be memorable or retrievable.

Soon I would come to know more about the visitors composing the Company, along with the self-sacrificing tailors, Elzivir, Jackie, and Dyno, who were, it appeared, always going to be somewhere else working on the curtains. I would also come to be intimate with a quantity of dogs and rabbits. But for now, I wondered if the big wind had brought them from a far shore—a country so opposite that the adults darted in and out of doors like children, and the children remained solidly in place; stable, sad, and concerned with solving the puzzles of the rooms in which they found themselves.

...

Not long after this Friedrich began to tell stories concerning the other four beds of the room, which were currently empty but, by the sounds of these stories, had not been that way for long.

"Cathy in bed three was a criminal," he told me, "AND an orphan." She knew how to swear, he insisted, and this had shocked the nuns.

"She'd been caught stealing so many times her parents didn't want her anymore, and they sent her to the reformatory," he said. "I've never stolen. But if I did, you could be sure I'd never be caught." He was reaching awkwardly across his bed, trying to get a stray, well-hidden cap gun out from between the mattress and the springs.

"Maybe she was caught because she was only eight and a girl?" he speculated. "Anyway," he continued, giving up on the gun, "at the reformatory, the other girls were bigger than her, and one of them pushed her down the stairs and broke her heart."

"Not her heart," said Sister Philomena, who had just appeared, majestically pushing the trolley with the tin basins and white jugs for washing up. "It was her ribs that broke, and her ribs, they ruptured her spleen."

"Same thing," said Friedrich. "And before she got better and turned nasty, she even *said* she had a broken heart. So there. Anyway, now she's gone back to the reformatory to kill the girl who did that to her or die trying." He seemed to enjoy picturing the murder. "That's what she said," he added, nodding in fellowship.

Bed four once had a cowboy in it. "A sort of cowboy in training" is how Friedrich put it.

I wasn't nearly as impressed by this. After we came to Saskatchewan, every boy in my class, including Danny, thought he was a cowboy. I wanted to ask what was wrong with him, this cowboy in training, but I was once again having trouble speaking, and particularly when it came to asking questions.

But Friedrich carried on without my question. "He had a disease called polio, and his case was so bad they named a whole strain of it after him," he announced with obvious envy. "This strain was SO terrible, it caused everything in his body to stop, except his heart and his lungs and his voice."

Sister Philomena interjected here. "We couldn't leave him in this ward, even though the virus had done its damage. Didn't want even the chance of any of the others getting polio. He was sent on to Toronto."

Voice. I thought about its persistence in the polio victim but not in me. My relationship with my own voice, though on the mend, was still uncertain. I believed that the wind had tried to knock the voice right out of me and had almost succeeded. Then I remembered that my voice had disappeared once before, when I was reciting "My Heart's in the Highlands" for the Master.

"The name?" I managed to ask about the special strain, curiosity having stimulated my reluctant vocal cords.

"The Grabowski strain," he said. "Antoni was Polish, though he said he didn't remember anything but Fish Creek, where he lived. He was here for the polio massages that Sister Editha had learned how to do, and that had got famous all over the prairies. They didn't work out, though, and Sister cried when Antoni's father came with a rolling crib to take him back to Fish Creek."

"And then to Toronto," Sister Philomena added.

Toronto was beginning to sound like the end of the line, the scrap heap. "It's where the old loco motives go to die," the Conductor whispered in my mind. I could see the words "loco" and "motive" in my brain, so I knew the Conductor was not referring to the engines of trains.

Both Friedrich and I fell silent after Sister Philomena's announcement. Friedrich looked distressed. I knew, then, that he had liked the Polish boy, Antoni, and had felt sorry about Sister Editha and her failed massages. Even though he'd rather give up his last cap gun than say so.

The fourth and fifth beds had been occupied by twin brothers who had been involved in a terrible accident involving logs from a barn their father was building. "Those logs rolled off the wagon, crushing one twin's leg and the other twin's arm," Friedrich announced with obvious relish. "They had parents who didn't live too far away, and who came in here and cried loudly," he stated with no little amount of contempt. "The twins got better pretty fast," he told me. "And then they had to go home with those sissy parents and live with them for the rest of their lives." Friedrich's tone suggested he felt they would have been better off dead or in Toronto, which now to my mind amounted to the same thing.

I was brought to tears during this story because of the word "twins." I missed my baby brothers, I realized, and I didn't know what had happened to them, how the big wind had dealt with their little frames.

"There was a girl called Lillian in your bed," Friedrich said, after a period of silence during which Sister Philomena had washed his back. "She had a wasting disease. But Sister Philomena brooks no nonsense when it comes to food," he assured me, "and Lillian stopped wasting lickety-split!"

Sister Philomena was holding on to Friedrich's hair and attempting to wash his neck at this point. "I told her she could waste completely away if she wanted to, but not on my shift," she said, with a tug at Friedrich's curls and a large amount of sternness in her tone.

"The sixth bed?" I found the strength to ask that one question.

"He didn't stay long," said Friedrich, in a quiet voice. The neck washing was finished, and he was no longer trying to squirm. He looked defeated somehow, which was uncommon. "He left after a few days."

After Friedrich spoke those words, the sunlight in the ward got much brighter, and everything—side tables, bed rails—winked and gleamed, as if all the objects in the room wanted to bring something to our attention. Because I couldn't figure out what that something was, I would forever connect the sixth bed with strange and forbidden narratives, and often at night I would see the cold Conductor sitting on that bed, swinging his legs and whistling a tune in a minor key. Various parts of him—badges, buttons, patent leather, and the whites of his eyes—glistened in the moonlight. At times like that, the whole ward would rock and sway, as if it were just one incidental car of a long, long train.

One June day, when we were outside after school hitting some baseballs in the yard, Danny said he did not believe in God. I was full of faith, as were most people of the time, and so I was shocked by his announcement. We had a long discussion on this subject, aware that we were outside, beyond the range of eavesdropping parents.

"So what does he look like, then?" he asked me, while tossing a ball from one hand to the other.

I described the great-uncle who sat grimly in a formal group photo on our parlour wall, and who had a similar look to the punishing Old Testament characters that were illustrated in the family Bible. "A bit of white hair," I said. "A long white beard. And very, very old."

"Nonsense," said Danny. "If God exists, which is doubtful, he is a general principal, not an old person."

He had collapsed on the lawn, and I was sitting on the nearby swing our father had built for us even before the house was finished.

Danny, being older, was never much interested in it, and now neither was I, except as a comfortable resting spot.

I visualized my great-uncle in full military regalia, as a principal general. This was soon after the first war, remember. Photos of generals were, at the time, even more plentiful than chromolithographs of prophets.

"I like the saints well enough," said Danny. "They're interesting. A bit like Greek and Roman gods, each with their own peculiar story."

All this from a thirteen-year-old boy. But of course, I didn't think this at the time.

I knew nothing about Greek and Roman gods.

"Master Stillwell," he replied when I asked how he knew about them. "He's been at the university in Toronto for such a long time, he knows everything."

I said nothing. I had been busily twisting together the two ropes that held the swing, and now I let go of them so that I could spin around and around.

Then I asked Danny what he thought Master Stillwell was doing in our classroom when he should have been in Ontario. Danny pondered this for what seemed like a long time. Then he said, "He is the boss, sort of. He is the inspector of the inspectors."

Research was what Master Stillwell was doing in our Saskatchewan school district, according to my mother. His research in our Ontario school had involved differences between what my mother called "the intelligence of urban children, and that of rural children." I remember his printing on the Ontario blackboard— things we were required to copy into our workbooks. "A big-city school has as many as twenty rooms," the blackboard read. "It has caretakers, a nurse, and a principal. A country school is very, very small. It has just one room. It has big children and little children all in one room." After we were finished with the printing, we were encouraged to draw what we thought a big-city school might look like. How this determined our intelligence, or lack of same, I now fail to see.

But this Saskatchewan research was about something altogether different. Sometimes, our ordinary teacher had to come back to our classroom while Master Stillwell went out to schools ten or fifteen or even fifty miles away. I asked my mother why.

"Because for his new book, he needs to compare your school, where the pupils are English, with the newer schools, where the children are not."

"But you are not English," I pointed out. My matrilineal grandfather, who was Irish, had made a great fuss about not being English. He had thumped his cane on the floor and shouted when the subject came up among the relatives. He could speak another language called Irish. And when he did, he explained, he was cursing the English.

"The parents of those children don't speak English," is what my mother said. "They speak a foreign tongue." She had begun to feed wood into the kitchen range and was banging down the iron lid after. "Everyone in this country has to speak English," she said, "and that is just the way it is."

I could tell she was getting hot from the fire in the stove because her face was turning red.

"Those people are foreigners," she said, almost to herself. "But maybe their children won't be. Master Stillwell is studying ways to make it easier for the children of the foreigners to become English."

Danny entered the kitchen at that moment, and after opening the bottom doors of the corner cupboard, he reached for the dented tin box where my mother kept the oatmeal cookies we always ate after school. He pried open the lid, then glanced at my mother with a surprised, questioning look when there was nothing inside. But he didn't say anything.

"Danny," my mother said—quite sharply, I thought. "Put that tin away and go out and bring in some more wood."

As he rose to go out to the woodpile, I remembered that neither his name nor my name was English.

Danny, I thought. Emer. And the names felt awkward to me. As if they wouldn't fit comfortably, anymore, in my own mouth.

The night after Friedrich told me about the history of the room, bed by bed, I saw the structure of the parliamentary system on the ceiling just the way the important Master Stillwell had drawn it on the cardboard blackboard. It was shaped like a tree, and like a tree, it had a crown at the top.

We had nature study at school when we had less important teachers, and we had learned about photosynthesis and how the crown of the tree took light out of the sun and turned it into oxygen. Master Stillwell compared the tree's leafy crown that we already knew about with the jewelled crown we had heard rumours of, and he told us that without those crowns, neither trees nor human beings could stay on earth. According to him, we would be thrown into darkness and would soon suffocate if it weren't for the British Crown keeping us alive. "It keeps our political system alive as well," he said. "And it protects the two houses." He then looked fiercely out at the class. "Danny," he said, "what are the two houses?"

"The House of Commons and the Senate," Danny dutifully answered.

"And what is the Senate's primary function?"

"The Senate is the watchdog of Parliament," Danny said, with less certainty.

"Would you like to be a senator, Danny?" Master Stillwell sat down behind his desk as if to give Danny the floor. "Or would you rather be an elected parliamentarian?"

"Neither," said Danny, with boldness. "I want to be a farmer."

Master Stillwell flushed at this, but courteously pointed out to the class (a repressed laughter had swelled and receded among us at the audacity of Danny's reply) that farming was an essential service. "But, Danny," he said, his finger instructively cutting through the air, "being a farmer does not mean you can't enter the political arena. Take me, for example. I am a teacher! But that in no way prevents me from entering politics."

He turned back towards the cardboard blackboard and wrote the words "The Role of Opposition Parties in Canada."

"I am a member of the opposition party," he told us. "Do any of you know what that is?"

A few days after the players and their dogs had spontaneously entered our room, Friedrich told me he had joined the Company after his mother died. As far as he knew his father had never existed, and he had no siblings, never mind a sibling old enough to care for him. For a while he had an imaginary brother, but he severed relations with him when he proved to be "unreliable." Without his imaginary brother, Friedrich soon ran away from the orphanage in which he was placed, though he liked the nuns who looked after him there.

"In fact," he told me proudly, "one of the nuns helped me escape!" She had given him food and a bit of money and had then stood guard while he sprinted down the long hall that led to the back door. "I used to be able to run like the wind," he said.

I knew he still liked nuns because the nursing sisters, who had taken such a shine to him, were of course nuns. I recall hearing one of them laughing, and then saying to Friedrich, "Only God, my dear, could love you for yourself alone and not your yellow hair"—something

I almost agreed with once I had been turned and could see that hair, lit by sun. It was Sister Hildegard who made this surprising pronouncement, her words coloured by the German language she had spoken until she came to this prairie world. During the part of my childhood that was lived in Ontario, I had never heard what was then called a foreign accent.

It is only now that the strangeness of Sister Hildegard's quoting poetry occurs to me, and not just because of her normally stout and practical manner. When was the moment that the Irish book containing that poem about yellow hair was placed in her hands, and who was the person who had placed it there? "Poetry sometimes walks through hidden rooms," was what Doctor Angel had remarked when I told him what the sister had said about Friedrich's hair. And then I explained about my own unlikely father, who learned to read in middle age and had fallen in love with the work of a popular American poet.

"My point," said Doctor Angel, though I could tell there was laughter in his voice. "Poetry has a life of its own."

Sister Hildegard was one of three cloistered nuns—the others being Sister Editha and Sister Philomena—who had come to the prairies before I was born. They were almost children at the time, and even now, they kept their childhood memories close to them, perhaps as a protection against the hardships in this place where everything was raw and new, where the temperature skated rapidly down to fifty below in the winter, and where the biting insects were as big as birds in the summer.

In and out of our ward they floated, efficiently performing unpleasant tasks, and taking on the roles of both nurse and parent for the children in the room. They knew what it was to be a child separated from home because, as I would discover, they had entered their cloistered convent very early in their lives. My most cherished nurse, serene Sister Editha, at nine, rule-abiding Sister Hildegard at eight, and strict Sister Philomena at only five. Poor Sister Philomena! She could never with any certainty even picture her pre-convent childhood—the visitors she stared at through a grille on Sunday afternoons would have been more like strangers to her than parents and siblings. The novitiates were permitted only twenty secular words a day, so questions were not an option.

Sister Editha, however, vividly recalled the girl she had been and the childhood she had lived before she entered the cloister. And quiet though she was, she was eager to talk.

The first time I saw her, or at least the first time I remember seeing her, I confused her with the Conductor and called out in alarm.

In my dreams, you see, the Conductor had been jabbering, laughing, riding around on a bicycle, and swinging the rope—the lasso, he called it—with which he intended to catch me. He was wearing a large white hat above his pale blue face and his dark uniform. He was telling me that my mother had abandoned me and was living in one of the palace hotels, and that she was wearing her one good dress every day and drinking wine and eating chocolates. "She knows you are finished," he sometimes said. "She knows you are broken into pieces and worthless, and she wants nothing to do with you. She wants you to come with me." He went on and on in such a vein. I knew in some part of my brain that I was dreaming. But also feared I would be unable to wake from the dream, even though I was trying and trying to do so. Those first nights I had no legs in my dreams, so I could not run away from the Conductor. Still, I was sometimes able to use my arms to hoist myself up into a passing train where Mister Porter Abel waited—a train on which the Conductor was not employed—and after I hoisted myself up into this train, I would awaken to the sound of Friedrich's soft breathing and the sight of the muted light coming in the door from the nursing station. And physical pain. The pain was almost always worse at night. Still, pain or not, it was always a comfort to board that train, to awaken, and to be released from the night terrors.

What a shock, then, when I realized that the Conductor was right there with me in the hospital ward, standing by my bedside, his small hand on my forehead and his high woman's voice speaking to me in soothing tones. Then I remembered that, while sometimes shrill and high, the Conductor had never spoken in the tones of a woman, and his hands were in fact large and blunt, not at all like these hands. The minute I realized these things, the Conductor laughed uncertainly, almost with embarrassment, then faded, as if he had played an elaborate trick that didn't quite come off.

And then Sister Editha came into view. "Oh, come now, Emer," she was saying. "What is so frightening about me?"

"It was the white . . ." I gasped, unable, because of fear and pain, to finish the sentence. "The white . . ."

"My wimple," she concluded, touching the starched band that ran across her forehead, and then her chest, which was also covered with white cloth.

Much later, when I told Harp about the hospital, he said that—in his mind's eye—he could see Sister Editha's face, and the white cloth framing it. Hers would have been the face of a medieval woman, he said, a face that Hans Memling or Rogier van der Weyden would have carefully and lovingly transferred to a canvas or an altarpiece. He had come to know such paintings and altarpieces well, the man I loved, as, according to him, looking at such things in quiet places was his only escape from public life. He read art history and, when travelling on speaking tours, eagerly visited museums.

"I've come to sit with you," Sister Editha said that night when for just a few moments I had confused her with the Conductor. "And I will tell you a story if you like."

I nodded. I was still in pain. But I was suffering even more from the suspicion that my mother no longer wanted anything to do with me, and that sooner or later I would be in the sole custody of the Conductor.

"Life is full of sorrowful leave-takings," Sister Editha said, as if she knew my thoughts.

In the darkest part of a moonless night, coyotes could occasionally be heard far off on the prairie. And now and then a train, the sound of which was like a long, slow exhalation of breath—a death rattle or a lover's sigh—that became fainter and fainter. I always waited for the sound of a whistle, but on this night, none came.

Sister Editha seemed to be made entirely of cloth, except for her medieval face, which sometimes, like the painted faces of the women saints she resembled, was filled not so much with pain, but with an acceptance of pain. Her habit looked as if it were fashioned by wind, though of course there was no wind inside our room.

The coyotes were singing in the distance. "Wolf," I said, frightened.

"Rogier van der Weyden was the most compassionate of painters when it came to women," Harp would later tell me. "Even in grief and disarray, his women are so pure, so beautiful."

"No, Emer," Sister Editha said. "Those are coyotes and are far away and will never worry us."

I wasn't so sure but relaxed, anyway, in the wake of her gentle voice in the night hospital.

"When I was a child," she said, "there were still wolf-charmers and wolf-walkers in my village, which might explain the lack of wolves. But the old people still spoke of wolves and crossed themselves when they did. Some of the wolves they spoke of had names and personalities: Der Terror," she said, "or Todesfall. But they were there only in memory.

"I was born in the village of Friesach, in Carinthia," Sister Editha confided, "in the foothills of the Gurktal Alps. Our house backed on the Metnitz River—we always had an old boat or two tied to our walls—and my father was a tanner, so having the water nearby was a blessing. The water was swiftly moving, though, especially in spring, and sometimes children were swept away and drowned in it."

I couldn't see her medieval face well enough in the faint light that came from the nursing station in the hall to know if some child she had been close to had been swept away. Or not.

"I was one of those children," she continued, calmly. "I loved to play in the old boats tied to the back of our house, and one day in spring I lost my footing and I fell into the river. I remember the town of Friesach passing by me while I was in that river. I recall seeing the shadowed underside of the Neumarkter Bridge while I navigated one of its three arches and tried desperately to attach my fingers to its smooth stone pylons. I did not know how to swim, and I was certain I was going to die. . . . I was already in mourning for the wonderful valley and the town that I loved and my parents and sisters and brothers. But I soon realized that my sobs only brought more and more river water into my lungs, so I forced myself to stop crying and to concentrate on keeping my head above the water. Soon I was passing the little gardens, each entirely different from the other, that sat along the river on the outskirts of the town, and I thought of how hard the old gentlemen, my own grandfather included, worked to maintain their flowers and vegetables and fruit trees, and the simple goodness of these gardens seemed so poignant to me that I could not agree to leave earth behind."

So Sister Editha did not die when she was a child, although she could feel what she called the dark curtain of death falling over her. Instead, she told me, she climbed out of the water and was guided through a gate at the river's edge into one of the small walled gardens full of fruit trees and roses, not by one of the old gentlemen but by a beautiful lady. The lady sang to the little girl Sister Editha was then, and then she gave her a peculiar kind of cake. When asked, the lady said she was Saint Elizabeth of Thuringia. Then she opened her cloak, and a fountain of roses flowed from the sacred heart on her breast.

I think now of this quiet young sister coming to my fretful bedside to gently distract me from my pain with stories of her own lost childhood set in a landscape she would never see again, and I am deeply moved by her kindness. Even now I believe every word she told me, in the way I believed the fairy tales my father used to tell the whole family on long, frigid prairie evenings such as these.

Sister Editha was silent for quite a while. Letting the memory picture form in her mind, I suppose. And also letting a similar picture form in my mind. I heard the coyotes again, but now they sounded like the smallest and most nervous of the Company dogs, and I paid them no mind.

"All of this," Sister Editha eventually said, "changed me profoundly. The world became both vivid and distant at the same time, as if there were polished window glass between me and my surroundings. And to this day, my hands and wrists carry the scent of roses and of that wonderful cake."

She held one wrist up to my nose, and indeed, there seemed to be a cinnamon-like perfume coming from it.

"The beautiful lady told me two things," Sister Editha confided. "One was that I must entreat my parents to take me to the convent as soon as possible—Saint Elizabeth of Thuringia had been a cloistered child herself, you see—and the other was that I should minister to the sick and lame. Then she led me to the opposite side of the garden, where there was a road leading into town, opened the old wooden garden gate, and bid me depart."

Sister Editha's mother had wept when her little girl returned home and told her story. But she had not disbelieved her. Her father had looked at his small daughter with awe, and then he had begun to pray. "They were both very beautiful and near to me, and I was very moved by them and saw them profoundly through the polished glass that separated me from them," Sister Editha told me. "But I could hear the sick and lame in the convent hospital calling and calling in my brain, like the largest of the three bells in the village church belfry." She looked towards the light coming from the nursing station in the hall, and for the first time, I could see her exquisitely translucent eyelids, the branching of the veins in them.

"Lame," a word I had not much considered until that moment, but one I would come to know intimately in the future. "Am I lame?" I asked.

"Not yet," she said. "Though if we can help you to walk, you may very well be lame in the future. Now you are still in the land of the sick." She delivered these facts without a trace of pity, something I was grateful for. It made me feel included in, rather than excluded from, her mind, and I wanted to know her better. Even at that very early age I knew that my self, in whatever state she was, would need to be available for friendship, and I could feel a relationship developing between me and the small spirit-struck girl that Sister Editha had been.

She resumed her story. "After I was cloistered, I saw my family only on rare occasions, and only through a grille: a prison of my own choice. They were somewhere near when I put aside my white novitiate clothing and accepted Christ as my true bridegroom, but I don't remember if I was able to see them."

As she spoke, I was imagining Sister Editha standing naked at an altar so ornate it included angels and devils and the baby angels my mother had called putti. I wondered if the neighbour's new-born baby, who had been blown right out of her mother's arms, had become a putti (the way I would have put it then and through adulthood, until Harp corrected me with the singular "putto"), and if so, whether she would have her picture painted on a ceiling somewhere. And wings.

When I asked Sister Editha if she had had no clothes on, she giggled like a twelve-year-old girl, then finally said, "Oh, Emer, I was never without my shift. I started wearing this habit and wimple at that time," she added, wistfully. "Or one just like it."

"Did you ever see that lady again?" I asked. "The one in the garden?"

"No," Sister Editha admitted, becoming serious again. "No, I never did. She was a messenger, I think, and once she had told me what to do, her messaging, her ministering—in my life—was finished. But I learned more about her in the convent, where we were taught how to read so that we could understand the Bible. Sometimes at night, when I was half awake, I became confused and thought that the lady, whom I dreamt about often, had performed a miraculous abduction and had really become my mother. But she hadn't, of course. I still had the strong memory of and my longing for my own dear mother. But the notion of this other mother, and the polished glass that stood between my real mother and me, was a sorrowful leave-taking for me."

Sister Editha drew her legs up under her and leaned back against the foot of the iron bedstead. There was something in this gesture that reminded me of my Ontario cousins and me, how we would exchange confidences curled up at the ends of beds, theirs or mine.

How young Sister Editha seemed at that moment! She was still hardly more than a girl.

"As I said, that leave-taking was quiet. I barely noticed it until later, until the final departure. I was busy with my studies towards nursing the sick and the lame." She paused. "And I was busy with my friends. We were all still children, you see, so we played in the dormitory at night. When the full-fledged nuns assumed we were asleep, and went to sleep themselves, we pretended to be the martyred saints we knew about. Often there was romance in this, and sometimes we felt as if we had fallen in love with each other. When one of us was pretending to be the abandoned lover or husband, for example, or when the saint was forsaking the ways of the flesh and the ways of men to devote herself to God and to her true bridegroom, Jesus. We allowed ourselves some passionate, tearful embraces at that time.

Everything we understood about that kind of drama came from the lives of the saints. Truly, it was all we knew of the variances of human nature." Sister Editha smiled. "All this was mimed, of course. . . . We never managed to save up our twenty secular words until the end of the day. And truly twenty words would not have been enough for the tragedies we were enacting."

"Danny, my brother, likes the saints," I told her. "But he does not believe in God."

Nothing about this information seemed to alarm Sister Editha. Nor did it cause her to stray from her story. There were two friends in particular, she told me: the children who had been cloistered since they were five and eight years old, and who would later become Sister Philomena and Sister Hildegard. "As you can see," Sister Editha said, "they became my companions for life. When nursing sisters were needed for the missions of the northern Great Plains, we all three—still hungry for drama, I suppose, or perhaps hungry for the wonderful and unlimited secular speech that would be permitted to us if we agreed to take the journey— put up our hands. And here we are." She sighed. "We were all only girls at the time. We knew nothing of the world, or of travel. Though we had heard and seen trains, we had never boarded such a beast, and the only ship we could imagine was the one that held Saint Ursula's virgins, and that we had seen in a very old painting on the convent wall. I will leave the story of our journey for another day."

She was quiet then and I imagined that she was thinking about the little girl she had been, and about the village in the beautiful mountains where she had lived so happily until a vision of gingerbread and roses had swept her out of those mountains and out of her childhood, towards the harsh life that awaited her in a cold, cold climate.

I looked at Sister Editha in the light that came in from the nursing station and saw her face, finely drawn and filled with the flawless crystal tears that I would later be told might have been painted on her cheeks by an artist like Grünewald or Dirk Bouts or Rogier van der Weyden. I thought about Sister Editha's mother and the second terrible, sorrowful parting and all the oceans and continents between them. And then I began to cry in a way that I had not cried since I was taken to the hospital. I was picturing the face of my own mother. I was weeping because for the first time, I realized I would never see her again. And I understood that I was alone.

So we remained there, Sister Editha and I, in that afterlife of piercing light or dark sky, the coyotes singing at night, and the blue and purple distances of the northern Great Plains.

A week or two of strangely foggy days followed Sister Editha's night visit. I was curiously interested in whether the window was misted on the inside or the outside of the glass, sometimes whispering the words "inside or outside" as if this were a question that I was required to put to myself over and over. On one of those days, I again was taken into the operating room by Doctor Carpenter, who said he needed to make some revisions to the bones that were inside me. I felt as if I were my mother's one good dress: in need of amendment. And I did not want to be a dress; I did not want to be altered. So I cried. But though two or three kind voices—including Doctor Carpenter's own voice—said, "Don't cry, Emer," the Conductor's voice said, "Prepare the ether," and soon I had been modified by everyone there into air and into darkness.

For two or three days after that, I was busy reassembling my body. In my mind, I was always climbing a tall, tall ladder, trying to get as far away from the operating table as I could. The Conductor's breathy laughter was down below. And was itself a kind of grey mist: I was also trying to get as far away from it as I could. Finally, I succeeded, broke through the vapour, and experienced a completely clear afternoon, during which I found myself coveting a colourful set of cards with which Friedrich was playing solitaire. He showed them to me, gleefully, happy in the knowledge that he could not bring even one of them over to me, and nor could I scramble to his bedside to snatch them.

Later that evening, Doctor Angel visited me and told me about a phantom palace hotel that had tried to get itself built in a city like the one where the hospital was situated. "Tried but failed," he said. "But its skeleton is still there. Oddly, it is named after a river valley, the Qu'Appelle. Very beautiful river moving through these northern plains. The river refused to be stolen by the hotel. Refused the hijacking of its name, I figure. Made a ghost hotel out of it."

"Qu'Appelle? Who calls, Emer?" Although he addressed me when he said this, I knew he was talking to himself, in that way he had that was not quite singing. "Did you know, Emer, that Qu'Appelle means 'who calls'?"

The next morning brought Mister Porter Abel. He was an astonishingly happy sight, talking and laughing and jangling his keys and tipping his buttoned cap to everyone he met. Including me.

I could still see the exhausted sorrow in him. But when Friedrich sat up and smiled, he smiled as well. And when he reached my bedside I held out my good hand, and he could tell I really wanted to give him a hug. We were both delighted to see him, and I could tell that he knew it.

"Who is this here?" he asked. "What happened to that little girl who used to be here?" He looked with surprise at the cast that now covered half of my upper body and both of my legs. He produced a velvet horse from one pocket and a seashell from the other. "This one," he said, placing the small horse near my hand, "this one is from one of those big fancy hotels you go on and on about—one of those gift shops in one of those lobbies." He paused and looked very serious for a moment or two. "I had my friend in the dining car get two of these for me. One for you. And one for Miranda. My daughter," he added in case I had forgotten. "The one just about your age."

"Why your friend?" I whispered. Each time my body was re-arranged, my voice receded. But then, oddly, it came back stronger than before within a few days. I wanted to know why Mister Porter Abel had sent the dining car waiter to the gift shop and had not gone himself. He seemed to understand my question.

"I can't just stroll around one of those lobbies or look around one of those gift shops," he said. "No telling what could happen in a place like that."

Why? I wanted to say again, wanting the reasoning behind this restriction, but I couldn't manage the sound. We both stayed quiet for a while, thinking.

"And this one is a sea urchin from Nova Scotia," Mister Porter said, breaking the silence and changing the subject. He placed a round object near my face. I studied the small balloon-like shell; it was like a miniature paper lantern. "Nova Scotia is where I would hang my hat if I were ever permitted to hang it anywhere for any period of time at all," he continued. "I picked up this sea urchin on the beach not far from where I might one day *permanently* hang my hat. Miranda herself has a hundred of these things in her room, so I didn't bother to get one for her. But I did ask her if I should pick one up for you. And she said you might like it."

I remembered now. The girl who was such a trial to her mother.

Friedrich began to sing something very sad and low and German. Sometimes he did this (as he had with the "Mein Vater" song) to try to keep people out. But just as often he did it to draw people in, as he was doing now. He would be interested in getting Mister Porter Abel's attention. I knew that.

"Who is that fellow over there?" the porter asked me now. "Why's he got such a broken heart?"

"I am singing something very beautiful," said Friedrich, feigning indignation, but pleased as punch that he had caused Mister Porter Abel to turn to him. "I do not have a broken heart."

"Abel," I said, recalling this porter's name, and wanting to draw him back.

"What can I do for you, sugar cake?" he asked. "Good for you for remembering my name is Abel," he added.

I wasn't ready to say anything else, so he carried on without me. "Look at you! You are so covered up with icing sugar I can't even find you. When did they cover you with all this delicious stuff?" He rapped his knuckles on my cast, then mimed spooning it up to his mouth and swallowing it.

I could not remember the resetting of my bones or the application of the cast. There had been rubber tubing, and a mask was held to my face by the Conductor. I remembered that Doctor Angel was saying one of his poems to Doctor Carpenter at the operating table, and they were each mirror images of the other.

"All sailors have broken hearts," Mister Porter Abel said suddenly. "It's all that constant going away to sea. In Nova Scotia there are a lot of heartbroken young men around. Either they are sad because they miss the sea, or they are sad because they have fallen in love and will have to be separated from their beloved in order to *go* to the sea. Often both these things are going on at the same time. Lots of heartbreak." He was drumming his fingers on my cast thoughtfully.

I could hear the Conductor whispering in my brain. "Some of them don't ever come back from the sea," he said. His pale blue face, tight with concentration, had begun to perspire along the edge of the silver-and-ginger-coloured hair that fell out from under his cap. It was as if he were trying and trying to solve a difficult puzzle that wasn't coming clear. "Sometimes the sea gobbles them right up," he said, smiling quickly, showing his grey teeth, then twisting away.

"I have two sons who are sailors," said Mister Porter Abel, who was pacing now and looking around the room. He walked to the corner, picked up a chair, and brought it back to my bedside. "I remarked to them that by venturing out onto the sea, they had chosen to travel in the opposite direction from me. Away from me." He settled into the chair. "My job is to rattle across this big hunk of rock and dirt. Could have got them both a pretty good wage doing the same thing. But they chose to splash around in the ocean. They make pictures of their hearts with seashells—they call them sailor's valentines—while they are out there on that ocean. Next time, I will bring you one of those pictures—one of those *valentines*—I promise."

Friedrich had stopped singing. I could tell that he was listening. Abel looked up quickly towards the door and then down again at me. I couldn't move but could imagine the exquisiteness of Sister Editha hovering in the doorway, then gliding off down the hall.

"Is that man your doctor?" Mister Porter Abel asked, proving my imagination wrong. "Think he was," he said. "You, cupcake, were delivered to me, then delivered *by* me. I have seen plenty of luggage and lots of packages on that train, but you were by far the most interesting. You were delivered to me, and I delivered you to him."

I recalled two doctors. The argument that ricocheted between them. "Two," I said.

He laughed. "You want two valentines?" he said. "Well, I guess I could arrange that, could get my sons to work on one apiece. I guess you want to give one of them to your friend here. And keep one for yourself, of course."

I could practically hear Friedrich listening, and I was mortified.

"I don't want one," said Friedrich. He had stopped singing the beautiful song. By now I knew that a good part of Friedrich's job with the Company had been to sing these heartfelt tunes. There were cycles of them, and almost always they were about winter. When Friedrich first told me about the song cycles, I thought he meant icicles because of something he called the Winterreise cycle. His mother had played the piano and had taught him how to sing such strange, haunting songs.

"Regularly," said Mister Porter Abel, "regularly, a man will very much want something he claims not to want at all." I was now not sure if he was speaking to me or if this remark was directed at Friedrich.

There was a long silence in the room.

Then Friedrich started to sing again. "*In stiller Nacht*," he began, those syllables hanging in the air.

I knew nothing of German lieder then, nothing of Brahms beyond the lullaby that my mother had sometimes sung, and that I believed was hers alone. Nothing of the icicles that Friedrich had talked about, which were so cold, and so sad, and were often somehow connected to a man called Schumann. Harp, who like me had taken piano lessons as a child, but in more recent decades had come to have access to more sophisticated forms of music, later told me that *In stiller Nacht* was the most beautiful love song ever created, and to hear a boy soprano spontaneously singing it would be one of life's most mysterious moments. It would be a wonder—more wonderful even than the child that Sister Editha had been when she encountered the perfect lady with the gingerbread in the garden. And he recited the words in English so that I would never forget them and would always associate those words with him.

But it was Friedrich who prepared me for adult love and its subsequent sorrow. Singing this song in a hospital room in Saskatchewan, he made Mister Porter Abel close his eyes as if in physical pain. Though I could not see this, I knew it was true. And in me were feelings of loss and helplessness larger than I had ever known, ones I would later recognize once I came to know the man I loved. I am an old woman now, but I have never become as ancient or as fragile as I was listening to Friedrich sing that song. I remembered the winter windows of our Ontario house, and then the drifts of white snow near the seldom-used white door of our Saskatchewan house. And while he sang, ferns made of frost unfurled on the wall I was once again facing, with my soft side pressing into the mattress and the hard carapace of the cast covering my other side like a shell.

Today I returned to Willow School. Thankfully the wind was down and the sky was clear, so the snow tires and chains moved me safely and swiftly along the road, and no snow was blown out of the ditches on either side. "'The sun has gone from the shining sky, bye baby bye,'" the children sang. "'The dandelions have closed their eyes, bye baby bye,'" they sang with such enthusiasm it was possible to believe they had murdered the tot. I follow a rail line for part of my way to this school. Though it is a section away, because of atmospheric clarity, on my return, I could see the milk train on the branch line. I can't even glimpse a plume of smoke from a locomotive's stack on the horizon without thinking about Harp. His offhandedness, his indifference; sometimes feigned, sometimes genuine.

To spend time with Harp, it was necessary for me to ride the branch line railroad to one of the three prairie cities where we could blend into a crowd and not be known—where, to be more accurate, he would not be known. I myself was not recognizable beyond the neighbourhood of the small town in which—as an adult—I had always lived, and where I continue to live, and the scattered school-houses that I visit with my triangle and tuning fork. Still, Harp argued, my limp made me more visible than other unknowns. He said this in a teasing sort of way, and I laughed and said, "Perhaps you are right. I can't exactly dart into bushes and hide. I can't really run away." We were sitting side by side on a settee in one of the hotel rooms, talking. "Like you can," I added.

The circumstances of Harp's life made it impossible for him to love me in an ordinary, daily kind of way. Or so he told me, and with time, so I came to believe.

There were his wives, of course—two during the time we were close to each other. But more significantly, there was the early fame brought to him by his enormous, and almost accidental, medical discovery; a discovery so brilliant it changed and prolonged the lives of countless people around the world. Ironically, it did not prolong his own life, though it changed it completely. He was a callow and often madcap young man when the idea that would result in the discovery visited him in the middle of the night. Suddenly his youth was over in an afternoon, and he would never be permitted to retrieve it. He was thrown into an adulthood of celebrity that no one could have prepared him for, and that nothing could save him from.

There it sat, this discovery, stubborn and impossible to ignore. It would be the source of arguments concerning its genesis and the vanity of the discoverer. It would be the cause of fist fights, broken glass, and broken friendships in the lab Harp loved so much. It would be the provider of honours he privately doubted he deserved, and it would be the reason for lecture halls filled with men twice his age, and with twice his experience, rising to a standing ovation when he entered.

Once the discovery had been achieved, it ran away from him like a taunting delinquent child who desired his attention but also wanted to discredit him. A few academics spent their entire careers combing through research files in order to find others who might have seeded his discovery, and whose achievements remained unsung. The heads of various scientific departments at the university where he worked claimed that the discovery had, in part, been theirs, and they used their connections to ensure some of the prizes he received were shared with them. In society, his wives were completely defined by it (whether they wished to be or not), and might just as well have been called Mrs. Discovery the First or Mrs. Discovery the Second. He himself would never be able to take pleasure from it. Thrown into a world where he was required to wear uncomfortable clothing and stand awkwardly at multiple public lecterns, he was ultimately embarrassed by his lack of speaking skills, and by what he believed to be a fraudulent version of himself on view for all to see. He took to drink. His marriages failed. His friendships weakened. He was humiliated by the fact that despite generous public funding, he was unable to discover anything else that came close to his original triumph. By the time he was forty, he knew he was his own ghost, haunting his own magnificent past.

And so, he turned to the study—and sometimes to the amateur practice—of visual art. He read the art history texts in various university libraries, or he purchased large tomes from academic presses. On his American and European speaking tours, he spent much of his time walking in what I imagine would have been an intense, purposeful way through one museum after another, memorizing the pictures of the artists he had read about and trying to puzzle out their techniques.

Never a bystander, he wanted a role in the game. And so, Harp began to paint. He was not a fantasist regarding his slim allotment of artistic talent. In fact, he was comforted by the knowledge that this endeavour, which gave him so much pleasure, would bring him no further notoriety. In the quiet, easy company of professional landscape artists he had come to know, he took the northern and western routes of railways and then the spurs of railways to mining settlements in the north or one-street prairie towns in the west. He had a hell of a time, he told me, and would continue to tell me, finding a week here or a week there. Once he found those weeks, however, he painted outdoors, furiously, without much originality or success, in all kinds of weather, and slept in a bedroll surrounded by the snores of his friends. Short of being dead, he was as distanced as he would ever be from the peculiar, unnatural life the discovery had forced him to live.

He was fresh out of one of those bedrolls when he walked in through the door of my schoolroom decades ago, when I was still a full-time teacher. He needed a shave, his clothes were wrinkled, he smelled faintly of tobacco and alcohol. The children, and the parents (for by now news of his impending visit had been telegraphed through the kitchens of my students) awaiting his arrival, were charmed by his lack of showiness.

We, the children and I, often wrote to public figures—the King, the prime minister, Lucy Maud Montgomery—and often, if they lived in North America, we invited them to visit our little school. In almost every case a standard form letter appeared after months in our mailbox, with the notable exceptions of Lucy Maud and Thornton Wilder, both of whom wrote a few lines in their own hand. And Harp, who not only replied but took us up on the invitation.

Later he would tell me that he had replied to the letter and the invitation because he wanted an excuse to be on the spurs of the railway with his pals. The children had not invited him but merely praised him, at my suggestion. Unlike politicians, he had nothing to gain by a visit. In fact, he had invited himself. I remembered this when I limped across the sunny schoolroom towards him and held out my hand, which he took in both of his.

He gave an honest and straightforward talk about the discovery to the children, good-naturedly answering their not always appropriate questions, and those of their parents. Then, after the adult crowd had dispersed, he settled into a vacant seat near the back of the room, where he laughed and joked with the tall boys who were lounging there.

At lunchtime he walked out to the schoolyard and dismissed Clarence Strong, the farmer who had driven him from the station, and who had stood patiently waiting near one small calf occupying the back of his truck, all morning long. Then Harp walked back into the schoolroom, ate more than half of my bagged lunch, and went outside again to use the privy.

When he returned, I said that surely Clarence would be coming back soon to take him to the Muenster Hotel, where he was staying. He looked surprised. "But you have a car yourself," he said, referring to my very old, rusted, and unreliable Ford, parked near the fence.

I had fended off the advances of a school board trustee in that car, and the memory of this came immediately to mind. I stood, leaned on my stick, and looked at this famous man with suspicion. The big boys had gone out to the yard for lunch, along with the rest of the class.

Glancing out the window, Harp said, "The sound of children playing is a beautiful thing. How does it happen so spontaneously? They are like crickets or cicadas: put a dozen of them in the right habitat, and this high-pitched trilling noise will occur, even during the shortest recess. There is no method of creating the sound without children. No one teaches them how to do this. There is no rehearsal."

Then, looking at me, he moved forward, took the hand that rested on my cane, steadied and straightened my shoulders as I recovered my balance after the cane's removal, and repeated, "There is no rehearsal."

I hadn't much experience with men. There was one young man during my teacher training. But beyond physical attraction that we both knew we could neither admit to nor satisfy, we hadn't much in common. I often wanted to be alone. I preferred reading and music. And the young man considered such things to be too womanly to engage in except in a mild attempt to please me. Eventually we drifted apart, and he found someone else.

But of course, I had always loved Danny, my brother, and Friedrich, with whom I had everything in common, including an interest in men. But despite my lack of experience, I knew this man, this famous man who had his hands on my shoulders, was about to kiss me. Then two small girls burst through the door, and the moment was lost.

Later I asked if he had meant to kiss me then. He denied it, of course. But by then there wasn't a detail so small that he couldn't deny it.

Still, in those early moments, his nervous laughter and how he stepped away at the entrance of the children had seemed human to me. And without being fully conscious of it, I had opened to him.

We ate a supper of mashed potatoes, string beans, roast beef, and gravy in the Muenster Hotel with all the other tables filled with townspeople and many more country people outside, peering through the windows. This was the first time a celebrity had visited the region—and everyone wanted a glimpse.

Harp, as I would come to call him, talked about art for two-thirds of the meal, the landscapes of Constable, I recall, and sometimes, to my shock, disparagingly. I later learned that he had picked up these opinions from the modernist painters who had admitted him into their circle entirely because of the discovery, not because of his knowledge or practice of art, something he would eventually sense and be hurt by.

Then he changed the subject to the naming of Saskatchewan towns. He had passed through the hamlets of Romance, Kandahar, and Wolverine, he told me, on his way to my school, which was five miles north of Humboldt. "Sounds like the emotional deterioration of one of my wives," he said, grinning.

I laughed. But, of course, wondered how many wives he had had. Not as many as he had pretended, as it turned out. But enough that he had become tired of the subject of marriage and was reluctant to discuss it. I would come to know that there were many subjects he was reluctant to discuss.

It was almost scandalous that I, a schoolteacher, should have dinner with him in the hotel dining room. Almost but not quite, the dinner being such a public experience, with the theatrical light of a blinding prairie sunset being poured in through the large and plentiful windows. And with no liquor present.

"I wish we were somewhere else," he said. A small-town boy himself, he understood the rules.

I was at the time unconscious of what I desired from him. But I knew I wanted more. I looked at his hands; the way his fingers opened his wallet and overpaid the bill lying in the wooden tray.

We held each other's gaze before I rose with my stick to leave.

"I know the name of your school," he said.

That was the beginning, then, right there. In the prosaic hotel of my own hometown, with the local gravy congealing on the plate.

I n total darkness, or in the frail light of dawn, I would drive to
Muenster Railway Station, where I would take a spur line into
one prairie city or another. I recall the red surprise of grain
elevators against bluish morning snow, churches that were either near
the tracks or so far away their crosses and onion domes seemed point-
less on such a vast horizon. And when I arrived, I would check into
a hotel so grand and large, it seemed like a madman's folly in the midst
of one small, tidy prairie city or another. Still, it was the faux glamour
of the hotel I was stepping into that, ironically, made me feel as if
I were a woman who mattered enough not to be taken to hotel
rooms for years and years without any kind of hope of a settled
relationship.

Each time I walked into the lobby of a castle hotel, I thought of
my mother. The interiors of these empire-building, developer-fuelled
palaces were essentially all the same, and likely remain the same to
this day. Harp and I met in their rooms for so many years, we were
witness to the way furniture becomes worn and faded, or passes out

of fashion altogether in such places, how the light changes when other nearby buildings are built or torn down, or when trees that had been saplings when we first embraced have grown to maturity and now throw watery shadows across the carpets. How odd to think that I spent what passed for my emotional life watching the lovely elms of new prairie cities thicken and strengthen from hotel room windows. I can recall the moment when I saw that two of the elms that lined both sides of the street—trees I had begun to know years before— were able to touch overhead: something I knew they had been trying to do for decades.

I pointed this out to Harp.

He made no comment, disliking the mawkish side of my nature and trying to ignore it.

Tonight, I am thinking of the only time Harp came to see me at my own house. It was high summer. Almost everyone in town was either at the beach or in the dance hall in Watrous, or they were sheltering indoors, trying to avoid the sun, the dust, and the mosquitoes. I had a cord of firewood in my back garden. It had been delivered in the spring by a farmer who lived just out of town, and when he stacked it for me, he unthinkingly covered up the back gate. Because I knew Harp would want to approach the house from the back, I moved every single piece of that firewood so that he could quickly gain entrance to my screen door from the lane that ran behind the yard. I hesitate to say this because it makes me look as if I am filled with self-pity. But I had to use the stick, of course, and that made it even more difficult.

Our arrangements were always as difficult and awkward as moving that cord of firewood.

But what I didn't know while I deliberately lifted one log at a time, then fitted each into place in a new woodpile as if I were Psyche carrying out yet another of Venus's categorization chores, was how much this upcoming visit would confuse me, and disturb the foundations of our love. Our love, you see, was like those castle hotels: full of private hidden spaces and beautiful velvet furniture, and no responsibility for tidying up afterwards. It had nothing to do with that kitchen where, after rising from my own bed, I turned towards the stove to cook his lunch.

After the task with the wood was completed, I stood at the screen door looking through its rusted mesh, waiting for him to arrive, and soon I saw him at the end of the lane. He walked quickly with his head down and the collar of his jacket pushed up high. The word "furtive" slipped into my mind for the first time, and it hurt me, regardless of the fact that I was complicit in everything that might have made him furtive.

This was many years ago—a different era, as they now say. There was extreme poverty and dust everywhere. All men's faces were shadowed under the brims of their hats, and most walked rapidly from place to place with their hands hidden in the pockets of their overcoats. Like anxious grey ghosts with a dusty wind of wariness and remorse trailing behind them. Extraordinary as I may have believed him to be, Harp, the man I loved, looked—from a distance—the same as any other man of the time.

But it was extraordinary to see him navigating the unmanicured lane behind my house, he in whom longing for the aesthetic was lodged so recently and yet so deeply. I had never seen him glance out a hotel room window without examining the placement of each tree on the boulevard or the curve of the avenue. Now there he was, walking through vernacular space organized around the principles of economy, utility, and chance.

Several years ago, after Harp visited me in the castle hotel of the capital city of Saskatchewan, I wandered outside the lobby and walked under those magnificent elms, which were draped—fresh and innocent—with the luminous green of late spring. I was heading towards a park that I hoped would be filled with lilacs, because I knew the combination of new lilacs and the soft green of the elms would last only a day or two, and I wanted to be able to look at something as easy and soft as that, something I could count on.

As always, the posturing of the park, which was indeed filled with lilacs, touched me in some way and made me long for a past that had never been mine, not even in the ancestral sense. There was the rose garden, the decorative scrolled underpinnings of the benches, the hint here and there of balustrade, the floral clock carefully rendered with yellow and orange chrysanthemums. Men who, were it not for the Depression, would have been working in factories or toiling on the land had brought all this into being in the most solemn way, without a hint of irony, and they would have been gratified by bringing England's idea of beauty to a stolen landscape. In winter, the men seeded these plants and kept them alive in glass houses. And now, in summer, they pumped water from the rivers to keep the same plants hydrated and free of the dust that was killing absolutely everything outside of the city limits.

I rested on a bench and was preparing to relive the hours that I had just spent with the man I loved. This always occurred: these moments of reflection after our meetings, during which I would carefully examine what he had said, or how he had responded to what I had said. I would also recall several of his gestures and try to measure the level of affection transmitted by them, usually with exaggeration. And I would wonder if he was thinking similar thoughts wherever he was now, and almost always concluded that he was not. I might have had an imagination, an inner life. But in the end, I was a realist after all.

I saw the boy first. He was of medium height and spare build, with beautifully shaped, strong shoulders and upper arms. His hair was black and curly and lifting in the soft, declining breeze of early evening. I was a hundred feet away, but nonetheless could sense how thick his eyebrows and eyelashes were, and how startling and green his eyes. A coil of rope hung from his wrist. After uncurling the rope on the ground, he tied the opposite ends of it to the trunks of two mature maple trees that were growing perhaps twenty feet apart. The result was like a clothesline at hip level. I assumed that he was one of the men who looked after the park, that something was being engineered, staked out. Then I noticed his bare feet.

At that moment I saw the girl. She emerged slowly from the shadow thrown by one of the maples and seemed a shadow herself. She hadn't his quickness, or his vitality. Or so I thought, at first. Nothing about her in the beginning was anything other than shadows. Her soft grey clothing, her vague brown hair, and her slow steps seemed the very essence of somnolence. The boy walked towards her, took her hand, and led her to the rope, where they stood quietly, not talking, not moving. Then the girl shook her head so that her hair lifted from her scalp. She bent over at the waist and arranged a ponytail at the back of her skull, the gesture alarmingly muscular in the midst of the quietness that returned to the scene the moment the task was completed. I had rarely seen young people stand so still. They were once more holding hands, but they did not look at each other.

The beautiful elms gleamed around the perimeter of the park. The lilacs were in bloom. Then the suggestion of a breeze came again, shaking the shadows of the maples. And the boy, as if unlocked by the air currents, leapt onto the rope, where he danced for a moment or two. Testing its strength, I decided. A couple of moments later he made the short jump back to earth, and it was her turn.

What a performance! It put me in mind of Friedrich on the days when he sat up straight in his bed and performed what he called the Great Memorizations. Shakespeare usually.

The boy walked beside the girl, holding her hand as she made the first tentative steps of that strange gavotte; one partner on the ground and the other unsteadily navigating the rope. I realized that were it not for that one spot where her hand touched his, her equilibrium would be gone.

It was during these first moments, when she was destabilized and awkward, that I saw how beautiful she was. And I knew that he saw it too: the tenderness between them became palpable. There was something about her now that I recognized—the quick turn of her head, the straightening of a shoulder, the enormity of unexpressed feeling—and I realized that she put me in mind of Tatiana, such a silent presence in our children's ward.

Beyond the girl's attempts to find balance in such an unfamiliar situation, there was no real tension in the scene. I knew as well as they did that the rope was near the ground, so nothing alarming could possibly occur. Even if he let go of her hand, which, like all teachers, he would surely do at some point in the performance, her fall to earth would be only a cause for laughter between them, not a tragedy. But I also knew the distance from the earth would steadily increase as time passed, along with the danger. Except for these carefully planned and infrequent duets, he would stop looking at her tenderly and holding her hand. For most of her life she would dance this gavotte alone. But her dependency on her love—so touchingly revealed at this moment—would become complicated and painful. And like mine, it would probably never end.

Friedrich and I became two connected, yet stationary, moon-like orbs occasionally visited by the increasingly mysterious and increasingly distant life around us. As we lay in that room, we believed everything and everyone beyond our door was in a fascinating state of flux, an unpredictable solar system that was always spinning while we remained still. Although married to our beds, and with little or no contact with the rest of the hospital, we speculated tirelessly about what might be occurring there; I would not be so vividly attentive to the lives being lived in distant parts of large buildings until much later, when I spent time in the castle hotels in order to be with the man I loved. And Friedrich, too, imagined and intuited the details and personalities of the hospital. He quite seriously believed that babies he had never seen were soothed in the nursery by the German lullabies he sang, and I began to believe the new-born baby who had blown away was in the nursery being fixed in the same way as I was being fixed in the ward.

Unless I was that baby, which I sometimes, confusingly, believed in dreams.

We begged to see the babies, or at least Friedrich begged to see them, and quite eloquently. All I could do in relation to babies was say the word "please." But not one infant was brought into our room. We never even heard a baby's cry. Those lullabies Friedrich sang brought the twins into my mind, though, and filled me with homesickness and remorse. Had I been kind enough to them when I had them? Had I loved them enough? Memories of their perfect faces and clear eyes—even when filled with tears—caught at my heart. And then I would want my mother.

One day, Sister Editha came into our room with Sister Hildegard to lift and turn me as Sister Editha had promised they would do. I was very much looking forward to this as I had been facing the wall for what seemed a very long time, and familiarity, plus a gradual clearance of my mind, had made it less interesting than it was when I first came to know it. Also, I could tell by what was being said by Doctor Carpenter and the nursing sisters that they had been encouraging Friedrich to sit up on the edge of his bed. Although I was deeply envious of such physical freedom and change of point of view, I wanted to see him sitting there and enjoying such things.

They turned me. Sister Editha praying the whole time because of the large cast Doctor Carpenter had placed all over my body, and not wanting to break it, and Sister Hildegard being bossy and practical about how to move me and when.

How long had I been in that hospital by then? Perhaps days, perhaps months. Mister Porter Abel had been to see me at least three or four times, and to do that, he would have had to cross the entire country. Though sometimes he visited on his return trip, after he had (his words) survived the mountains once again. "Those mountains," he had said recently, more to Friedrich than to me, because I had not yet been turned that particular morning, and was facing the wall, "those mountains, which are like candy to a tourist, are pure hell for a porter. Train is always on a curve, so you are always bracing yourself. Your left leg is strained on the way out. Your right leg is strained on your way back.

You have to *ride* a train," he confided, "like a wild horse when you are on your feet all the time. You have to *ride* it like a bucking bronco."

We felt sorry for Mister Porter Abel, but as we confessed to each other weeks later, we still wanted to be in those mountains. Me more than Friedrich, who had already seen them and could therefore boast about that.

So this was the time of the day I was to be turned. It hurt and I cried for a while and Doctor Angel came and gave me a needle that made me cry harder, but a few minutes later that needle lessened the pain and I fell asleep. When I awoke, I was facing Friedrich's profile. He turned to look at me and blew an enormous pink bubble from the gum that the Company members brought to him on their visits and the nursing sisters regularly confiscated. "As much," Sister Hildegard had frequently said, "for its vulgarity as for its safety problems."

"You could choke on this," Sister Philomena told Friedrich when she was on the day shift. "But also, and importantly, a gum-chewing man is the opposite of attractive!"

"But I'm not a man!" said Friedrich. "I'm a helpless child."

"Helpless you are not," said Sister Philomena, groping under his mattress for further buried treasure. "A complete menace to the female world is what you will become."

Friedrich did not become a complete menace to the female world.

I fell asleep again after seeing Friedrich and his bubble, and when I awoke the second time, he was sitting up on the edge of his bed in his white hospital gown with a white sheet wrapped around his legs, looking for all the world like the infant Jesus on my Sunday school cards, though admittedly a little older and a little bigger. On those cards the infant Jesus is surrounded by swords of piercing light and always looks as if he is sitting on an invisible chair, or as if the lap of the Virgin Mary has been magically erased from the surroundings.

Harp, when I told him about this vision of Friedrich, said that the presence of the two nursing nuns, hovering anxiously on either side of Friedrich, would always bring to his mind European altarpieces because the clothing of nuns had not changed much over the centuries. I knew nothing of European altarpieces at the time, and still know very little, beyond what Harp told me about them and showed me in books: the pieta, a Madonna and child, or a crucifixion at the centre; the saints and angels presented on each arm in order of height or some other hierarchy; the mortals—monks and nuns and donors— small, humble, worried about mortality—kneeling uncertainly at the edges of such magnificent pageants.

That afternoon, when I was fully awake, Friedrich and I examined each other guardedly. We were both in pain because of the change in our positions, and that put tension between us. Pain, you see, always demands privacy, whether it gets it or not. Pain does not want witnesses because it does not wish to be remembered and refuses utterly to take responsibility for the humiliation it causes. We were embarrassed by our individual suffering, and we were concerned that evidence of this suffering might cause us to lose what little power we had in relation to each other. Or at least that's what I think looking back. Added to this, the nuns were attempting to convey some information—not to me, exactly, but for certain to Friedrich. "She will be here soon, Friedrich," Sister Philomena was saying. "Soon you will have another little friend to keep you company."

Another little friend. I felt the beginnings of envy. Would Friedrich prefer her to me? But that uncomfortable feeling was interrupted when Sister Philomena lifted Friedrich's knees to help him lie down again, because, as she said, "the sitting up was tiring," and he was "losing colour, and might faint." As she did this, the sheet around his waist was taken away, and I saw his thin white legs.

He did not have a right foot.

And Sister Philomena was inspecting the end of the footless leg and commenting on how nicely it was mending.

I was horrified. The Conductor, who, though dressed in his

uniform, bore a striking resemblance to Doctor Carpenter, roared like a passing train through my mind's eye and my mind's ear. Then he blew his whistle. But before anyone could get on board, he spun around, danced up the three stairs leading to the parlour car. And closed the door with a bang.

...

Shortly after this, a girl we would come to know as Tatiana was wheeled slowly, ceremoniously, into our room and taken to a space to the right of the door. She neither moved nor made a sound on her gurney, but I was certain that a veil of sun-shot snow followed in her wake as surely as if it had been part of a costume.

Doctor Carpenter was with her, walking alongside with a slow, steady pace. Two other men in white, men whom I would later learn to call the orderlies, pushed her bed and steadied the medical apparatus that surmounted it. Behind them, rendered silent by the gravity of the situation, were some members of the Company, including the daily clown, who had intended to cartwheel into the room but had met up with Tatiana's conveyance before his high jinks began. They now looked first at the child on the gurney and then at Friedrich. The clown, who today was Burt Simpson from Swift Current, began to cry quietly, his very real tears turned into black tears by the oily tear that was painted on his face. Two nurses who were not nuns and who followed the Company into the room were also weeping.

"This is Tatiana," Doctor Carpenter told us quietly, so quietly I could barely hear him. "She has been badly burned."

That explains the veil of snow, I thought. Though how it explained it, I did and still do not know.

The solemn journey that took Tatiana and her retinue to her place in the ward seemed to take hours. A bed had been removed across from me so her gurney could be wheeled into the vacant spot. There was the now familiar whispering of rubber wheels on tiles, and yet the arrival of that gurney was attended by such a tender slowness, it reminded me of the arrival of the bride in the only wedding I had witnessed as a small child back in Ontario.

Badly burned, I thought. I saw her dark blonde curls on the pure white pillow. I saw the fronds of her eyelashes and eyebrows. She looked as perfect as that faintly remembered bride had when her veil was lifted. The top sheet of Tatiana's hospital bed was not resting on her body but was tented over her and gathered at her neck. I later came to know that the cloth could not be permitted to touch her burned flesh. But without this knowledge I believed that she was suspended in the air just above her gurney, that she was floating on cold yet soft upward breezes, breezes that also held her clothing in their hands. Sister Editha, who still stood beside Friedrich, began to pray, as if knowing she was in the presence of a fellow saint. Had I understood her prayers I would have prayed alongside her, for suddenly I knew, for the first time, that Sister Editha had sainthood in her.

Much later the man I loved said that at that moment I had been witnessing one of the great processions, and that those processions always seemed to unfold in the slowest of tempos. "You were looking at a processive rendering," he said. "It could have encircled a Grecian urn," he continued, "or it could have been painted on the wall of an Egyptian tomb or an Aztec temple."

I wanted him to stop talking like this, and to pay some attention to my story of poor Tatiana. But he was in full flight, looking away from me, filled with his new knowledge of art history.

Since that moment I have come to know that the figures in these processions are often hunting. Sometimes they are fording a river on horseback or sacking a city, then bringing home the spoils from victorious campaigns. The great reproaches of crucifixions and other capital punishments, the castings out and banishments and expulsions. The panoramas filled with regal arrivals.

"The Medici returning to Florence," the man I loved had said. "A maiden being carried towards the place of sacrifice." He stopped suddenly and looked away from me towards the window of the castle hotel. And the winter trees outside. "A duke on a bier, attended by pleurants and the clergy." This delivered quietly.

"What are pleurants?" I asked.

"Mourners. Weepers."

"You mean it could have been a dance of death?" I said, hoping, in fact, for some medical information.

But no, his mind had gone elsewhere. "Sorry," he said. "I suppose I was showing off." I was the only person to whom he could talk about all the things he was learning in the academic libraries, he told me.

I softened once I understood that. It meant he needed me in some way.

"I was thinking," he said finally, "about illuminated manuscripts and about all the processions in them." There were so many that it was hard for him to recall the few he knew about. How did such manuscripts survive? he wondered. Then he told me about the word "provenance." How dukes bequeathed the precious books to their granddaughters, who married foreigners and took the books to foreign lands where they—the books—were carried off in wars and reformations. Or how Vikings attacked monasteries full of men bent over wonderfully slow, brilliantly coloured pictures, pictures painted with the tiniest of brushes, and how those Vikings knew enough to take the wonderful books with them after they murdered their creators.

...

That day the people in the Company, including the daily clown, stood huddled and silent near Friedrich's bedside. They were looking at Tatiana's bed, which was secured to the opposite wall. So extreme was her presence, so vivid, and so cold was the electric yellow-green of the aura around her that the members of this theatrical group—normally flamboyant and charismatic—seemed like any other group of ordinary adults, like a small crowd waiting for a train, or even their own audience of humble townsfolk queuing up to buy tickets to the show.

Tatiana remained motionless all afternoon and into the night. Safe under her white tent, she was like a swimmer in a cotton sea; we saw only her curls and her pale face. The next morning, however, she moaned the word "thunder." Friedrich and I, whispering across the space between us, then became certain that she had been struck by lightning, and that this explained everything.

Having myself been a victim of weather, I favoured this hypothesis. My father had told me that glass was made from lightning and sand. I thought that perhaps Tatiana's body had been turned to glass, and that this was why she didn't move.

I imagined her breaking apart, the physicality of her scattering like diamonds across the terrazzo floor, light bouncing from the facets of her bones.

Suddenly I wanted to tell my brother Danny all about her and the mysterious sensations she was causing in all of us: nursing sisters and orderlies, doctors and children. But Danny was so far away I couldn't reach him. Still, my imagination, my inner self, abruptly knew that there was a mystery associated with Danny. I almost understood what the mystery was before the darkness came and put me back to sleep.

It was because of Tatiana that I became familiar with degrees as a form of measurement of things both bad and good: degrees of temperature and distance, degrees of happiness, sadness, desire. That night Doctor Angel once again entered my room. It was he who told me about degrees of burns.

He had been thinking of a poem, he said, about a town where he had grown up, and how that town had degrees of the river. "Not its speed, exactly," he said, "but like a burn, its depth and width and general temperament," which, according to him, was described in terms of "flowing" or "pouring."

"Tatiana's burns," he said, "are of the third degree. I have no intention of letting her die," he added, shaking a glass thermometer, which he had taken from its silver case. He explained mercury to me, and what the numbers meant. I remembered that my mother had always just felt our foreheads with her cool hand when she wanted to know our temperatures.

"How much does Tatiana hurt?" I asked.

"Well." He sighed. "Thankfully not much at all, the nerves being gone. A burn like that is like snow falling into water." (I thought of the frosty veil I was convinced she owned, somehow.) "After it has achieved itself, at least, it is like that. Still, other bad things can get into the burns, and water can evaporate out. And that is the problem."

"Tell me again about your mother," I said. Then I changed my mind and asked, "Does she . . . does Tatiana have a mother?"

"Yes," he said, slipping the thermometer into my mouth. "But her mother is now wandering, and we cannot find her." He paused and ran his hand through his hair. "Not yet," he added.

Tatiana and her family were Doukhobors, he explained, and sometimes they were known to just stand up and walk away from their settlements because of their penchant for spontaneity. "They believe they are carrying the truth, you see. And maybe they are." He rubbed his temples with both hands as if the truth were lodged there and could be activated by this gesture. "It's extraordinary," he went on, "how they sense that they must constantly modify to be a part of whatever truth there is. They don't like to write things down, for instance, because of stasis."

I understood very little of this. "What is stasis?" I asked as soon as he took the thermometer away.

Doctor Angel didn't answer. "I am trying to write about the river," he confided. "And I am trying to write about its fluidity and lack of predictability. Lately I find I sometimes can't remember people's names. But I have never forgotten the name of a river. Could this be a mistake, this trying to nail down a river, trying to trap the river with words?"

"Why didn't Tatiana go with her mother on the wanderings?" I asked as my doctor squinted at the mercury in the glass tube.

"Tatiana stayed in place because of the school. She just wanted to go to school," he said while he returned the thermometer to its case and screwed on the top. He had forgotten all about me and was really talking to himself.

I thought about Tatiana being in the school, about my mother standing by the window in her own school, trying to coax more light onto the page.

I thought about Danny. How he was different from the rest of us, but also the same.

Then, while everyone in our ward breathed with the steady rhythms of sleep, Doctor Angel seemed to remember me and asked, "Have you ever thought about this hospital? Do you understand the physical structure of it? About the land on which it is built?"

I did not completely comprehend the question. But I was pretty sure the answer was no. Still, I stated what I knew. "Sister Editha and the others built this hospital," I said.

"Ah yes," he said. "Without them, it could not have existed. Remarkable! And they themselves only girls at the time." He shook his head in wonderment. I noticed that his face sagged a bit, that skin hung in a limp way below his jawline. "But we should not lose sight of the trees that were felled to make the floors and beams and clapboard of this building. Those trees are gone now from the region that they came from."

Poor Doctor Angel, I thought. He is getting old.

My own great-grandfather, on becoming old, had cursed the trees he and his sons had been forced to clear before they could have even the scantiest of pastures. "Like weeds!" he had purportedly said. The women, he complained, had never fully appreciated the labour he and his sons had endured grappling with those trees and then winching the stumps, huge and many-tentacled, out of the ground. And after the trees were cut, they began to work on the roads.

"And the wildflowers and wild grasses," Doctor Angel said. "They are quickly disappearing and will not come again to this landscape."

I remembered then the diary I kept when I first came to Saskatchewan, piercing the pages with the stems of the wildflowers and grasses I had picked. Then, once I found out what they were, I added the names that people called them. "Orange hawkweed," I whispered now, "rough pennyroyal, meadow blazing star." Was I responsible for the demise of such plants?

"Yes," said Doctor Angel, "their names in themselves are poems. Showy lady's slipper, smooth blue beardtongue, false dragonhead. They talk about breaking the prairie when they plough. But it's these colours they are breaking, these names. And the names that came before."

"The Indian names?" I asked.

He nodded. "Entire languages have disappeared. And the stories and knowledge passed on by the sentences those languages made."

I heard a fainting mewing noise in the distance. "A baby!" I gasped, thinking I had finally heard one.

Doctor Angel sighed. "No," he said, his voice low and sad, "it is only someone in pain. Someone far away, perhaps someone who is not even in the hospital anymore . . . they are that far away. Those cries always remain. Those moments when you cried or called out for your mother? Those moments will be caught in these timbers forever. Buildings made from forests can hold such things. The people who were already here when we came knew this. They knew how forests hold the memory of life."

I thought about that for a bit, remembering how the wood that built our house flew upward and broke apart, even as I had broken apart. Would the splinters of it remember?

"Did you know that when the sisters first founded this hospital, all the medical devices and tools had to be sent to Regina for sterilization each time there was an operation? They would be loaded on the train and would come back twenty-four hours later." He was thinking aloud again. "We hadn't the equipment then, but we do now," he said vaguely.

What I took from his words was that I would have to have another operation soon, and that was why Doctor Angel was thinking about surgery.

I wanted to be turned back to the wall then. I wanted to at least be able to seek out and find that stain that so resembled my mother's one good dress. I thought about my father breaking the wildflowers and grasses of the prairie. I didn't care that he had murdered those flowers. I wanted him near me too badly to care. I recalled him and my brother carrying me on the much-prized front door through the tall grasses. I wanted Danny and his otherness and his closeness.

Doctor Angel was now saying a poem. "Hospital where / nothing / will grow / lie cinders," he said. Or at least that was all I heard or could retain.

I was moving away in the train's noisy interior with its warm porter and its icy cold conductor. The cold conductor started to take shape just behind Doctor Angel's left shoulder. He was the palest shade of blue. "You will never see your family again," he whispered. "Especially now that your mother is dead."

Friedrich stirred in his sleep. Tatiana kept her secrets beneath her white tent. The stars moved from one side of the prairie sky to the other.

"In which shine / the broken," Doctor Angel said.

I remember us lying face to face in an untidy bed. The sheets smelled of bleach and were hard and rasping to the touch. Our bodies were soft and sensual on this unforgiving platform, as if we were two smooth, slow rivers moving over sandbars. Even Harp's three o'clock shadow felt pliable under my fingers. "Three o'clock shadow," I said. And then, "Perhaps that's what you should call me, the Three O'Clock Shadow." I was studying his long rectangular face: prominent nose, the rise of his brows, forehead with three dissimilar lines etched into its surface. Eyes an intense shade of green, perhaps on the small side, but surprisingly clear, given the cigarettes. Though now vague, almost drugged. "The usual term is five o'clock shadow," he said, unsentimentally.

"My brother is a monk," I whispered. "He does not have a three o'clock shadow."

Harp's eyes, which were beginning to close, flew open when he received this information.

"His name is Danny," I added.

"Anglican? Catholic?"

"With a name like Danny?" I laughed.

Harp had grown up in the Presbyterian kitchens and small churches of rural Ontario. His first wife, however, who had a nose for social class, had insisted he become a member of the congregation at Saint Simon's Anglican Church in Toronto. "High Anglican," he said to me now. "I do love the singing of Anglican choirs." He touched my hair. "Did you ever think of becoming a nun?" The question was quiet, serious, but there was that laughter in his eyes.

"No," I said hesitantly, after some mental searching. In fact, being mateless and childless, I might have considered the cloistered life. But that was Danny's world. Ultimately, he was the one elected to serve.

I told Harp, then, about Sister Editha. And the other sisters. And he told me about the altarpieces, as I've already mentioned. His hand covered the scar on my hip while he spoke.

And then, though I was in the trance that follows love, I talked about Danny's choir, that odd combination of farm wives, truck drivers, children, and monks who sang the music of the Middle Ages.

"I wanted to be in the choir," I told him. "But instead, I play the piano or the organ when they need me to." Danny had asked if I would accompany them, and I could never say no to Danny. "Born to be an accompanist," I murmured to Harp. I was drowsy enough that a realization of this sort seemed a profound epiphany to me, though it was not.

I rested my hand on Harp's face, hoping for a reaction to my cleverness. But by now he was fully asleep. A muscle in his thigh jumped, and I wondered if—in his dream—he was taking the stairs two at a time up to his beloved lab.

And Danny was also running and laughing in my mind, just outside the house, with a dog called Rex. I too was falling asleep. I had evoked Danny, the mystic, while I lay in Harp's arms, and so Danny remained, just on the edge of my consciousness. When I think of the scene now, my legs braided with Harp's, my head on his arm, speaking about my brother, it seems to come from a country so far away and visited so long ago, no memory can recover its shorelines. Harp's long body. And that woman who was me, not young, but so much younger than I am now. What of her? How did she manage it all? The man, his body. No one before or after.

I was helpless and adrift. He was unknowable. And that meant there wasn't any part of me that I didn't want him to understand, to know.

A few days after Tatiana's arrival, I was taken to the surgery by Doctor Carpenter. He arrived at my bedside, and in a crisp manner, he explained that my left hip was not mending in the way it should. There might be bone fragments that needed to be removed from the joint, he said. It was necessary that he go in "to take a look around." To "go in," he would need to saw through the cast that was already there, he said, tapping it two or three times with his knuckles, discard it, and after "fishing out" the bone fragments, make a brand-new cast.

As before, I began to cry when he told me about the operation. I could not completely remember the earlier surgeries but vividly recalled their aftermath. Now the surgeries themselves seemed part of an ongoing calamity that was arranged, I believed, by the blue-skinned, grey-haired Conductor, whose nearby pacing I could often sense, even if I couldn't see him. I was also crying because Mister Porter Abel had signed my cast with a lovely CPR fountain pen. He had inscribed it with his first and last name and his porter badge number, and then he had drawn a seashell to indicate that he came from the Nova Scotia seashore. Now all of that would be gone. Unlike Tatiana's tribe, whom Doctor Angel had described to me the previous night, I favoured stasis and stability. Once something was written down, I did not want it to be smashed up.

I also did not want the blue-skinned Conductor to get a crack at signing the blank page of my new cast. I had felt safe from this threat as long as Mister Porter Abel's signature was firmly in place as a charm, an endorsement, and an antidote. But he, the porter, was often far away on those trains. I could not predict when he might return, or whether he would return in time. And the Conductor, who, like a malign virus, seemed to be able to make copies of himself (one for the train, one for a prairie farm, one for the hospital), was omnipresent. And even more so when you couldn't quite see him.

This same Conductor had taken to quietly singing "Lavender's Blue," the first verse of which my mother had often sung to us, and especially to my younger siblings. "'Lavender's blue, dilly dilly, lavender's green,'" she would sing. "'When I am king, dilly dilly, you shall be queen.'" I had always loved those words, and the tune, which I had never tired of playing on the piano. But the words the Conductor used were unfamiliar to me. "'Call up your men, dilly dilly, set them to work. Some with a rake, dilly dilly, some with a fork,'" he sang.

He is taunting, not teasing, I thought. And I knew the difference.

They wheeled me out of the room, with Friedrich looking solemnly on, and took me down the hall. Sister Editha was holding my hand. "You are going to the operating theatre," she said, "and after that, things will be much better." She withdrew once I was in that room and under those lights, but not before kissing me gently on the cheek and brushing back my bangs. "We'll have to trim your hair," she said, "when we get you back to the ward."

I knew then that it had been at least a month since I was carried to this place. My mother was fastidious about our grooming. She never would have allowed my bangs to grow long.

Because everyone in the room was masked, I couldn't tell whether it was Doctor Angel or Doctor Carpenter who put the rubber cup, for what Doctor Angel had called "the ether," over my nose and mouth. It was held in place with a pressure that was not quite forceful, but not soft either. I saw something I would now call a spiral vortex. Then, ding dong dell, I fell down the well.

After the fall into blankness, I awoke to a dream concerning something else Doctor Angel had explained the previous night. He told me that a famous Russian author called Count Tolstoy had arranged for all the Doukhobors—including Tatiana's mother and father—to come to the northern Great Plains. The count had arranged this because he was filled with empathy concerning the terrible persecution of the Doukhobors in Russia, a land of unimaginable hardship, where the serfs, who were workers living in poverty, were so numerous as to be uncountable.

Later I would learn that the writer himself had hundreds of serfs on his own estate and was torn with anguish about this, though, it was true, he had come to this state of anguish later in his life. After spending a long period of time writing novels and achieving fame in European cities, and an equally long period of time carousing with poets and painters with whom he constantly discussed the meaning of life, Count Tolstoy had arrived at the conclusion that life and its meaning was unconsciously and sometimes consciously understood only by the millions and millions of working people, who, of course, did not discuss life and its meaning at all. The meaning of life was not at all understood by parasitic people such as he and his friends, he had decided, who lived off the labours of others while concerning themselves with pleasure and vanity. And so, he returned to Russia with its great empty regions filled with nothing but deep, frigid winter, unstoppable blizzards, and uncountable serfs who knew enough about the meaning of life not to discuss it.

The Doukhobors had kept themselves quite separate from the serfs, and stayed apart, as much as possible, from the masters as well. As gifted agricultural workers, according to Tolstoy's reasoning, they would have known—consciously or unconsciously—all about the meaning of life. Unlike the serfs, however, who kept their knowledge to themselves, the Doukhobors often discussed their theories on this topic. Apart from stasis, which they abhorred, and the flux of life, which they adored and considered to be the essence of Jesus, whom they worshipped, they knew with certainty that the meaning of life was such that it was opposed, and so were they, to killing fellow humans in wars or otherwise. With this in mind, the Doukhobors had burned the load of weapons that were delivered to them by the tsar of the Russian Empire, and as a result of this action, they were considered enemies of the tsar and empire ever after. Tolstoy, who was also a pacifist but would never be considered an enemy of the tsar because of his nobility and fame, felt that the least he could do for these people who clearly, consciously or unconsciously, understood the meaning of life was to get them away from a Russian Empire determined to annihilate them.

"Oh, the journeys by foot, the sea journeys, and the locomotive journeys these people had to undergo!" Doctor Angel had exclaimed on the night he told me about them. "Just to move from one frozen landscape to another." He shook his head. "But at least," he continued, "they would have known how to manage the short growing season of a northern country. Their agricultural skills had been taught to them by Russia."

While the ether continued to have its way with me, I dreamt that I was lost in the vast, empty regions of that land called Russia, caught up in a wind full of snow, a wind that howled "RUSSIA, RUSSIA, RUSSIA" all around me. Sometimes I could see the count's castle through the snow. Sometimes I could even see the count himself, lit by a single candle and sitting at a desk near a window of the castle, with the fields of his estate unfurling, white as paper, around him in all directions. I knew he was inventing a story at that desk in his cold castle, and that the story he was inventing would hold Tatiana's fate, and my fate, in its inky hand. At one point the wind shouted the word "RUSSIA" with such force that the count's candle was blown out. And I knew that without him continuing to write the story of our fate, neither Tatiana nor I would exist.

He lit another candle. And continued to write. Perhaps about life and its meaning. We existed. I opened my eyes.

W hen I awoke after the operation, I was again facing the wall, and the only part of my body that was able to move was my heart, which I could hear pounding in my brain and, more palpably, against the sheet under my ribs. There was no longer a map of the railways of Saskatchewan on the wall, and my mother's one good dress had also disappeared. Perhaps Sister Philomena had scrubbed it off during one of her ongoing sessions of spiritual cleaning. But if so, what had been revealed in the wake of such sessions was a picture of the apple tree my mother had brought on the train from Ontario, and on which Danny had discovered all those dollar bills. She had planted it in front of our house-to-be even before the house itself was built. Tiny and fragile, it had withstood two bitterly cold prairie winters and had grown to shoulder height under my mother's care. As I later discovered, it had also survived the big wind. But of course, I didn't yet know this.

Once, when I was quite small and still in Ontario, I swallowed an apple seed. When I confessed this to my father, he jokingly said that an apple tree would now be sure to grow inside me. I was terrified at the thought of this. Each night I prodded my stomach with my fingers for evidence of twigs and sticks: sometimes, as fall approached, I even searched for the shapes of the apples themselves under my skin. In spring I was certain I could feel a malign sort of blossoming in my bones. And then quite suddenly, I was old enough to know that all this was nonsense. Now, though, the thought of my mother's deep connection to the little tree she had nurtured in the pot and had carried with her to the northern plains suggested that I had not been entirely wrong about the beginnings of an orchard germinating inside me.

I knew the Conductor was a few rooms down the hall—perhaps conducting others—and I was on high alert because I sensed he was in the vicinity. My ribs were broken. The tree that might have been under them was on the wall instead—sometimes confused with the diagram of the parliamentary system. It was not growing the way it should, that tree; its roots had been torn from the ground, and its limbs were tangled and askew. The shape of its branches changed often, swelling on occasion, then twisting into thin wiry cages that seemed ready to inhabit my mind if the tree trunk were ever to succeed in its plan, which was to install itself in my body.

During the passage of the following few days, while my fever rose higher and higher and Doctor Angel hovered nervously near my bed, I was possessed by the tree. I began to see that the tree itself was a map, not of the railways but of the rivers of Saskatchewan. I began to believe I could paddle up the tree or float down it. I could swim in that tree. I knew it. Some people, men mostly, might want to build bridges over the limbs of that tree. Others, children mostly, would be baptized in it. At dusk, when the sun was just about to set, the tree became something else altogether. Bathed in the intense red of those last rays of light, the tree became my bloodstream, fevered, bright, branching poisonously from one or another of my organs and infecting the others. It was hot, hot, and I was hot, and there was a thirst in me, though I could not find my voice to ask for water.

In the fevered evenings, the cold Conductor, with his blue skin and grey hair, would drift in from the other parts of the hospital, and enter the room. I could hear him whispering and shuffling, but because I was facing the wall, I couldn't see him. He was a subtle character, and very discreet; it was often difficult to understand what he was saying. I was able to grasp a few words, however, because they pertained to me. "I am the only one who can break your fever," he said, "the only one who can cool you down." Then suddenly he was quietly singing his usual song:

> You're going to die, dilly dilly, as time will tell,
> You will be buried, dilly dilly, under the well;
> Why is this so, dilly dilly, please tell me why?
> So you can drink, dilly dilly, when you are dry.

Now and then shame would make me not want to begin the journey to see the man I loved. I believed that we were beyond the ordinary, as everyone who has been in love must believe. But on days like these, a more ordinary kind of shame, one perhaps from my grandmother's or my mother's generation, would stand waiting for me on the platform near the rails. Sometimes Count Tolstoy stood waiting as well. A snow-ghost.

Especially after a day when I had visited the classrooms, where the children, ill-behaved or well-behaved, were so innocent. And then there was the singing: their voices still rang in my mind as I boarded the train that would take me to one castle hotel. Or another.

The train that would take me away from the town of Muenster would seem like a death train then, and the skin of its employees would become the pale shade of blue that the Conductor had favoured all those years before. They walked like him as well, with the same soft yet deliberate steps. Sometimes they whistled vague tunes. There were no lovely porters on the branch lines I took from the open prairie to one or another of the two or three small cities where Harp would be arriving on an airplane, or first class on a train of his own.

Despite the castle walls that kept the real world at bay. And despite the elms with their green veils in summer and fine wooden bones in winter, the staff at the desk of the castle hotels where I checked in would look old and knowing. Nothing—not the crests on the walls, not the crowns and escutcheons, not the oak panelling—absolutely nothing, no one, would be eager to greet me. They would thumb with great care and slowness through the files that held the reservations, then sigh and reach towards the shellacked wooden wall on which hung the keys. I would lower my eyes and accept the key with its wooden fob and engraved number. And then I would limp with my cane towards the elevator.

Behind the room's closed door, I would sit down on the bed and wait, and every cell in my body would resist what I knew was about to take place. These were the moments when I wanted to stop, to return to my daily life, when I wanted to be fully claimed by the classrooms and the children, and Danny in his monastery. And if the man I loved couldn't, or didn't wish to, love me in a daily way, then why did he hold the key to this room? This saved life?

For mine was a life that had been saved, coaxed, kept alive; a heart that was encouraged to keep beating. A life to be cherished and grateful for.

Mister Porter Abel and Sisters Editha, Philomena, and Hildegard, the whole troupe of the Company, the innocent children who had lain in the beds near me, Doctor Carpenter and Doctor Angel, my own dear father and brother, the neighbours in the exploding farmhouse, the vanished baby, and everyone who had worked so hard to save me would shake their heads sadly at what I had become, then turn away from me, and fade. And yet I would continue to sit in that room and wait for the man I loved, as he knew so well that I would.

Harp would enter the room and I would rise to meet him. He would run his fingers over the uneven ridges of what had been my broken ribs and collarbones. He would kiss my scars, including the long scar that rode over the hill of my hip. Doctor Carpenter had made that scar, trying to rearrange bone fragments. My scars are like a railway map, I said once to this man I loved, while he laughed with delight. Then I told him about the wall of the hospital and the railroads and rivers I had seen there. Harp then said my scars were works of art whose canvas was my skin, my bones. I laughed, dismissively, and told him this was nonsense. Still, he was tender with this torn canvas. "You are a work of art," he told me—and in return, I rose to meet him.

One day Harp began to talk about the subject matter of Western art, rather than specific works of art themselves. In particular, he spoke of what he called the paraphernalia of martyrdom: the crosses and pyres and various instruments of torture. The decapitations and amputations, the starvations and imprisonments, the piercings and whippings and burnings and lashings. The caves and cages and dungeons and castles: all this delivered cleverly and with humour by the man I loved. He told me that when he was self-educating in European museums, he realized that most collections could be divided into two almost equal subject categories: the great martyrdoms of religious art, and the excessive gore of the battlefield. He chose to focus on the martyrdoms, he told me, because he could not bear to look closely at the agony of horses.

"Isn't that a bit ironic?" I asked. "You, the scientist with your research lab full of animals."

He did not reply at first, but offered me a cigarette instead, which I accepted, though I rarely smoked. Then he said, "All dying honourably and for a good cause, like soldiers."

I wished then that I had not brought this up. I knew Harp did not believe that soldiers died for a good cause. And I have never been able to stomach it, the idea of animals suffering. But now there it was, vivid and present in my mind.

He had changed the subject of his art history focus, he told me, after all the depictions of suffering, human and animal, had put him off. Too many crucifixions, he had decided, not to mention female saints with their breasts on a platter.

He raised his eyebrows after this pronouncement. Any man of the time might have done so.

He was now more drawn to landscapes, he insisted. "When it came to the *Agony in the Garden*," he said, "I abandoned the agony and kept the garden."

I thought a remark like that was very clever and laughed in appreciation.

I told him about Friedrich and his songs about wandering through winter landscapes.

"Seems especially sophisticated for a child," he said. "Debonair!"

I assured him that Friedrich was still debonair, even more debonair than he had been when he was the most elegant child ever to grace a hospital bed. "And beautiful," I said. "He is still beautiful.

"Beautiful and debonair," I said. "You should be happy about that."

Friedrich, who was often on tour with his theatre company, always came to see me when he could. Sometimes, but not always, he brought his partner, Antony, with him. I would always remind them both about the Polish boy called Antoni, whose polio had not responded to Sister Editha's famous massages. I did this because of my brother Danny. My one little note of revenge.

Friedrich always asked about Danny, however. Or at least allowed him into the conversation. "I always knew Danny would become a monk," he often announced. He didn't know anything of the sort, of course, but pretended, like a stubborn child, to have always been aware. I would look at him then, full in the face, knowing the heartbreak. He would meet my gaze then lower his eyes. And, really, there wasn't much more to be said.

Harp, when I told him he should be happy about Friedrich, looked at me over his glasses and raised his eyebrows in an expression of bewilderment. He had been reading the hotel menu, looking for a sumptuous meal for one that we could share. I knew from experience that he would eat most of this meal, not because of greed but because I had no appetite for anything but him when we were together.

"You made him better," I said. "You saved his life."

"I did?" His focus returned to the menu. But before that, I noticed a faint trace of boredom in his expression. He was experienced in concealing such things, keeping his face neutral and pleasant. When it came to the notion of being a saviour, however, he had heard it all before. I knew this. And yet, I wanted him to save me as well. I wanted him to make me, to make everything else, better.

"Is it boring being famous?" I asked.

"You bet," he said, snapping shut the leather-coated menu. "It reduces everything to a central point. No one can see you clearly afterwards." He placed the menu on the table beside him. "The prime rib," he said. "You want that?"

"I can see you clearly," I said, believing I knew what I meant.

Tonight, however, as I write this, I wonder if I spoke the truth. What did I see? A man who wanted me, who made me feel desired. I saw that. But I did not examine why I was, of so many women, the one he would return to. Now I wonder if it was the private anonymity of my life, the smallness of it, that attracted him.

Or is smallness just another name for a life that is lived in an ordinary way, with attention paid to an ordinary past as well as an ordinary present? My own past assertively haunted the series of rooms where Harp and I met. And he listened closely, chin down, eyes hooded, to the smallest anecdote I recited to him from that distant kingdom.

Yes, in the end, Harp knew the whole arc of my life, for who else, since I had come to adulthood, had examined my body in such a careful way? A body with the scars of childhood still vivid on its surface.

Sensing somehow that he may not have paid much attention to the rooms he inhabited in a daily kind of way, I was surprised by his fascination, real or feigned, with the minutiae of my daily life. "I grew up with those things," he told me when I described a kitchen table painted white, a linoleum floor. "Tell me what else is around you, what else you know."

What I knew then, and know now, is this landscape, the changing colour of snow and sky, the faces of singing children, my own kitchen, my own hallway, my own bed. The familiar knife and fork in my hand. And the dish I eat from.

Perhaps Doctor Carpenter should have sent his instruments to Regina for sterilization, rather than relying on the in-house system, because after the operation, I developed another infection.

My fever peaked each evening after sundown. Sister Editha would come to my bedside then, with a tin basin and a clean cloth to bathe in cool water the parts of my body that were not covered by bandages or casts. Afterwards, she would call Sister Philomena into the ward, and the two of them would turn me towards the room so she could hold cold compresses to my forehead.

In the daylight hours, I fell into long sessions of sleep, waking only to drowsily examine the wall and think about the little tree that was pictured there, trying to puzzle out its meaning in relation to the parliamentary system. At night, however, after Sister Editha and Sister Philomena had turned me over, and Sister Editha had quieted my pain and had left the ward, I was utterly alert.

Everything in the room—brass fixtures, night lights reflected in black window glass, a drop of water on my skin—was both bright and increasingly intensified by my fever, combined with the fact that I was now facing the world rather than the wall. I was thrilled by it all, shivering with delight in the face of everything I saw. The steel clasp of a clipboard lit by a flashlight, the embossed gold lettering on the side of a pencil: all of this was significant to me. It was as if these random objects were placed in such a way that they revealed a secret code, one I believed I could crack if I concentrated long enough.

One night I was certain I saw my mother's palace hotel sailing like an ocean liner through the quietly desperate winter landscape that Friedrich so often sang about. Fully lit, like a ship coming into a harbour, it hove into view outside the hospital window, stood majestically still for an hour, and then slowly, silently withdrew.

Had it picked up more passengers?

The next night, at the peak of my fever, I told Sister Editha about the hotel. "It had towers, like a palace," I said. "It had staircases and elevators and glass mail chutes. My mother said that the designs were European, and that Europe was a place far away where people knew more and had more artistic tastes." I explained all this to patient Sister Editha, who herself had talked about her childhood in such a place.

"My mother spent only two nights in hotels like this," I said. "And one of those nights was in faraway mountains that we will never see."

It was then that Sister Editha described leaving the old world of the many-towered convent, the town that was gathered like a skirt around it, and the surrounding mountains that she would never see again, and coming to the northern Great Plains, which now spread as far as you could see outside the hospital window. I understood that she wanted to tell the story of this departure, but I also knew she feared it would hurt her to tell it. For a while she appeared to be weighing these two possibilities, and a small frown line could be seen just below the forehead band of her wimple.

I waited. And eventually she began.

"Not one of us," she said, referring to herself and her fellow nuns, "not a single one of us, had been farther than a quarter of a mile from the convent in our remembered lives. I was the only one, you understand, who could recall—even faintly—a life elsewhere. We were all, in many ways, still children because of this. And truly, none of us had reached twenty years of age, though, I suppose, innocent and inexperienced as we were, we would have been considered young women at the time."

I was surprised by this. The idea of the sisters as children was somehow easier to accept than the idea of the sisters as young women.

"Weren't you excited?" I asked. "By getting out and going away?"

Sister Editha did not answer my question. "When we left the carriage," she said, "my mother's cries were still alive in me."

I knew that my own mother's cries were still alive in me as well. Or at least her crying. It would never leave me, never ever not be a part of me.

"Father Ambrose escorted us into a place that was as big as a *cathedral*," Sister Editha continued, "but full of noise in a way that sacred places never are. We were convinced that the loud sound rumbling up the stone staircase towards us was the thunder of hell, and we wanted to go no farther. But the priest motioned towards us and told us to descend. He said that we were in a railroad station, and that we were about to get on a train."

Sister Editha took the poultice from my forehead. I could hear the comforting sound of dripping water. Then the poultice came back to my face, cooler than before. She dried her hands with a linen towel that was hanging on a thin bar on my side of the bedside table.

"Nothing had prepared us for that railroad journey," she continued. "No one we knew had ever ridden on a railroad, and we were mortally afraid of the locomotive, which, with its steam and noise, looked to us like the Devil's own invention. Not one of us wanted to climb on board, but Father Ambrose pulled us up the three metal steps and told us to go behind a glass partition to two soft benches, each facing the other. He sat on one bench and we three sat on its opposite. We were timid in the presence of this big, loud priest who barked things at us we couldn't quite hear over the noise. None of us wanted to sit beside him. We stayed awake all night, sitting upright, paralyzed with fear, while Father Ambrose lay flat on the facing bench, sound asleep and snoring."

It was the first time I had heard even a whisper of disdain for another enter the tone of Sister Editha's voice.

Because I could picture the three young nuns on a train now, I wondered if there had been a conductor. Then I thought of my own Conductor, how efficient and bossy he was, how he often said things that I couldn't quite hear, or that I didn't understand. Sometimes it was as if he spoke a peculiar language made only of train sounds. "Clickety-clack, clickety-clack. Woo-woo!" he would sometimes chant, sarcastically.

Sister Editha was telling me about being in the bottom of the ocean liner in one small iron room, and how they were abandoned by Father Ambrose, who was "on an upper deck." "He came once, after we had slept for two days," she said. "We did not understand about ships' refectories, or how to find them—and so we threw ourselves on his mercy. He agreed to find food and bring it back to us. He also said that he had been playing something called shuffleboard. We spent the rest of the morning trying to figure out what that might have meant. I still don't know. Do you?"

I did not. I guessed it might be a kind of performance, though. Sometimes, just before they left Friedrich's bedside, the members of the Company sang a couple of lines of a song about shuffling off to Buffalo. "Maybe a show?" I offered.

Sister Editha did not respond. By now she had come to the part of the story where she had arrived in North America with her companions, and she was describing the new landscape, the new trains, and the new people speaking the new language. "It took us days and days on more and more trains to arrive in the northern Great Plains," she said. "Delegations of priests and nuns met us at train stations and took us back to their quarters for meals and sleep, but each delegation seemed to speak a different new language—though to us this did not matter, as we spoke no language except German. We had lost our bearings: we did not know what direction we were travelling in. One day on a train (our big priest had parted from our company at some city or another), we wondered if perhaps one of the delegations had played a trick on us by putting us on the wrong train, for, although we knew we were supposed to be going to the plains, we saw nothing but forests around us for what seemed like many days."

I remembered Danny crying on the train because of the trees. I remembered how frightening that had been.

"We were coming to the plains to start a hospital," Sister Editha said. "Can you imagine that? Three small terror-stricken children who had left everything, including their language, behind? Now we were certain we could never start a hospital because of the trees being everywhere, and we imagined the horrible wild animals, the likes of which we had never seen. I recalled all the stories about wolves that I had been told as a child. And I wished the wolf-charmers of my village were with me on the railroad."

Some of the trees suddenly appeared in the middle of the room near Friedrich's bed, where he was sleeping with a solemn expression on his face. But none of the animals came into view.

"We had to take a bus to Muenster." It was as if Sister Editha were speaking from a long way off. I was busy with my brother and the trees. Danny's sobs were shaking the branches inside my head, as well as the branches that appeared just behind Sister in the room.

"And when we arrived," she continued, "there was no delegation to meet us. We had to walk the several miles to the abbey carrying our suitcases. The monks were very happy when they saw us at their door. They had been praying for a cook, you see, and now, to their minds, God had replied by sending them *three*."

Sister Editha was leaning her elbow on my bed. My mattress shook a little with her silent laughter. "They were quite downcast when we told them we had come to start a hospital."

I was starting to take sounds apart into their various components, as I had learned to do the previous evening when my fever peaked. I could hear both the sound of water falling into the bowl and the sound of a wrung cloth as moist air escapes from it along with water. But it was as if these sounds were not connected to each other.

"We gave in, of course," Sister Editha confessed, "as one so often does with men when it comes to cooking. We helped in the refectory, though less so after we moved to our first convent, a tiny farmhouse with two rooms above and one below. And no water within; just a pump in the yard, too near the outhouse for my liking. Still, we had a stove that burned coal. The temperature was forty-nine degrees below zero on our first winter."

I was unsurprised by this, having lived through a couple of prairie winters myself.

"And then began our mission. We would be sent off to attend to the sick and the dying in the farmhouses of the parish. I can still see Father Bruno trudging through the snow, bringing us news of the day's patients. There were always more and more patients. Sometimes, if someone was very ill, we would be forced to stay in their home for days and days."

"Hospital," I said. I wasn't quite sure why I had said that one word. It may have been because Sister Editha was bathing my free leg at that moment, and I was trying to express my knowledge that attention was being paid to the healing of my body. And that I was grateful. Or it could have been because of what Doctor Angel had told me about the structure of the building, and the poem that he said about it.

But Sister Editha took the word to be a prompt. "Oh yes," she said. "The mercy visits to the farmhouses were in the divine plan. Always, even without our asking, the families would give what little they had to us—to the hospital—as we departed." I sensed she was smiling. "For the building of the hospital," she said.

I could hear Tatiana whimpering. "Poor lamb," said Sister Editha, who had heard her too.

We were both quiet for a bit, listening, until the whimpering stopped.

The Conductor whispered in the radiators. And I could picture him down in the basement. The sentence he was saying breathed out of him in a blue banderole. It had slipped into the basement boiler and from there into the pipes.

"You will scarcely be able to believe this," said Sister Editha, with the sound of hidden laughter in her voice, "but in the beginning, we did not want to go out to our patients. We were so shy, you see, and we had concluded that some of our patients were bound to be men. Abbot Bruno, sensing our discomfort, told us that all his parishioners were good, God-fearing people, and that most of them spoke German. Still, we were timid. Among ourselves, we eventually decided that Sister Philomena should be the first to venture forth because she was the largest and the strongest, and could perhaps fend for herself were she to meet a bad man who, whether ill or otherwise, might want to do her harm. It was to be just an afternoon call. She would be back with us in our small house before dark.

"But Sister Philomena came running back to us well in advance of the setting sun. She was utterly dishevelled; her hair had fallen out from under her wimple, and her habit was torn in many places, as if by a wild beast." By now Sister Editha was truly laughing, which alarmed me somewhat as I believed poor Sister Philomena had met with an unhappy accident. "But the only wild beast that had attacked Sister Philomena," Sister Editha continued, "was the barbed-wire fence she had been attempting to cross. She told us it had her in its clutches for at least an hour, and she claimed that there was no possibility of crossing the prairie, and that she wanted to go home."

The next morning, however, all three nuns had gone forth, arm in arm, to confront the wire fences of the prairies. Eventually they had come up with a plan that suited both their large unwieldy garments and their small size. They wrapped themselves up in their habits and rolled under the fences. "And in this way," Sister Editha confided, "the hospital where you and I are together this evening was eventually built.

"I myself had only one uncomfortable experience when I went out on a call," she continued. "One of the remotest families, in which the mother was tragically dying, did not offer me food. After two days, weak with hunger, I finally asked the two oldest daughters for something to eat. The whole family set down their knives and forks and regarded me with shock. 'But angels don't eat human food,' one of them said to me. No one, you see, had ever paid any medical attention to them in the past, and they honestly believed that the abbot had sent an angel to their home."

"Angel. Thunder. Wandering!" Suddenly, and with such a note of urgency, Tatiana was talking. "I can read," she said, in a much more ordinary voice. "Rolling over the prairie," she added, letting us know she was listening. Then she became silent again.

"She has gone back to sleep," said Sister Editha, who had straightened her back and lifted her head when Tatiana began to speak. Now she relaxed and placed a fresh cool cloth on my forehead before picking up my free hand. Her own hand felt like the paper of one of my mother's important letters, which we were never permitted to read, and which were locked away in a drawer, a drawer to which only my mother had the key. I had seen my mother standing by the bedroom window and using its light to read one of those letters, and the light itself moved through the paper as if it were translucent. It looked in my memory the way that Sister Editha's hand felt in the dark of this night hospital. This hospital that was built by three small nursing sisters who rolled out under the wire fences of the region to their patients on the prairie, thereby building with their own arms the very hospital that was trying to heal me.

"**I**n his youth he wandered much, and wept beside rivers," said Tatiana the following morning. Now I know she was speaking about the first Doukhobor leader, Peter Verigin, who had come to the prairies with Tatiana's people. But then I thought she was referring to Friedrich, and as I was still facing the room, I looked straight at him for a reaction.

"Lots of words," he said.

This was the largest number of words we had ever heard Tatiana speak. These sentences were so strange, and came from such a quiet source, that were it not for Friedrich being so solidly in my purview, I might have believed I was dreaming. Or that I was recalling one of Doctor Angel's poems, which I never completely understood even though some prelingual part of me was haunted by them.

"He threw the golden book and the church keys into the water," she said. "He threw the books into the Volga River. Wooden heart and stony soul," she said. Then she sang something so softly we did not know what the words were. Friedrich, however, commented, as if to himself, "That is not a language I recognize." And in that way, I knew she was not singing in German.

"Russian," I told him, experiencing a brief sense of superiority in the knowledge of this. He did not answer. This was because he had fallen asleep again. More and more he slept in the daytime, and then all night too. In the beginning, it was me who did the most sleeping. Now it was Friedrich. When I had a fever, I believed he was sleeping my sleep.

...

Friedrich received from the Company letters out of which colourful balloons and stickers and bits of ribbon sometimes fell. And gold stars like the ones my teacher would affix to an arithmetic test if I had done a perfect job. For a child, rather than a teacher, to be in control of something with as much currency as those gold stars amazed me and made me reconsider everything I had learned in my short life about the balance of power, and all that I believed was unattainable.

I recalled that Mister Lysenko, my piano teacher, had also made use of some of those stars. Sometimes I got blue ones, even silver. But he never gave me the gold stars, which I glimpsed once in his satchel, and which I thoroughly coveted.

But Friedrich didn't ask the sisters for paper to use the stickers and the stars, as he would have in the past. And this startled me.

During one of the times when Friedrich was awake, he told me that the company was in Truro, Nova Scotia. Then he told me they were in a place called Friedrich's Town in the province of New Brunswick. "They've named the daily dog after me," he said, slowly turning the page of his letter to read more. "They've named the daily clown after me as well," he announced, smiling. He read aloud, "What could we do in Friedrich's Town but name all new characters Friedrich, since the town in which we were performing had already taken this extraordinary measure concerning the naming of itself?"

"The members of the Company will not be back for a long time," he said, sobering. I could hear the tears trying to get into his voice, and him trying to stop them.

This was because they had to visit all the smaller towns between here and there. Friedrich claimed that he himself had visited those towns when he had what he now called his sea legs. (He had heard Mister Porter Abel use this term when describing how he kept his balance on a train.) There were tiny towns, he told me, named after the great European capitals, and big, bustling towns named after the wind or a flower or a tiny tributary of a secondary stream that now ran through a culvert under the highway. There were plenty of towns, he confided, named after old dead soldiers with hats shaped like boats and lots of brass buttons on their uniforms. Five islands in the middle of a wide river with the name of a saint were called by the names of British generals. The Quebec French, he maintained, were obsessed by rivers and lakes and animals, and called places names such as Rivière-du-Loup, Cap-Chat, Baie-de-l'Ours, Portage-aux-Rats, and Lac Saxophone.

"Not an animal!" I corrected, about the final name.

"But strange, you have to agree," Friedrich said. "Whose saxophone, and where, and why?"

I thought about those earlier Indian names, and wondered whether they were lost for good, or if they would ever come back.

Friedrich was speaking softly. I considered this might have been in deference to Tatiana's plight, and I supposed, to a certain extent in deference to mine. Or perhaps even to his own plight, which had become a reality for everyone.

Tatiana had become very still while Friedrich talked about Friedrich's Town. She made me recall the poem about the Lady of Shalott that Master Stillwell had made the whole schoolroom memorize. Even the big boys at the back who snickered at such poems had become strangely sombre as the story unfolded and placed itself in a permanent way in their minds. As old men, I suspect, they would recite it to their grandchildren, surprising the youngsters by the quaver of sentiment in their voice. Had the curse come upon Tatiana? I wondered. Had she looked down to Camelot?

"Professor Davidson is often speaking now," Friedrich told me. Davidson, he had explained earlier, was a sage who toured with the Company in order "to make the common people understand the drama." Sometimes the plays were pure fun, with jokes and dancing and lots of falling down. But sometimes the plays were what Friedrich said his mother had told him were gifts from long ago. Shakespeare or even Euripides! "He instructs those who come to see the plays. You know," he said, in his usual explanatory way, though I had not asked for an explanation. "He tells about how the plays are like what is happening in the world today. The character of Ophelia," he confided, "was created to show how sad it is to be a woman. In a way that goes all through time."

I did not think it was sad to be a woman but was too tired to say so.

Hamlet, Friedrich announced, was completely guilty of absolutely everything, and that meant he could see that everyone else around him was guilty as well. Macbeth was like that too. Except that he was weak, in a way that men have always been weak and wreak havoc as a result. "I have listened over and over to many of Professor Davidson's lectures, and believe me," he added, philosophically, "weakness is a real problem." Lady Macbeth, he maintained, was a witch. "You have to look out for women who are too smart," he told me. "Those women have been around through all time. They are dangerously universal." He nodded sagely as he concluded.

I was exhausted by all this information. But I wasn't about to take that. "You have to look out for boys who are too smart as well!" I shot back.

Friedrich began to respond. "Well!" he said, with a superior tone in his voice. "I would think that . . ." Then he fell silent for a bit, absorbed by the last few pages of the letter. "Lots of good garbage dumps in New Brunswick," he told me.

I had already been made aware that because they travelled so constantly, the members of the Company depended on various nuns for stage furnishings. They also had been known to scour the local dumps for props. "What is the point," Friedrich had said, "of carting props from place to place when perfectly good objects are to be found in local town dumps?" At the very least, they could always find some broken pieces of furniture. But it was not unusual for other treasures to reveal themselves. Sometimes, entire plays and programs were hastily composed around the random discovery of, say, three bright blue bottles with the word "poison" written on them, a parlour pump organ, and a shaving stand with a broken mirror. In Friedrich's Town the trash discoveries had been surprisingly nautical in nature, given that it was fifty miles from the sea: emerald-green glass fishing floats, a couple of broken oars, and most wonderfully, a naked wooden mermaid who had obviously been a ship's figurehead. This had resulted in a spontaneous play called *The Captain's Dream*, in which a humble fisherman (who uses emerald-green glass fishing floats, and who first sees the figurehead from beneath) and the captain of the ship both fall in love with the ship's figurehead, who comes to life at noon and midnight, and who must choose between them. At noon when the figurehead comes alive, she dives from the ship and swims around the rowboat in which the fisherman plies his trade. At midnight when she comes alive, she swims up to the porthole of the captain's night quarters and sings to him.

"What finally happens?" I asked.

"I don't know," he said. I could hear him shuffling through the pages of the letter. "They don't tell me. But I bet there is a storm. No point having a ship scene if there is no storm."

There followed a lecture on how to create a storm by shaking thin tin sheets behind the stage, and by unfurling long bolts of blue silk and then waving them up and down. I was barely listening, thinking instead about my own storm, how inland it had been, and how devastating.

Then suddenly Tatiana was speaking, shouting almost, with great strength in her voice.

"Joy," she said. "The living book." Then she said the word "joy" one more time.

Friedrich, who could now do so but seldom did, sat bolt upright in his bed in astonishment. I merely tensed up and felt the long arm of pain move through my body. Perhaps that is joy—the reminder that always there is pain, the reminder that we are living beings.

"Joy?" Friedrich gasped. "We are youngsters in a hospital. Where is the joy in that?" He had never, in the days that I had known him, admitted to the fact that we were shipwrecked, ruined children, in need of constant medical care. Even when we were both crying in pain, he had never admitted that.

"It's life," I told him. "It is being alive. It's being alive." I had no idea where these words of mine came from. But much later, I would recall them being said by my mother, while she wept and talked about pain. And my brother, saying the words years later, referring to my sad liaison with the man I loved, and as I would come to know, referring to his own heartbreak as well.

I have thought about this often since. How pain situates us and makes us present in our lives. I thought about it every time I met with, and then separated from, Harp. And I think about it whenever I remember my mother. I recall also how often physical pain shook me awake in that hospital.

"Upside-down world," said Tatiana. "Spontaneously!" she said. "And often we were all walking together to migrate with the whole truth, for the whole truth never stays still."

The window was open in the ward that day. The sound of the trains was stronger, and the prairie breeze came across the room and touched Tatiana's tent so that it made a faint snapping noise. I was afraid that this would hurt her in some way, but she made no sound to indicate that this was so.

Friedrich began to sing about his father again in German. He did this through clenched teeth. But not for long, because soon he turned his back and went to sleep.

He is sleeping too much, I thought. "Ah, sleep," whispered the Conductor in the wind that came in through the windows. He coughed, and the air near the window turned into a blue-tinted vapour.

I wondered how old Tatiana was. I knew she was a child because she was in the ward with us. But I couldn't see the length or width of her body, which made it impossible to guess her age. I thought about Mister Porter Abel, trapped inside the velocity of those long steel horses galloping past the fields of wheat and curving through mountains. It was Tatiana who had made me associate machinery with horses because she had said one more thing when she heard the whistle blow. "The white horse," she had said.

When her high-spirited cousin Fiona died, my mother inherited her sewing machine. I expect it was my father who had selected it to be among the essential things that we would take with us to the northern Great Plains, as my mother had retained her suspicion of such a contraption. It sat in the attic of the new house for a few months after that house was built. But later it was moved to the parlour and assembled near the piano. There it crouched, looking feral, while I practised scales. Because it had a treadle, which resembled the pedals of the player piano, and because it required the use of both hands to make it work, it seemed like a small, malign copy of a piano gone angry and wrong and about to spring. Like my mother, I had no desire to provoke it.

Then one day, I came home from school to be greeted by its halting whir on the one hand, and my mother using the word "damn" on the other.

I found her in the parlour with one piece of white cloth in the machine, and several more on the floor around her feet.

"I've joined a women's club," she explained. "Sort of like the church group in Ontario."

I was happy about this and hoped new friends (who, as it turned out, were simply her old friends with a new purpose) would take away her sadness. Her old friends were sad like her. They were sometimes in the kitchen when I came home from school, brooding over their tea and none too pleased to see me, I thought. It was beyond my imagination at that point to understand that such ordinary women could have been discussing something I was not meant to hear. Apart from these few glum women in their lisle stockings and faded house-dresses, my mother seemed to have no friends except for my father.

"I'm the only one with a sewing machine," she added, with just a hint of resentment in her voice, as though somewhere in her was the knowledge she was being taken advantage of.

"Do you know how to work it?" I asked. The whole house smelled of pine because there were no rugs, and because, as I realize now, it was only two years old.

She was so intent on a diagram in her hand, she did not answer. I stepped closer and looked over her shoulder. The garment she was trying to make looked a bit like a dressing gown on the piece of paper. It had a rope belt like those I'd seen at the abbey. But it was shorter than the robes the monks wore, and a pair of slim female ankles, ending in surprisingly fashionable high-heeled shoes with straps, were revealed beneath it. On the woman's head was a weird conical hat that also came down over her face as a mask.

Scattered around the room were the paper pattern pieces that my mother had drawn from the diagram and from measurements of the women.

"Are they—the women's group—going to dress up as clowns?" I asked. I was envisaging a skit like the kind we had sometimes seen adults play-acting in at the town hall. One time my father was Santa Claus. And another time he was a town crier with a bell.

"I have to make five of these," she said, waving the piece of paper in the air impatiently and ignoring my question.

Seeing my mother so absorbed by a domestic task made me want to remain in the room with her, and I took a book out of my leather schoolbag, sat down on the piano stool, and pretended to read so that I could linger nearby. Usually, she performed her household duties distractedly. Even the twins could sense that while her body was in the kitchen or outside in the garden, where she grew vegetables, her mind was often in some unfathomable other place, and something about that place was being turned over and over by her thinking about it. Now she was at least present in the house—not paying attention to me, it is true, but somewhere in the vicinity. I felt the warmth of her, and the wholesomeness of her conventional concentration on the task. Her slight frown as she pinned the pattern pieces to the white cloth, the fact that she had joined with other women for some good work or another—all of this pleased me with its ordinariness.

I rose when I heard Danny's familiar footstep on the porch; I always liked to talk to him after school. As I left the room, my mother raised her face from the machine. "Emer," she said, "the women's group is a secret. Don't tell your father."

I assumed that this group was made up of women she had met, or had come to know better, when she went visiting. For my mother was often out visiting now. It had got into her, this idea of visiting, and she was seldom in the kitchen when we came home from school. Once, she passed me on the road as I was riding Bruno back to the farm. Either she didn't want to see me or she didn't recognize me. On her face there was a look of great concentration, great absorption. And her steps were the quick steps of someone with a purpose. She was losing weight now, what with all this purposeful walking from one farm to the other. Sometimes, if our father was in the fields, she left the little twins alone to fend for themselves. Sometimes they were both crying when I walked in through the door.

On the day of the sewing, when my mother was preparing dinner in the kitchen afterwards, I went back into the parlour. The vicious little sewing machine was now draped in the white cloth that had been lying on the floor. It still looked like an animal, but covered as it was, I was free to imagine whatever was beneath it, and it seemed more benign. Maybe there was a white horse under there, or a unicorn. Something mythical anyway.

Later, in the night ward, I would think about this sewing machine, how it had looked like the clothed white horse that Ivanhoe rode in the one beautiful illustration in my brother's book of that name. In my mind's eye, I could conjure Danny reading that book and looking again and again at the picture. I realized I had forgotten how much Danny liked Ivanhoe, and had only just remembered. And then my eyes filled with tears for my steadfast brother.

Years later I would be told that Tatiana was likely referring to a Russian philosopher and religious leader when she said, "The white horse." Surprising enough in itself. But I could never disassociate the term from my mother's inherited sewing machine, those funny conical mask-hats. And only much, much later came to understand more completely why this was so.

Doctor Angel and Sister Editha were standing near Friedrich's bedside, talking in whispers. He had been sleeping since the previous afternoon. Sister Editha had in her hand a letter from someone in the Company, and when she wasn't talking to Doctor Angel, she was trying to get Friedrich to be interested in that letter.

"Look," she was saying, "there is a postmark that says 'Quebec.' Do you think they are performing in French, Friedrich?"

He didn't answer for a long time. Then he said, "No."

The adults continued to whisper at that point, assuming, wrongly, that neither Friedrich nor I could hear them. But of course, we could. Children depend on their heightened listening skills to avoid conflict and to get what they want out of life.

I once waited a long, long time for Harp to write a letter to me. I had written to him, you see, in that unwise storm of desperation women sometimes experience when they are in a helpless state of mind. I felt

I could not bear the fact of losing him. Because I knew I would lose him. More educated, better placed, more cultivated, he would take himself to someone more his equal, someone else. Not that I saw it that way until a long time afterwards. What I saw was veiled. But I knew that I loved him.

He had gone with his artist friends to New Mexico. He was still on the central plains of the continent, but far from me. "Physician, heal thyself," he had explained in the last telegram I had received from him. He favoured telegrams and the occasional postcard. He was always careful not to say too much. Brevity, I used to say, was his middle name. Secrecy, Brevity. Harpocrates, Brahitis.

It was towards the end. When he wasn't with his artist friends, he was working for the war effort. I saw him rarely, and I wanted long days of him. I always wanted more. Especially when he wanted less.

I confessed my love for him in that letter. He did not answer. It wasn't love he sought from me. My letter neither moved him nor put him off, however, so although he did not answer, he also did not shy away. It wasn't domestic love I wanted from him, either, though I couldn't comprehend that; not yet. I thought I wanted him to fall on his knees and ask me to share his life. But in truth, I wanted to be aestheticized, made beautiful, by everything he knew. And I did not.

My mother knew things. She knew, for example, that were they laid end to end, the foundation pilings of a single castle hotel would have stretched for a dozen miles, and the concrete used in their construction could have formed a single column that was five miles high. Although she spent every Christmas Day that I can remember labouring over a turkey in our kitchen, her face red with exertion, she knew that the festive dinner served to guests at a castle hotel would be attended by waiters in Elizabethan clothing, and that the head of a wild boar would be carried in on a platter.

Her pursuit of knowledge was perhaps less steeped in self-delusion than mine. Or so I thought. She had, after all, earned her third-class teaching certificate in one of the makeshift model schools set up in rural counties for this purpose. In order to do this, she had to walk four miles through swamps and forests. And at the end of the trek was what Master Stillwell would have called "a handful of bush brats." And Master Stillwell himself, sent from the city university to prepare, and then examine, one country schoolteacher after another, most of them only just emerging from childhood, only a few years older than the bush brats they were being trained to teach, only a few years beyond being bush brats themselves.

But my mother knew, as I did not, that a third-class certificate—I have one myself—in no way guaranteed you would be treated differently as a woman. And so, she prudently managed her desires. She wanted only an intellectual connection to a "great man." Sadly, and ironically, narrowing her desires made her more fiercely blinded by their pursuit. I wanted—why not say it?—I wanted, impossibly, to be a great man. It was the impossible part that was comforting. I knew it was out of my hands. So I exchanged that desire for one that demanded a permanent place in the life of the man I loved, and in his mind. And I would fight like a wild dog, once our connection was established, to maintain it.

I would accept any conditions.

What was my mother thinking? As she boiled the water. As she stirred in the oatmeal. As she chose her one set of good dishes—a few of which remain in my possession to this day. As she nursed her twins—her little surprises, as she called them—and fed the fire, the one in the stove and the one in her mind. There was the pure physical labour of her life, the chopping, and pounding, and scrubbing, and peeling, and pouring and pushing, the sweeping and polishing, the digging in the vegetable garden, and then the creation of the one row for the zinnias that came in August. That almost obscene eruption of vibrantly coloured flowers, so out of place in the world that surrounded them, must have echoed something deep in her. I never knew her to bring them into the house. When I said that I wanted to make a bouquet for the parlour, she objected. "Those flowers don't want to live in the house," she said. "It wouldn't be right." And then, surprisingly, "They are a gift for the bees."

I now know she was always thinking about that one important letter. Perhaps her mind was like the locked drawer with only darkness and the contents of that letter inside it. A small geography, yes, but one that contained multitudes, for the letter would have taken her to many conclusions and to the opposite of those conclusions by the time she had finished reading it. But in fact, she would never finish reading it, and would never finish examining her own reading of it, which would change from day to day. Sometimes she thought the letter was instructive, and that she understood its instructions. But just when she was on the verge of carrying out those instructions, she would wonder if she had understood the letter completely, as if the letter could have changed in the night, as if it were subject to seasons and weather.

"Gather money," the letter read, "to support this cause. For in supporting it, you will be supporting everything you cherish. The poetry of our culture, the great scientific discoveries, the faith of our forefathers, the gifts of our ancestors: all this could be annihilated by great numbers of them."

Part of the letter contained an answer to a question she herself had posed in a letter of her own. Some days she would have felt at least satisfied, if not happy, with this answer. But on other days she would have been troubled by three further questions: Did the writer of the letter fully understand the question she had asked? Did she herself fully understand the answer? And ultimately, could she trust the language of the message that was on the page in front of her? Perhaps she was seeing in the letter only that which she wanted to see. All this would send her back again and again to the pages, to all the possibilities they contained and to everything that could be destroyed by them. Or to everything that the letter destroyed and to all the possibilities it unleashed.

Was there any room for her children, her husband in the locked drawer alongside that letter? Certainly, we felt loved by her, Danny and me. And the twins are living measured, comfortable lives with their families in two separate Ontario cities. Could this have been possible had they felt emotionally abandoned by their mother in early childhood? But like that letter, life is difficult to decipher. Happiness, when it arrives, is often hard to recognize, and unhappiness is invariably not what it seems. Both are impossible to verify in any real way.

"There are beautifully clear streams in our northern plains. The trout flourishes there, all silver and light. And the water is clean. But when the foreign fish come to these streams, the very water itself becomes unwholesome. The lakes and rivers and lesser tributaries fill with parasites and disease, until we turn away from our own murky waters in disgust." That was the part of the letter I would remember when I was a child in that ward.

In my parents' prairie bedroom, between the wall and the dresser that contained the locked drawer, was a shadowed space just large enough for a child to stand in. And this is where I always stood when I wanted to look inside my mother's jewel box, to touch her three brooches and her jet beads and then those other beads with the cross on the end of them that I had been told were part of her religion. This is where I was standing when I saw my mother, a mature woman, no longer that young teacher she had been in the forest school, open the drawer with her key, remove the envelope, then draw close to the window of her winter bedroom and search the pages of that letter for something, something. . . . I saw my mother, but I knew she did not see me. The intensity, almost ferocity, of her search, the way her eyes slid back and forth as she read, the way she almost clawed at the pages or turned them over impatiently, completely erased not just me but anything else. Then, as if to intentionally bring her back to the present, the twins began to squabble in the kitchen. One shouted, the other one howled, then cried louder in the way that children cry when they want adult intervention. And my mother looked up, turned her face towards the real world, and hurried away to the other end of the house to resolve the dispute, leaving that one important letter on the windowsill not four feet from my hand.

"Disgust," it read. "Gather money," it instructed. "Our tender love," it promised.

I didn't understand. Did I refuse to understand? I put it back on the windowsill.

As for the letter from the man I loved, I waited for it in vain. It did not arrive during the year of my humiliation, or any of the other years of our long connection. Telegrams appeared, and the kind of postcards one could purchase at the post office, ones without any telling images. Occasionally, he used the telephone. And there were, of course, the hotel visits at his convenience. But no letters. What with scandals and divorces, he was far too clever to put anything in writing.

I was hurt, of course. But in the end, I admired him for this.

In the very early evening, after I had read the letter, my father came in from the back acres smelling of grain dust and manure. The stewpot was simmering on the stove, the kettle was sending a ribbon of steam into the air, but the sun was still in the room, and it was not yet time for dinner. My mother brought her hand up to the back of her neck and moved her head against it in a way that suggested strain, fatigue. I could tell she was trying to break out of her preoccupation. "It's early yet, John," she said, without taking her hand from the back of her neck. "Supper won't be ready for an hour."

He sat down heavily on the daybed and unlaced—but did not remove—his boots. "I was thinking of a lesson," he said.

My mother looked at him but did not immediately respond. Then her hand dropped down from her neck, and she crossed the kitchen to a shelf where the only books in our house were kept. Among them were the *Ontario Readers* that she had brought with her when we travelled west. I remembered being introduced to the earliest of these. Or at least I thought I remembered the sheer joy of being introduced to it. But I was particularly fascinated by the little school-book that was not a reader at all but a book called *Picture Study* in which there were smudged and dim black-and-white reproductions of famous European paintings with intriguing fragments of English—and very occasionally American—poetry printed adjacent to them.

"Show me the book with the paintings," my father said now, as if reading my thoughts.

"There's nothing but poetry in them, John," my mother said, trying to dissuade him.

"I'm of a mind to try to read the poetry," he said. "I know you are fond of it," he added, softly. Although a quiet man, my father had his pride. Currying favour with his wife was not his customary style, and I winced with embarrassment for him. Even the twins, who had been chasing each other around the house, sensed the change of tone in the kitchen and stood together near the door, strangely quiet. Danny was somewhere out of doors, but had he been in the kitchen, he would have fallen silent as well. We all knew about these sessions, and the tension that resulted.

"Oh, John," my mother said, raising her hand in the direction of his arm but not touching him, "you're not yet ready to read those poems. You know that."

His forearms were resting on his knees. He did not look at her when he said, "I'd like to make that judgement for myself."

There was a beat of silence. And then I could see he felt the presence of his children, our increasing wariness, and as my mother reached for the book, he glanced at me and winked. But there was neither play nor fun in his expression.

My mother had been teaching my father to read for as long as I could remember. And still he struggled. She had begun with the *First Reader*—he knew the alphabet and some simple words—but he took an aversion to the rhymes. "These are for children," he had said, throwing the book down in exasperation. "Ding dong dell," he had chanted, shaking his head. "Fly away, Pip."

So she moved him to the *Second Reader*, and that is when his exasperation turned to anxiety. Still intended for children, this book had words that were longer and more complicated. The rules my mother had taught him about the sounds connected to the letters revealed their exceptions. Though gentle by nature, he sometimes lashed out at his wife in frustration, and swore. In a more temperamental man, these outbursts would have been less alarming. But coming from him, the surprise of his anger terrified those of us who were children. My mother, on the other hand, seemed to take it in her stride, and occasionally even turned her face away from him and smiled, as though it brought her secret pleasure.

He opened the *Picture Study* book to a foggily printed picture that I now know was one of Fra Angelico's panel paintings and began, haltingly, to read aloud the words of the poem adjacent to it.

Listening was painful for me. After the line "Wrap thy form in a mantle grey," my father's voice cracked while he was trying to sound out the term "star-inwrought." "Star," he recognized once he had the "st" sound. But "inwrought" utterly defeated him.

In the quiet that followed this setback, the whistling kettle began to scream unbearably on the Quebec heater. A log had likely come apart in the stove box and sent up a pillar of flame under the element on which it sat. I ran across the room, seized a tea towel, wrapped it around my hand, and removed the kettle from the hob.

When my mother told my father what the word was, he was loath to believe her. "But, Laura" he said, "it doesn't make any sense."

She was not smiling now. "John, this is Shelley," she said tersely. "On a deeper, more important level, each word makes wonderful sense."

"Deeper than what?" I could see there was a bewildered, almost hunted, expression on my father's face.

My mother could see it, too, and suddenly, a more benevolent notion seemed to take hold of her. "You can't understand it," she said slowly, as if discovering this for the first time. "You'll never understand it." She stood and moved to the window, then turned and smiled at him. "It's not your fault, truly."

She crossed the floor again and lifted the book gently out of his hands while he looked at her suspiciously. "There might be something . . . something—perhaps about farming—that should help you understand?" The statement was couched as a question, as if she were addressing herself on the subject. "Perhaps this?" She turned the book around and displayed a picture of several oxen accompanied by a drover. The twins scampered over to her side to look at the new picture, but she nudged them out of the way so that my father could examine it.

My father was fond of animals. He loved them singly and admired them collectively. I never knew him to pass a neighbour's herd or flock without stopping the wagon, stepping down from it, and strolling over to lean on the fence for what seemed to his child-passengers an interminably long time.

"*Oxen Going to Their Work.*" He had read the title printed beneath the painting with surprising fluency, and he knew it. He glanced in my mother's direction, perhaps seeking her approval.

Her expression remained neutral. "Try to read the poem on the page opposite," she said. "Those oxen will be in it."

His own father had had a team of oxen back in Ontario, and perhaps my mother recalled that, and knew that my father would recall it too. I, however, was familiar with this poem, having taken it in school, and I was terrified that he would not be able to manage the cumbersome language that accompanied the cumbersome beasts it described.

But my father persisted. "'In the furrowed land / The toilsome and patient oxen stand,'" he read. The words emerged slowly. He pronounced "toilsome" as "toe-il-so-me," but accepted the correction from my mother without frustration or embarrassment. "I know what it means," he told her. "It means someone has been ploughing."

He grinned, pleased with himself. "It wouldn't be harrowing," he added, "because of the furrows." He bent back over the poem and, with great effort, sounded out the next two lines, and then the next.

"'Rain in Summer,'" my mother said. "It's not the whole poem that's there, but enough, perhaps?" She framed this remark as a hopeful question. "It's by Longfellow," she added. "You see, John," she explained, rising to walk to the other side of the kitchen, "poets can make the ordinary, extraordinary."

The bar of late afternoon sunlight in the kitchen turned the skirt of her brown dress red.

My father did not reply. He dropped his gaze to the book instead and continued to sound out the words. His mouth was moving, but he didn't even whisper. I could tell he had decided to keep the poem for himself.

My mother was looking out the window towards something, or someone, only she could see. She had been present for the few moments when she had searched for and then presented my father with a string of words that might connect him to poetry: the best part of teaching. But now she was absent again.

Outside a breeze picked up and shook the small apples on the little fruit tree. I could see this through the kitchen window. But it seemed to me that the breeze was also touching the pages of that letter, causing it to shift ever so slightly on the bedroom windowsill or, if my mother had gone back to it, in the darkness of the drawer.

I t was night again in the children's ward, and we were very quiet. But all three of us were awake and I knew this. Sister Philomena was on duty, and as she had told us many times, she "brooked no nonsense." Tatiana was incapable of nonsense, only intensity. And I hadn't the heart for nonsense yet. But in the past, Friedrich liked a joke or two. He had been known to use his pea-shooter to frighten the night nurse on occasion, or to let the air out of a balloon in an undignified manner in order to shock. I knew he was intending to shock because of what Sister Philomena said one night when he had been doing that repeatedly, and she marched in the room to take the balloon into custody.

"If you think you can shock me with rude noises," she had said, "think again, young man. I spend half my life in the company of a bedpan—often *your* bedpan—so there is little left in that department that can even surprise, never mind shock, me. Now hand over that balloon and go to sleep."

But this night there were no more rude noises now that Friedrich was so tired all the time. Just his mind racing in the dark alongside exhaustion, as if it were filled to bursting with all the running and the dancing he could no longer do. I could also feel Tatiana's mind flowing and wandering, like the creek not far from our house in Ontario, just gently touching one subject and then another so as not to be imprisoned by whatever that subject held in its hand. My own mind was caught by something I could not push away, and I envied Tatiana if what Doctor Angel had said about her people was true, for then it would be true of Tatiana as well. She would resist settlement and stabilization, is what I thought much later. But then I only understood that her mind would not be caught in the way that my mind was sometimes caught.

It was something about my important schoolteacher—Master Stillwell—that had caught my mind. Sometimes at night I imagined I could see him pacing back and forth in the dimmest sections of the schoolroom, where all light seemed to be absorbed by that opaque blackboard except where the white numbers of times tables were written. And sometimes the rote learning of times tables became all mixed up with the poems that we all memorized, those poems that moved him in the way my mother wanted to move him.

That night I could hear him whispering to me through the sounds of the radiators.

"Two times two is four, three times three is nine," he whispered as he paced. "Do not close the door, until I make you mine."

Finally, just before I went to sleep, he walked away from me and shook hands with the Conductor, who had been watching from the other side of the ward. "Train number two-two-four," that pale blue railway employee reported coldly, and in a matter-of-fact tone. "Train number three-three-nine. All passengers will continue to snore, right 'til the end of the line."

"People like them have *leaders*," one or the other of them said. "They wait for their leaders to tell them what to do. They want to be educated in four hundred different foreign languages. We can't allow it!" There was a pause.

"Agitate, agitate, agitate!" exclaimed the Conductor. I knew it was him because the sounds of the words were like train sounds. "Agitated, agitated, agitated," he added, with irritation. "The white horse," he said, with a snort of dismissal. "Foreigners and white horses!" He laughed, and his laugh was like slow coughing, like a tolling bell, or like a train pulling into a station. "Ha . . . ha . . . ha . . . ha."

I could see some of those words written on the white, almost translucent paper of my mother's one important letter. *White. Horse. Foreign.*

I began to cry then, but somehow I knew my sobs came from the throat of my mother, and the sounds I made were those I had once heard her making when I approached the quiet house in mid-afternoon. My teacher had started putting me in charge of the class, recently, when he had to leave for an early afternoon appointment or for a meeting with a fellow educator. That's just the way he said it: "fellow educator." One day after he left me standing at the front of the room, I told the children to stay as quiet as possible until the wall clock reached three thirty, and then I walked down the centre aisle towards the back door. I could see Danny looking at me quizzically from the back, but I ignored this. I said I was sick, and I needed to go home. Then I ran and ran. It had rained the night before and there were puddles on the road. You could see reflections of the prairie sky on their surfaces. I remember how the clouds exploded as I ran through them.

I had been absorbed by *Peter Pan and Wendy* until the moment the storm came. Unlike the architecture of my life and the blood network of my family, this distant world, invented by a well-placed British author, remained intact when everything else had been torn apart. I often imagined, therefore, and sometimes dreamt that the ward was the night nursery of the Darling family's home in faraway London. An orderly and a night nurse going about their business could metamorphose into George and Mary Darling sweeping regally by our bedsides in advance of their departure for a dinner engagement.

A flashlight being turned on near a clipboard could be magic. Anything was possible. Sometimes I could swear that the face of the tower clock called Big Ben was rising like an ominous moon outside the window. At those moments I could sense palaces nearby. Not just my mother's palace hotel, but real palaces with a king and all the king's horses and all the king's men.

One night I became aware of the entrance of Peter Pan himself. I had not seen him slip over the windowsill, but his presence was so sudden in the room, it was the only way he could have entered. He was sitting cross-legged on the empty fourth bed, tapping one knee impatiently. Suddenly he was off the bed and moving around the room in a restless, awkward manner that suggested he was not as good at walking as he was at flying. When he reached Tatiana's bedside, he asked her several whispered questions that I could not hear, and she did not answer. Getting no response, he headed for Friedrich's part of the ward, where he began to read aloud one of his *Boy's Own Adventures* by the light of the prairie moon that had recently climbed up the window. This roused Friedrich, who lifted his head and snatched the book out of the boy's hands. In doing so he, Friedrich, knocked a glass with a spoon in it off his nightstand. The resulting sound of clinking metal and shattering glass was magnificent! It suggested magic and Tinkerbell, but brought instead Sister Philomena, who took Peter Pan back to the empty fourth bed and instructed him to "lie down this instant" and go to sleep. When he said he would not, she sailed out of the ward and returned with a glass of water and two pills, which he also refused.

"See here, young man," she said. "Cooperate or I will bring in the orderlies and have them strap you down, and then you'll have no cake in the morning."

I knew there was never any cake in the morning, only rapidly congealing oatmeal, which, because of my infirmities, I had only been required to eat for the last day or so. But apparently Peter Pan was innocent of this knowledge. He accepted the bribe quietly, lay down, and took his medicine like a man.

There were a hundred questions I wanted to ask him, but I couldn't fight sleep any longer. I was looking at the full moon/Big Ben in the window. I knew there would be blue shadows on the snow that I could not see from where I lay, and coyotes on slight rises in the prairies, but I suspected there might be the River Thames and Houses of Parliament as well. The trains would have exchanged their cow-catchers for ploughs, by now, and would be sending up clouds of snow as they progressed across the land. But there would be barges on that famous river, and ships heading for the ocean that I had never seen. I wondered if Peter had viewed all this from above, and whether he had used the prairie train tracks as navigation devices when he flew towards the hospital. Maybe he had used that river, I thought sleepily, or the frightening face of Big Ben.

The next morning Peter Pan had vanished. He was nowhere to be seen. A boy called Eli Cohen had occupied the fourth bed, whence he was sharing his considerable wisdom with the whole room. "I have basic human rights," he was saying. "No one can keep me here against my will. Where's my cake?" he was asking.

Friedrich was, I think, too tired to take to this chatty new boy, and to be fair, Eli was even more of a know-it-all than Friedrich— something I would have considered impossible until he (Eli) appeared. Given to philosophical remarks such as "Space never stops," and "How do you know that the colour blue is the same colour to me as it is to you?" and other rhyming social questions, like "Where does all the garbage go when it goes away? There's going to be a mighty pile-up on some future day." Or, "Top hats and tails and talcum for top dogs, Torn rags and sweat for those who aren't free, The bosses and owners will gaze on in wonder, When Russia exports its Communist thunder, From far away over the sea."

He announced to Friedrich that out on the farm collective, they had the biggest spiders in the world, and that those spiders covered all the fields with webs every single night. "They are like the working class of spiders," he said, "selfless and productive." He had seen those webs shining with dew and alive with spiders the size of dinner plates. "Hard workers," he said. "Good workers." He turned to look directly at Friedrich, who was pretending not to hear him. "Undervalued," Eli added.

Friedrich continued to feign indifference. Then, exhausted though he was, he couldn't help but join in the contest. During his short stay at the orphanage, he told us, he had seen huge spiders that could cross the room in one leap. "They inspired me," he said grandly. "They made me the dancer I am today."

I was feeling irritated. Having lived with twin boys who had begun to compete verbally almost before they could walk, I considered masculine boasting to be both annoying and boring. I was on the verge of pointing out that Friedrich's dance career was over anyway, and that Eli was really Peter Pan, but I felt that might be cruel to Friedrich, and I hadn't the energy for cruelty. Especially towards Friedrich.

Friedrich persisted with the subject of spiders. "Each generation of orphanage spiders was bigger than the one before," he said. "By the time I was captured, there were three generations: the great-grandfathers, the grandfathers, and the grandsons. Some were the size of millstones."

"Granddaughters, I think you mean," said Eli. "The male spider is smaller than the female, and once they mate, she gobbles him up."

Sometimes I could feel Friedrich's feelings. Now I could feel his humiliation in the face of this boy who seemed to know as much as—more than, I suspected—he did. There was nothing for it but for Friedrich to quote Shakespeare. "'Spider-like, Out of his self-drawing web,'" he declared, turning his head in the direction of Eli. "That was Shakespeare," he explained. "I know everything about Shakespeare because of working in the theatre."

But Eli was unperturbed. He told us proudly that before his family decided to come to Saskatchewan to join the farm collective, he had spent one year at a socialist elementary school in Winnipeg, where he had played both a vile capitalist and an oppressed worker in the school's annual winter pageant. He told us that as a vile capitalist, he was required to make a large drawing of a gold pocket watch and cut it out and attach it to a long gold paper chain. All this was pinned to his rich man's formal attire, which came with a bowtie and a top hat as well as tails.

Friedrich scoffed when he heard this. "None of that was real," he announced. "You never had a real gold pocket watch. I bet you didn't even have gold paint. I bet you coloured it yellow." He was sulking now. "Also, you weren't a real actor," he said, "like I am."

"Anyway, if I had had real gold," said Eli, eager to establish a moral high ground if nothing else, "I would have given it away to the poor, who suffer more than we do."

"You speak 'an infinite deal of nothing,'" Friedrich said. "That's from *The Merchant of Venice*," he added, but a little weakly, I thought.

"Who speaks nothing?" asked Mister Porter Abel, swinging around the corner, into the room, and over to my bed. "I don't hear your voice in the discussion, sugar cake, so I expect that's you. When do you suppose these boys, here, are going to let you into the conversation?" He wheeled the nurse's chair across the room and sat down on it backwards, with his arms resting under his chin. "So," he said, "here are some gold uniform buttons, for keepsakes. To remember me by." He opened a small paper bag and spilled four buttons onto the sheet, where I could see them. They were about the size of a nickel and had the shape of a shallow bowl turned upside down. I touched each of them in turn with my one good hand.

I looked at the braid on Porter Abel's cuff and saw the two buttons that were still there. "Happy!" I said as I was delighted by his arrival, also.

A friend was retiring, he told me. When Abel asked for his buttons, the friend, whose name was Stan, said, "Take them all! I never want to see them again."

I did not understand what he was telling me, so I simply nodded.

Suddenly I was aware that Eli was at the porter's side. "These are vintage CPR buttons," he was saying, "in good condition."

"Take one for yourself," said Mister Porter Abel.

"No," Friedrich and I said, right at the same time. Why we did that I'm not quite sure, but it had something to do with Eli being the newcomer and not having earned the right to these gifts.

"Please," said Abel. "Take one for yourself, and here." He placed two buttons in Eli's palm. "Hand one to your friend Friedrich over there."

"Not friend," whispered Friedrich. But Mister Porter Abel either didn't hear him or paid him no mind.

Friedrich snatched the button out of Eli's extended hand. "Now this"—he lifted the small brass object aloft to examine it in a bar of sunlight—"this is true gold."

No one disabused him.

"Where is your whistle and your flags?" asked Eli, bouncing unevenly back towards Abel.

"Signalman has all the flags," said Mister Porter Abel. "I don't get that much permanent paraphernalia, you see. Lots of baggage, but not much permanent paraphernalia. The Conductor, now, he has the most of almost everything. The metal stool so passengers can board, access to lanterns. The ticket punch, a decent living wage, the whistle. It is very uncommon for us to become conductors."

"All aboard!" sang Eli.

I turned my face away. The room was slowly filling with a cold blue mist. It curled around the feet of Friedrich's bed, then moved over to the corner where Tatiana lay so quietly. There was a faint smell of blue spruce and camphor in the air, as well as the smell of creek water from the kinds of streams they'd had back in the forests of Ontario.

I knew the Conductor, with his decent living wage, was in the building, and I closed my eyes so I would not see him if he came into the ward.

"Come on back, Buttons," said Mister Porter Abel. He had taken off his cap. "I'll leave you my Twenty-Five Years of Service appreciation badge in my will," he said, "if you'll just come back. Look." He shook my arm. "Here it is, right in the centre of my hat brim. The conductors come and go," he assured me. "Very rare for them to get anything like this."

But sleep, who had been tapping me on the shoulder all afternoon, now began to tug on my one good arm in earnest, and I had no choice but to go with her.

"The Conductor comes and goes," he repeated as I drifted off. "Don't you pay him any mind."

I awoke just fifteen minutes later to the sound of an announcement in the hall. "Introducing the Dog of the Decade, Aerial the standard poodle," the announcement declared, "and her lovely companions, the talented Vandalistics!" With that, a white dog the size of a small pony pranced into and toured the room, visiting each of our beds in an alert, confident, and brief manner. She stopped only once, to lick Mister Porter Abel's outstretched hand, then exited as swiftly as she had arrived.

"Oh," said Eli in disappointment. "Why did he leave so soon?"

"It's part of the act," said Friedrich, undeniably the expert on this occasion. "And she's a *she*. Just wait."

Shortly after this we were startled by the cacophony of three fair-haired girls—about my age—tap-dancing their way into the room. They wore the kind of pink party dresses I had always wanted but had never achieved, and the kind of black masks favoured by the robbers I had seen illustrated in the books Danny liked to read. They also had stunning tap shoes topped with black bows. Accompanying them was a fourth girl, dressed in exactly the same outfit but playing an accordion and not dancing. The tune she played was stirring and caused my heart to beat so hard, I felt it move the mattress under my ribs. (Friedrich later told me the music was something called "The Gladiator" march by John Philip Sousa, not that I had a clue who that was at the time.)

The Dog of the Decade re-entered the room and pranced around them on her hind legs. It was almost too much for me, and I could tell by his absorption that it was almost too much for Mister Porter Abel as well.

"I know you want to be one of those girls," he said after they had finished and were gathered in a giggling scrum near Friedrich's bed. "But you never will be." He took my one good hand in his large warm hands. "They will disappear into adulthood and will never be seen again, you understand." He put his cap with its twenty-five-year pin back on his head, stood up, and pushed the nurse's chair to the spot it usually occupied in the room. When he returned to my bedside, he picked up my hand one more time. "You will take everything you are right now with you into womanhood. You will keep the injured child that you are now alive in your mind so you can know yourself better. She will sustain you. She will never disappear. Adulthood will never extinguish her."

A few nights later the terrible pain began again. Accompanying it was a fiery desire to get up and move around the room the way I sometimes moved around the yard at home. My father called it "cavorting," and I was so taken with that word that I looked it up in the big dictionary that was open on a lectern in one corner of the schoolroom. It said the word "cavort" was a combination of the words "curvet" and "gavotte" (which did not enlighten me in any way), and that it meant to leap and caper about.

I wanted to do cartwheels across the room and chase the twins and make them squeal, and I wanted to run after Danny and tackle and tag him, but I wanted to do all that in the night ward, and this wanting presented itself as a kind of penetrating and painful flame that was burning through my muscles and even through the tendons at the back of my knees. I knew my body strove to twitch but was incapable even of twitching. In my bed at home, I sometimes had what my father called restless legs. He said that I was growing too fast, that I would have long legs, and that the restlessness would disappear once my legs were the size they wanted to be.

Now I was worried that this extreme form of restlessness in my useless limbs might never disappear. How could my legs, fractured as they were, ever grow enough to be as long as they wanted to be? I thought about growth then, about everything that is growing and how that growth could be cut off, brought down, interrupted, or entirely cancelled.

My mother had once showed me something in the family Bible that had filled me with dread, and now, with the desire to cavort upon me, and the physical pain, and the memory of what she had shown me suddenly fresh in my mind, I was in a terrible state. The last few pages of the large Bible, wonderfully surrounded by colourful intertwined climbing flowers, were dedicated to the family register, with the birth and death dates of all up to the fifth generation in faraway islands off the coast of faraway Europe. It was while reading this register that I came to know about the terrible numbers of dead children in the families of my mother's generation and the generation just preceding hers. Aletha and Noreen and Violet and Evelyn, all dead before they were ten. Gladys and Herbert and Newbold and Bridgit, who died in the first one or two years of their lives. I suddenly understood with absolute clarity that all these children were present in my blood and in my broken bones, that they wanted to run and play as much as I wanted to run and play. I was their host; their running and playing, their cavorting, was my responsibility. It wasn't as if I believed that I was doing the running and playing *for* them, exactly, but that they simply could not do it without the conveyance of my body.

An involuntary spasm visited my spine then, and for the first time since the accident, I began to move without the aid of another human being. My one good arm shot out and swept all the objects off the bedside table, causing a silver waterfall of metallic items to cascade noisily to the floor; kidney and wash basins, a bedpan, a small tin water jug, and a glass thermometer filled with mercury. The children inside me were playing, cavorting, but the feeling was powerfully unmanageable, and the pain rang like a bell in my bones. Doctor Angel, who had mysteriously come into focus through the games that were being played in my legs and spine, laid a steadying hand on my shoulder as he inserted a needle into my hip.

And then I became quiet. The children turned back into the ghosts that they really were, and dissolved, coming apart in the air in the same way that the winged seeds of clustered milkweed separate and depart from the pod. Or prairie clouds sometimes become stratified and then disappear, devoured by the clear blue sky.

I told Doctor Angel about the children. "Dead children," I said. "In the family Bible," I explained.

"Yes," he replied, as if making an admission of something he already knew and felt responsible for.

"Living in me," I said. "Playing in me."

"Now?" he asked. "Still?"

"No," I said. "Now they are all . . ."

"Gone?" he said.

"Yes. No, not gone. But quiet," I whispered.

"The needle settled them down."

I supposed that was the case, though I didn't say anything.

"Did you know," he asked, putting his hand back on my shoulder in that steadying way he favoured, "that a scientist called Father Mendel discovered how our eyes and arms and legs and hair are formed by patterns that repeat themselves? Those children may have had a mouth like yours or an eyebrow. Some of them may have had hair the same colour as yours, or a thumb the same shape. So in some sense, it is true that when you play, they all play. Their potential for play was brought into the present by you—you are their heir—and even though they died when they were very young, parts of them are alive in you."

Someone passed by in the hall, and he turned his head to see who it was. He raised his hand in greeting, then put it back on my shoulder. "And those parts," he added, "are eager for play."

He became silent. I sensed a poem was forming. Through the partly opened doorway, I could see Sister Editha dozing at her post in the triangle of light shed by her desk lamp.

"He observed flowers," Doctor Angel said, "in a monastery court-yard. I expect he walked in the cloister every day and assessed the blossoms at the centre. There would have been one bright rectangle of blue above these blossoms, and stars moving over them at night."

I was attempting to sort through the mystery of what Doctor Angel was telling me when suddenly he spoke again.

"Genetics and light," he said, with conviction, as if those two words explained everything. Then he stood up to leave me. "Genetics and light," he repeated. He sighed. "Sometimes it was almost too much for him—the patterns, the beauty—sometimes the noon of night . . ." He didn't finish the sentence. He touched my shoulder one more time. "Goodnight, little Emer," he said. "Keep playing tag in Mendel's garden."

I think of Danny now when I remember this. How hopeful he is, and how curious about life in his own monastery, and his own garden, how interested in and in love with the world despite having to give up romantic love. When, before he took his vows, I cautiously mentioned this to him, he reminded me that his most significant attachment had come and gone before the vocation tapped him on the shoulder. "You know I've been deeply in love, Emer," he said. "I am able to keep the memory of that while still carrying on with a life here." He was quiet for a moment. And then he surprised me by saying with a grin, "How lucky is that?!"

He loves weather, the birds, the toothed cogs and the wheels of the printing press that publishes the parishioners' newspaper, prayers, sheet music, debating, snowshoeing, and skating on the outdoor rink he creates each year. What a sight he is with skate blades flashing and robes billowing! With his penchant for enthusiasm, he is more like Harp than he knows, though the subjects of their passions differ.

There was sheet lightning far out on the prairie the night that Doctor Angel told me about Mendel's monastery garden. It lit the darkness of the night ward. As I began to dream, I could see a full day, and then another, and then a summer sweeping speedily over the zinnias in my mother's flower garden, and how the shadow of the house touched the blossoms, then moved on.

During the quietest hours of the winter night shifts, when she was not dozing at her post or ministering to the sick, Sister Editha worked on her book of saints. I knew that this was true because she told me once. And, also, because I could hear pages being turned in her notebook and the irregular scratches of her pen on the paper. Sometimes there were long pauses in the scratching, and I knew that Sister Editha was thinking in the silence of what her next sentence might be. When she had told me about the book, she also mentioned that sometimes the sentences flowed as if they were being dictated by God, and sometimes they halted as if the Devil himself were trying to interfere.

She was writing about the saints that the artist from Europe had chosen to paint on the walls in the nearby Saint Peter's Abbey church. The artist from Europe, she admitted, had not been in Europe for a long time because he was so busy painting the interior walls of the churches and cathedrals that were being built in the Americas. Saint Peter's was one of those churches, but one that the artist from Europe had taken such a shine to that he had decided to set up his studio in Saskatchewan. "The railways of Saskatchewan can take you anywhere, so he could travel for business," Sister Editha reminded me. I did not need reminding, having seen my Ontario teacher, Master Stillwell, reappear like an itinerant ghost to haunt our lives, even though we were so far away that our Irish relatives had an immigration wake for us when we left the province.

"To think those railroads brought me from Austria. One of God's great miracles! I have never been inclined to climb back on board, mind you." She shook her head and shuddered at this point, as if trying to rid herself of the noise of trains.

She told me about Saint Benedict, for whom the monastery and convent were founded. She told me about Saint Bruno, who had spent time in the desert and, when called to Rome, had also built himself a small hermitage in the ruins of the baths of a Roman emperor. I thought of him putting a roof over a tin bathtub like the one we had at home for our weekly baths, and splashing about therein. She told me about how the painter had decided to include the Irishman Saint Donatus because of the small Irish colony that had been founded in the vicinity by Father Sinnett. She said that while she was writing, she sometimes prayed to Saint Donatus because he had taught grammar and had written poetry. "He knew that words could sing," she told me. "And knew as well that they very often don't sing. When the words no longer sing, I summon Saint Donatus." She was silent for a moment, thinking. "To be perfectly honest," she said, "I very often pray to Saint Gertrude as well. She was a copyist in the scriptorium of her own convent while she was still a little girl, but she also wrote many books herself after Christ became her bridegroom." Then there was Saint Isidor, the farmer, whom the artist from Europe had included in his wall painting because so many of the people in the region were farmers, and Isidor was a simple farm labourer. "A humble profession," Sister Editha observed. "And one filled with grace. The artist knew that someone like Isidor needed to be among the saints in the abbey church."

Very quietly she crossed the room and looked down at Tatiana, who was as still as Snow White on her bed. "Saint Agnes, the youngest of all the saints, still a child at thirteen," she said. "Tatiana is like her. Almost the same age, but also like her in her beauty and her suffering."

On an early winter morning, when the dawn was no more than a thin red ribbon intersecting darkness, I saw the saints and prophets Sister Editha had spoken of passing by the door of our ward. Saint Agnes carried the palm of martyrdom; Saint Gertrude carried the long feather pen with which she copied the gospel in the convent's scriptorium. Their gait was restrained, and their steps were so quiet I understood the slowness of their approach rather than heard it. But I could feel a soft joy pouring from them, then flowing, almost by accident, across the floor in my direction. The men had crooks and staffs and mitres upon which they leaned, and which gave them dignity, but also a heaviness and sombreness the women did not possess. Everyone had an abundance of long white hair—quite unkempt but lovely nevertheless—and the men all had the long beards favoured by various kings I had seen in the half-dozen illustrations decorating the Old Testament part of the family Bible.

They stood at the doorway for a while as if struck with wonder, or as if they themselves were the wonder—a vision of visionaries— then moved soundlessly into the room, where they drifted among our beds, sometimes touching us on the hair as if anointing us before moving over to the window, where they stood silhouetted against the now pale orange sky. They were all speaking at once, but in whispers, or at the very least in tones so low I could not make out what they were saying. Their speech was like the sound that is made by that one branch of tenacious dried November leaves, or like the pedals of a pump organ when you have failed to press a key. I thought I heard one of them say, "Help her heal, help her heal," but then I realized that almost every sound they uttered was filled with breath in the way that "h" words are. Eli woke up. Then Friedrich. But Tatiana lay as still as she might have had nothing at all changed in the room. They began to move back and forth at the window. Some of them made noises that were like chanting or singing, or even like crying. Eli sang a few phrases then, in the minor key that I would much later discover was associated with a cantor in a synagogue, then fell silent. I held my breath. I knew that Eli and Friedrich were holding their breath too. Tatiana breathed in the beautiful regular way she always did.

Then Sister Philomena bustled in, hands in the air in distress. "How on earth did you get DOWN here!" she exclaimed. "One fall on the stairs would have been the death of all of you!" The saints and prophets proved to be very uncooperative as she tried to round them up, moving off vaguely in all directions. But eventually she succeeded in restoring order. As she led them out of the room, she announced, to no one in particular, that getting them to behave was just like herding cats.

I thought her statement was very disrespectful and said so. "Saints and prophets," I announced.

"Those were the old people," Eli said, his voice quiet in the silence they had left behind. "They come from the old people's part of the hospital." The room was pink now, and I imagined Eli's face, rosy in the glow.

"What was the old people's part of the hospital?" I wanted to ask, but my sleepy voice was all used up by articulating the word "saints," followed by the word "prophets."

"What old people's part?" Friedrich asked, as if speaking for me.

"It's at the very top of the hospital," Eli said, with certainty. "They are tremendously old up there and will soon be dead. So they may as well be on the top floor, closer to heaven."

My breath came back, and my voice came back too. I recalled the very aged Old Testament prophets. "Are they on the roof?" My mother had told me that her cousin Ella, whom my mother claimed was "saint-like in her suffering," and who died of tuberculosis, was often put on the roof in winter, to air out. Perhaps the very old prophets needed to air out as well. My question seemed reasonable to me. But Eli laughed his highest laugh, which was followed by a falling arpeggio of laughter. Even in the dark, I knew that it would be accompanied by a lot of rocking and head shaking. Very humiliating for me.

"How do you know they are going to heaven?" Friedrich asked. Then, "How do you know there even IS a heaven?"

"They are not on the roof," Eli said, suddenly serious. "And there are several heavens. One for scholars, another for angels, a third for the decent men and women of the working class, and so on. Oh, and the throne of God is in another heaven. Or maybe the same one as the angels. There are seven in all, I think."

I remembered my mother saying that when she was in the castle hotel, she felt as if she were in seventh heaven. I thought the murmuring saints and prophets should also have been in this seventh heaven, which I now visualized as the castle hotel. They might have been sitting in one of the tower rooms at the right hand of God.

I remembered the old people in our Ontario family, how they had been seated, not in a tower and not at the right hand of God, but rather in the corners of kitchens in various farmhouses. Thin, spent by child-rearing or agricultural labour, or a combination of both, they bore absolutely no resemblance to their younger selves, who were often to be found in the unheated, distant parlours of such houses, staring out from daguerreotypes. Sometimes those same parlours sported an example of something amazing and superfluous that those old people had done when they were young: a fine hooked rug on which you must never step or a bowl made from applewood. Occasionally there was even an oil painting of an improbable landscape with tropical trees and mountains. The same old aunt who had, in her youth, painted the tropical trees and mountains would inevitably be laid out in the parlour, possibly beneath this very picture. Perhaps that landscape had been her idea of seventh heaven.

Just as the castle hotel had been for my mother.

The sighing saints and murmuring prophets were completely unlike my aged relatives. There was an inexplicable strength and direction in the soft, tender steps these dawn prophets so tentatively took, a startling imagery in their stance against the orange sky, and purpose in the mysterious sounds they whispered. Encouraging my Ontario elders to behave would have been hardly worth the effort, they sat so passively and silently in their corners. It would have been nothing like herding cats.

There must be a moment when you suddenly know the comfort of those corners, however; a moment when your hard-backed seat at the table is filled by someone younger and stronger, someone who just yesterday was a child clinging to your skirts, and who now crosses the room with a plate of soft food for you in their hands. When will I sit in a padded armchair with cushions at the small of my back? I still drive the frozen roads and deliver the music to children who so eagerly want to receive it. But for how long? On these winter nights, while I am writing this, I can feel those shadowed corners preparing for me, anticipating my arrival. Except that my own farm kitchen was long ago destroyed by change and weather. And the small community of wounded children that temporarily replaced that world is frozen into the past. The man I loved is gone and can no longer come to me. Danny, my brother, is cloistered in his world, and I in mine.

I am left alone and willing to bargain for the comfort of strangers, for a life that matters, for human companionship.

Wishing there were another breath in the house.

Oh, the evening games played by lamplight! The hiding and seeking. The tower of blocks that the twins built, then destroyed with the subtlest nudge of a hand. *The Lost Heir* board game that Danny was so keen on. The games with shadows. How we made silhouettes of each other's profiles, standing in the light a fire makes on a wall.

Sometimes I saw those silhouettes on the hospital wall. Other times I saw the cracks in the glaze, or the deeper cracks caused by human carelessness, across the silhouetted pavilions and bridges and song-birds of my mother's Blue Willow dishes.

My mother had one good set of dessert plates, handed down to her from her own mother. Its pattern was green, not blue like her other plates, and encircled by a gold border. Decorated, at the centre, by a small scattered still life of the palest of pink roses and apples and pears, not one piece of it was exactly the same as another. It was seldom if ever used, even on special days such as Christmas or my father's birthday. Very occasionally my mother would remove two or three pieces from the sideboard, lay them on the table, and point out to me that if you looked closely, you could see the differences in the painting at the centre. Sometimes there were two pears and an apple, sometimes two apples and a pear. On one, there were several roses and only one piece of fruit. This, she said, proved that they were painted by hand, or as she said, "hand done."

Doctor Carpenter would use the same phraseology when justifying his version of treatment. "I heal by hand," he said. "I don't cure diseases. I fix the broken things instead. By hand."

The Blue Willow pattern was not hand done. An Englishman's idea of a Chinese landscape, mass-produced and meant for everyday use, it was more interesting than its Spode cousin. It was casually strewn across the pine table in the kitchen. It jumped and possibly cracked when my father's fist hammered home the iambics of a poem by Henry Wadsworth Longfellow ("Pegasus in Pound" comes to mind), and it fell to pieces in the dishpan. But it was alive, and we were drawn to its pavilions and bridges, its people and softly swooping birds. The only thing I do not remember about the willow-pattern plate is the willow itself. I recall instead a monk beckoning from a temple door, a sugges-tion of foreign mountains, a meeting on a bridge.

S ometimes during his frequent absences and silences, I drifted away from Harp. He became indistinct, a shadow, a stranger glimpsed out the window of a train. He was not replaceable, so he was never replaced. Still, I was coaxed away from him and towards life by my singing children, the way all their faces turned towards me as I entered their makeshift schools. I was even drawn away from him by the material structure of the schools themselves, how they had been pounded into existence by unrefined, agricultural men, many of whom could not read, but who were determined that their children would do so. Without personal ambition, they had done what they knew how to do, and had built the schoolroom in which their children would learn how to be ambitious. They did this by hand.

"Let the stonecutters be stonecutters," Hippocrates, father of all doctors, had said. Doctor Carpenter told me this, or he mentioned it in my presence. Perhaps he was speaking to someone else, excusing himself for his bone cutting, his brutality, which was often the only way to save a life. "You have to have the stomach for it," he said. "And the results are not guaranteed. You have to be willing to take the risk."

Surely I overheard this. Who would say such things to a child?

In fact, the Conductor had said something similar a few nights before in my mind, but much more casually and cheerfully. Of course, once he got everybody aboard, he knew *his* results were guaranteed. I heard him say it once. He was laughing softly and pulling up those iron stairs that meant no one who got aboard could ever get off without his cooperation. He winked. "You *have* to have the *stomach* for it," he said.

Then he laughed in that train-like way of his. "Ha . . . ha . . . ha . . . ha . . ."

Now it was Eli who was crying out in the night. Having had his foot "corrected" by Doctor Carpenter, he was in tremendous pain.

"At least his foot *could* be corrected," said Friedrich, peevishly and sleepily. "What's he crying for?"

Sister Hildegard was on night duty. Unlike the other nursing sisters, who wore the tokens of their religion lightly, Sister Hildegard sported a large wooden crucifix that bounced against her habit as she walked. When she came to Eli's bedside to comfort him, the wooden crucifix, with her flashlight behind it, swayed into his line of vision, and he cried out in terror.

Sister Hildegard tried to calm him, but he wouldn't be calmed. "On fire," he said. "A cross on fire."

Finally, Sister turned on the tin lamp on his bedside table, and he settled somewhat. "What is troubling you, Eli?" she asked.

Now fully awake, Eli was coming back into his own. In a shaky voice, he said, "Jesus was a Jew himself."

"True," said Sister, a bit taken aback.

Then Eli told those of us who were awake that some bad people had come to the farm commune dressed in white, and they had banged together large crosses and set them alight while everyone was sleeping.

"And they tried to burn down our houses," he said. "They smashed our windows and threw lit torches into our kitchens."

None of us in that sick room were strangers to the persistent life of hallucinations, which we believed in, often more passionately than we believed in that which is visible.

We all believed Eli.

But Sister Hildegard did not. She stroked his forehead and said, "All will be well."

He cried longer, but the energy had gone out of his crying and finally it subsided, then stopped altogether, though the sinking silence it left in its wake was more disturbing. After a little while, Sister rose from the chair beside his bed, turned off the light, and began to tiptoe towards the door.

Just before she left the room, Eli sat up and called after her. "It's true," he insisted. "There were crosses burning. My mother and even my father cried because of them. And there was firelight, and broken glass, and the noise of horses."

And then he added, almost in a whisper, "And all the windows were broken."

Sister Hildegard did not answer him. She just smiled to herself instead and shook her head from side to side as she left the ward. I could hear her talking to someone in the hall. "What those children won't imagine!" was what she said.

I could see that firelight in my mind. I could see Eli's face in it, and the tears coming out of his eyes. I could hear the stifled adult weeping of his parents, so different from the deliberate orchestral crying of a child. I wished I could roll over to the wall, to free myself of the thought of those unhappy mingled sounds, and the inner pictures I had of the white clothes that covered the torchbearers, their tunics and hoods, the pattern and stitching, the labour behind it and the burden of it, which I knew so well.

I had found my mother in front of an uncooperative sewing machine, weeping in frustration while trying to make those complicated garments.

"I have been in love," she had said to me, yanking up the white material towards the machine, then pushing it under the cloven foot and needle tooth of the Devil's instrument. "I have been in love," she insisted, in a choked, almost strangled voice. "And that is life. That is being alive."

Harp has been gone for almost a decade. And yet the idea—and the mystery—of him stays with me.

But not the graceful mystery or the pleasurable haunting that was present when I knew for certain I would see him again. Then I would find myself, stock still with my hand on the door before going out into the yard or motionless in the middle of the kitchen floor because a moment from one of our previous meetings had unfolded itself in my mind. Harp, though far away, was very near to me at those times, a benign presence, as if his breath were near my heart.

Now, at night, I see him differently, as if in his definite absence he has become a perplexing and vaguely malicious spirit, bent on causing bewilderment, shame. I question and interpret every sentence I can remember him saying in one palace room or another. Who was included when he used the pronoun "we"? I ask myself. Why did he use the distancing demonstrative pronoun "this" to sum up all the complexities of our entanglement?

Sometimes I am shaken out of sleep at two or three in the morning by inner inquiries to which there are no conclusive answers. At these moments I haven't a drop of Danny's philosophic saintliness. Added to this is the suspicion that Harp is only pretending to be dead and has, in fact, joined some collective, a fraternity of "those in charge." On the edge of consciousness, this coalescence seems a magnificent betrayal. "You owe me an explanation," I say, angrily, to him or to nobody in the dark. "We need to talk this through!"

We. This.

"You wanted those like you to prop you up because you are weak," I whisper, climbing out of sleep, slick with sweat and anger. Whether this slur was meant for him or someone else, or possibly for myself, was all the same to me. It was his fault, his betrayal. It was where loving him had brought me. It was cold and empty, all its wild grasses and flowers were gone, and the wind had murder on its mind.

And then, as dawn comes and I am still fully awake, I always begin to soften. What was it about him? Surely my life was enlarged by knowing him. I recall his humour, his playfulness. His enthusiasms. His intermittent tenderness.

And his heartbreaking ambition: this need to prove that the great discovery had been just the first of many, which even I could see was not going to be the case. And, as always, his unconvincing denial of ambition.

They want the impossible, the men who—essentially on our behalf—carry our human ambition into the world. They believe, with touching sincerity, in the dailiness of the work. There is little poetry about the process, as they would be the first to tell you, and something noble and ironically selfless in their aspirations, which ultimately lead to the enlarging of the self. And they are patient—in the way that workhorses are patient—with the implausible outcome this ambition demands.

By mid-morning I have stopped whispering to Harp and he has ceased to haunt, and I cannot remember what it was he was required to explain to me in the night. I remember the importance of the discovery, how its annunciation shook *him* awake in the night as certainly as it would have had there been an annunciating angel in the room delivering a heavenly proclamation.

Harp was surprisingly intuitive and feminine in his reception of this annunciation. Normally driven and determined, he was nevertheless unsurprised that his monumental breakthrough came to him as a dream. He literally jotted it down, then let the experiments prove the point. The lab work was there, of course, before and after the instant of semi-conscious thought that led to what he called "the moment of truth." But in essence, he blundered into the fire of discovery, then burned into greatness. And paid for that blunder, that burn, for the rest of his life.

He was "through with wives" by the time we met. His first wife (the one whom he claimed had been out and about being Mrs. Discovery) was unable, he insisted, to cope with his success—the speaking engagements, the extended absences—as well as his infidelities, which were not as frequent, given his schedule, as she may have imagined. In the end she herself had taken a lover, and in an opportunistic bid to save the reputation of their famous client, his lawyers, or someone hired by his lawyers, had burst in upon a tryst with a young man barely out of his teens. Harp had known nothing about this plan, he assured me, and was shocked by the vulgarity of it. And he was made uncomfortable, he said, by the idea of the humiliation he knew she would have to undergo in the divorce courts. I knew he was lying. But, had I suspected he was a complete cad, it would have made no difference to me then. Kindness, I later realized, was another one of the things that I did not want from him.

I wanted him to be confident and steady in his care for me, even when that confidence pertained to my believing all the lies he told with such panache. I loved him for his knowledge of science, his rich understanding of anatomy, including the unsettling thought that he knew everything about my own anatomy, its beauty and its unsightliness. I wanted him to talk about medicine, about science, but it was in him in such a cellular way, he seldom spoke of it. I also wanted access to the world of culture that he cared about so deeply. He did not take his access to culture for granted and, as a result, would enthuse about it in my presence. He knew the painters who painted untarnished northern landscapes in the mode of the French impressionists. They sometimes painted forests on the banquet room walls of castle hotels built in the very cities whose growth and greed would destroy such landscapes. He knew the sculptors who made the memorials to war, commerce, and ambition. He himself had already been memorialized by such sculptors.

I knew none of these people.

And it must be admitted that he did his best to see me as he sped through the northern plains on railways destined for more important places. With a full roster of speaking engagements, advisory board meetings, and international public health panels, Harp was almost always on the move. Hence the more important places. To see me, he took the spur lines from more important places to less important places: those two or three castle hotels I could reach on a spur line of even less significance.

He was concerned about media discovery due to his celebrity (due also, I am certain, to the memory of the surprise arrival of the detectives in his ex-wife's hotel room), and he disguised himself accordingly with wigs and costumes—once even a tartan kilt complete with sporran and bagpipes. He used Russian and French camouflage—hats and scarves—repetitively and successfully. He was once followed by the hotel detective, however, when he dressed as a prairie farmer in rubber boots and overalls. This was very suspicious; farmers were never seen in the lobbies and elevators of castle hotels. After that, he let such extremity of masquerade go. Bellboys and desk clerks seemed unfazed by his journey to the elevator. They knew about his achievement, his great discovery, but despite the bronze portrait busts and statues, or perhaps because of them, they did not know his face.

Harp was a tall, rangy man, with a narrow head and a mouth too big for the territory it occupied. His hands were large and bony, with long, tapering fingers. There was something in his slightly stooped posture that, despite his height, put you in mind of certain failed lightweight boxers, or the kind of clowns who never make you laugh. As he once said to me, whenever he appeared in the flesh, he never failed to disappoint.

But his flesh did not disappoint me. I loved him. Physically. And in all his disguises.

Still, I wonder now if perhaps that was part of the explanation I demanded when half awake, years later, in the middle of the night. What was the unlovable part of me that made him so unwilling to see me whole?

In the years towards the end, when he had been single for over half a decade, his fame waned, and he became calmer. It was at this point that he began to break the secrecy rules he himself had put in place. First, we went for short walks in the park across from the palace hotel of the moment, or we strolled around the block it occupied. Sometimes we stepped out the door arm in arm. On some occasions we went downstairs to the dining room, where we sat across from each other, infrequently speaking, and almost as relaxed as the married couples who were at some of the tables surrounding us. Like them, we were not bored, simply contented. After years of tension, we were beginning to be comfortable in each other's presence. This was a surprise—to both of us, I suspect—though neither of us spoke of it. Either we were frightened of breaking the spell, or we knew the undeniable truth of what had been lost: this calmness was evidence that we had settled and cooled.

One evening, after we finished a steak dinner and a bottle of red wine, Harp squinted at me thoughtfully through a cloud of smoke from his interminable cigarette. "I think I would like to take you out," he said.

I laughed and said, "What took you so long?"

There was a movie theatre nearby. Sometimes, on a late afternoon in winter, one corner of a room we had rented might start to flicker with the acidic colours of a blinking neon sign. I wondered if that was what he had in mind, and tried, unsuccessfully, to conjure an image of us sitting side by side, staring at a screen.

"Perhaps," he ventured, "you could come with me to a reception when I'm back next month."

"A reception? What kind of a reception?" I was digging in my handbag, trying to extract a miniature mirror with which to examine my face, as women did in those days. Why did we do this? I wonder now. We were never satisfied with the picture that was revealed in our palm.

"Political," he announced, with a casual wave of the hand holding the cigarette. "Aren't they always, in some form or another? Usually I decline, but this involves a friend." He had been shaking the ice cubes in his glass, and now he tossed back the water they had created and a fair quantity of ice as well, judging by the crunching that followed. "A friend from college," he added. "I often see him when I pass through these parts."

I abandoned my search and stared at him. I could tell he was serious. He was looking out the window to his left. A wrought-iron fence. A park under sodden trees. It had rained all afternoon even though it was August. Harp never made eye contact when the subject being addressed was important to him.

"I don't see why we can't attend together," he said, becoming a bit defensive under my scrutiny once he noticed it. "You could just as easily be my assistant." He pushed his cigarette into the ashtray. "Or something like that."

I knew he had several assistants. All were scientists who worked alongside him in the lab, and two or three were women, unusual at the time, or for that matter, even at this time.

"I've never been to a political reception," I said. I doubted that town hall meetings would count as experience in this matter.

"Do you have a good dress?" he asked. Condescendingly, I thought. I knew he meant a cocktail dress and decided right then to purchase such an item before I left town tomorrow.

"Of course," I said. "It's how I dress for funerals."

He laughed, though this remark had left him considerably less comfortable. Perhaps he recalled, as I did, that a few short hours ago we had been in each other's arms, not trading ironic remarks about fashion.

As a broken child I had seen the shape of my mother's one good dress on a hospital wall, and I had remembered its story. Only now do I make the connection. The dress I would buy for that one public occasion would be my one good dress. It still hangs, all these years later, in my closet. I have never worn it again.

Suddenly I was thinking about high-heeled shoes, so I must have been flattered by the idea of Harp's taking me out. Otherwise, I, the lame child, could not have considered such things. I would need to buy a pair of those as well, and I would have to practise walking in them, cane and all. I also worried that once I put these shoes on and stood beside this man whom I adored, I might be taller than he was. I doubted he would like that.

As it turned out I was not taller than him. Nevertheless, I have not worn the shoes again either. They did nothing to improve my posture or my gait, and for weeks afterwards, the hip pain they were responsible for kept me company on sleepless nights.

"Where are we going?" I asked him once we were back in the room. "Where are you going to take me?"

Years later disquiet would stalk me. But at that moment I was experiencing that combination of apprehension and excitement a much younger woman—a girl—might feel in anticipation of the kind of dance I felt I never could go to because of my limp.

"A party fundraiser," he said. It was an evening in early August and the sun had not yet gone down. The shadows of the elms were moving in the light that had pooled near his chair. The sun was hitting one side of his face, and he held his hand against it in a half-hearted salute to block the light. The surprising fragility of that gesture startled and moved me.

It wasn't like him to agree to appear at events such as these, or to even faintly suggest support of one political party or another. I pointed this out to him now. "You never do this," I said.

"I have a friend or two," he said, "in the place where the fundraiser is being held." He looked at me and smiled. A bit sheepishly, I thought, but with affection. "My college friend is a former premier. And there will be a chief justice—that sort of thing. They are hoping to get more money from the province."

"And this money is for what?" The sun abruptly vanished from his part of the room. It was about to get dark, though we were still in summer.

"The Saskatchewan School for the Deaf. The former premier— my friend Walt—is its director. We were at university together in Toronto for a year or so. I told you that, right? I can't even remember how we met—he was in English or education. Or was it history?" He thought about this, frowning for a bit with his face turned down looking at his shoes. "Education, I believe," he said, without changing the angle of his face, so that even though we were both seated, he appeared to be looking up at me. "I think he may have taught at one time or another." He mulled this over. "Doesn't matter," he finally said. "We became pals."

So that's it, I thought, catching the allusion to education. He can take me with him to this event because I am a teacher. Added to this, the oddness of my body, my limp and cane, would make him appear to be kind. Another bonus. These were the thoughts I sometimes had, uncharitable, self-involved. Still, I was certain Harp was an opportunist, and to this day I believe he never went anywhere, or did anything, without two or three motives. All genuine.

It took a moment or two, but I came round to thinking about the children. "Do the students—the deaf children—live there?" I asked.

"I believe so." An emotion he wouldn't confess flickered across his face. He was fond of children, I knew, and was sensitive to any handicap they had been unfairly dealt.

He had untied his shoes after we returned to the room. Leaning forward now, he pulled the laces tight in his fists, on one foot after another. Then his fingers became busy with the oddly feminine task of making two bows. "Some are as young as six, according to Walt."

"Six," I said. "Sophie was only six."

"Who?" He stood and pushed his arms into a pale yellow cardigan. August evenings on the prairies cooled quickly. The garment was too small for him and pushed the shoulders of his shirt up towards the collar in a way that resembled the ruffs of the European explorers I had seen in the *Picture Study* book when I was young.

I rose from the chair to kiss him goodbye. "It's nothing," I said. "Just someone I knew when I was a child."

"School?" he asked.

"No, a roommate from the ward."

"Ah," he said. "Did she have . . . ?"

"No," I interrupted, "only Friedrich. You remember, the boy soprano."

"Of course," he shot back. But by then he was looking for his hat.

"Sophie had another disease," I said. "Leukemia," I added.

We looked all over the room and in both the bathroom and the closet for that hat. But then suddenly, he remembered it lying on the restaurant floor beside his chair.

I called down to reception to ask.

Always prepared for departure, I thought.

Harp was staying with his friend. The one who had studied history or English or education at his university. He would be heading over there now, after he retrieved the hat.

Soon after he closed the door, I would prepare for bed: teeth, face cream, flannelette nightwear.

We rarely spent the night together. I had begged him for this— this one concession—in the beginning. But I didn't beg for anything anymore. As Danny pointed out, didn't even pray for anything.

My train did not leave until midday, so that would give me plenty of time to stop by a dress shop on my way to the station. I would look for a navy-blue silk dress with the slenderizing waist of the period, short sleeves, and a white lace collar. I wouldn't be back in the city until our next meeting. But I could buy the high heels in the little shoe store once I was home in Muenster.

Then came the day in the children's ward when I could sit up by myself against the pillows. Sometimes the pain returned and made me gasp. But sitting up was worth any amount of discomfort. I could see the whole room now. Doctor Carpenter stood by my bedside, having insisted that I let him prop me up. He smiled, but never lost his sternness. The other children, except for Tatiana, had their gazes fixed on me. Friedrich looked both fascinated and a bit irritated. There was worry in his expression as well, but I could tell he was trying to hide that. When I looked towards him, he dropped his plentiful eyelashes over his eyes and became absorbed in removing a game of jacks from the package that held it. The tiny red rubber ball, the lovely star-shaped multicoloured counters.

"You see," Doctor Carpenter said to me, "you can do this sitting up just fine. A few more interventions"—I now knew that "intervention" meant surgery—"and we'll have you on your feet."

I was not certain that I still was in possession of feet. I had achieved a seated position, but I couldn't remember what was entailed in the act of standing up. The knees lifting, the arms pushing from behind. But I sensed that standing up was the ticket to the rest of my life. I was very wary of the "interventions," however.

At that moment, with Doctor Carpenter's attention on me, and the curiosity of the other children in the room aroused by the suggestion that I might soon be standing, Sophie entered our lives and diverted all attention (including mine) to her glorious self. She was conveyed into our ward by a wheelchair piloted by Sister Philomena, though everything about her looked both healthy and mobile. Her black mop of hair was messy and shiny and beautiful. Her eyes were brown and questioning. "Who is *he*?" she asked, with some disdain, I thought, as she was wheeled past Friedrich's bed. And then, "Why is *she* asleep at noon?" as her chair passed poor silent Tatiana.

"This is Sophie," Sister Philomena announced. "Let's hope one of you gets well soon, as Sophie here will be occupying the last bed in the ward."

What about the *sixth* bed? I wondered.

"I'm ready to leave *immediately*!" Friedrich made no eye contact as he said this. "My public awaits me!"

I stared at the new arrival. Eli stared at her. But Friedrich, who was still playing with his set of jacks, appeared to be unaware of her presence.

Sister Philomena ignored him. "Here is your bed," she said to the newcomer. "Let me help you into it."

Sophie in turn ignored Sister Philomena. "But I am much better now," she said, "and don't have to be in bed while the sun's up, that's one thing for sure." She stood up nevertheless and let Sister lift her up on the mattress. I had not realized how small she was until this moment, how young. Her tiny feet, the shortness of her shinbone. Maybe not as young as the twins, but still a small child. The youngest in the room.

Her hair, backlit by prairie sun, made a halo around her head—a dark nimbus—that also shone with light and air.

"So what's the matter with her?" asked Friedrich, without missing a beat in his game. The morning would be filled with the muffled, repetitive *thwock, thwock, thwock* of the tiny red ball hitting his bedclothes.

"None of your business," said Sophie, suddenly lying down and turning her back. Then she flopped over on her other side to stare at this dismissive boy.

"My sentiments exactly," said Sister Philomena.

Friedrich finally looked at her, then glanced quickly at me, his face filled with surprise. "Is she Mister Porter Abel's daughter?" he asked.

"No," I said, with satisfaction. This was one of the few times I had the information, and he didn't. "Mister Porter Abel's daughter is my age. She is too little."

Just then, and for the first time, a half-dozen members of what I assumed was Tatiana's family stepped over our threshold. Solemnly moving across the floor, they presented a stern collective countenance. The three women wore kerchiefs on their heads, and large grey overcoats, under which a few inches of generous, brightly coloured skirts could be seen. Two of the three men were bearded and had cylindrical black hats on their heads, making them seem very imposing. The one without a beard was not as tall as the other two. He had a cap on his head. There was a restrained energy around him that suggested he was young. He stood somewhat apart from the rest of the group.

From where I lay, I was able to see his face, which was bright red with embarrassment or some other extreme emotion. At first I thought that, though young, he was a man like his bearded companions. But when I looked again, I realized he was a boy, about Danny's age or maybe even younger. His hands were large; he kept clasping and unclasping them the way I had seen some restless boys do when we were lined up for activities in the schoolroom and they did not quite know what was going to be expected of them. I decided that he must be Tatiana's older brother. And then I missed my own older brother in the most terrible way, and envied poor Tatiana her visitors, despite her terrible trouble.

When they reached Tatiana, the women began to weep loudly in the way that children weep, with great gulps of air and rapid sobbing, and then, after several minutes, when the women had collected themselves, the men began to sing. The men, I thought, had known they were going to sing when they came into the room—otherwise, there would have been some discussion in advance of their tremendous song. Perhaps they were waiting to begin until the women's sorrows had abated.

Sophie sat bolt upright on her mattress so that she could see the singers. Friedrich stopped playing jacks, stilled by sound.

"I like the singing," Sophie said. Then she tried to sing along. I could see that she was doing this, her small mouth opening and closing, but her child's voice was overwhelmed by what was happening at Tatiana's bed.

All three men, including the boy, had bass voices and sang in a catastrophically arresting harmony. Their song may have been a type of prayer, but I would not have known that then, and still am not certain. As it was, I could hear the rushing of lush, surging rivers in their song, and the kind of wind that muscles into your life and changes it forever. There were mountains hidden under cloaks of rain, and now and then the suggestion of persistent thunder in vast, unimaginably wet valleys. But the prairies were in the song as well, I thought, how they stretched out in winter around all of us like a giant's bedsheet. Even Doctor Carpenter—who, it seemed to me, completely dominated every room he entered—was reduced to a secondary position, and was visibly overwhelmed by the sound. He stood with tears in his eyes, something I could barely believe and had to look at twice to confirm.

Sophie was howling or singing. Sometimes I couldn't tell the difference.

Only Sister Philomena remained unmoved. When they had finished singing, she inspected the group with thinly disguised alarm. "No nonsense here," she said to them. "No nonsense here in the hospital."

Doctor Carpenter, who was still beside my bed, looked at me and, quite uncharacteristically, winked. A tear he was paying no attention to slid down his right cheek. I thought of the sadness of the daily clowns, how they painted a tear on one cheek for effect.

What had Sister Philomena meant? I wondered. These solid, humble individuals, who entered so quietly and sang with their hands clasped in front of them, could not possibly have caused a fuss beyond the shock of amazement inspired by their song. But Sister Philomena stood like a battleship in their wake. She was clearly trying to prevent something, but who knew what? Was it the singing? The monks singing in the abbey were the only precedent—and a soft one at that—for the power of their song. How could Sister Philomena object to powerful singing?

The whole group wept and embraced when they saw Tatiana open her eyes. She woke long enough to say, "The white horse!" then sank back into sleep. They all repeated her statement with a brief relief and joy, in English and then in their other language. It was a profound moment. I could see the steadfast white horse in my mind, the strength of its neck and torso, and the hair of its white mane being tossed by a ferocious wind, a wind that, despite its ferocity, was irrelevant to this animal's sense of purpose.

Then one of the women took off her overcoat in the overheated ward, and Sister Philomena was on her like a bat that gets entangled in your hair. "Don't take anything off! We'll have no undressing here," she said, with panic in her voice. Then, as if sensing her own vulnerability in the situation, she added, "Don't think I've not seen nudity before. I see it every day. You can't shock me!" It was then I knew.

What Sister Philomena meant was "Don't take *everything* off!" Tatiana must have been a child of the much-talked-about Sons of

Freedom Doukhobor community, whose members had been known to respond to stress—and to stasis—by wandering naked out of one village and into another. With anxiety and wonder mixed with sorrow, my parents had spoken to each other, and to us, about these spontaneous events. "The Doukhobors who live here," they said, explaining the world to their curious children, "came from a land so far away that none of the arithmetic you have learned in school could measure its distance from us. And this may very well have been a land," they conjectured, "where taking one's clothes off was just as ordinary as keeping them on is here."

I knew they were as shocked as we were. But they were trying not to alarm us.

"Also," my father added, "they speak Russian, which is a language so different from ours that we will never, ever untangle it, and they will never, ever decipher English." Furthermore, he said, the language had an entirely unique alphabet that had too many characters. "Think of it!" he exclaimed. "A completely different alphabet! With an impossible number of letters!" Exasperated by the thought of this curious and unruly alphabet, even more than by the suggestion of nakedness, he threw up his arms in disbelief and went back to reading Henry Wadsworth Longfellow.

But a tendency to disrobe was terrifying to Sister Philomena, even though, as she had pointed out, she was well acquainted with every corner of human anatomy. It was equally terrifying to the police of the various prairie regions. They had no idea how to respond to a crime so embarrassingly lacking in the usual violence. The Doukhobors would be arrested, jailed for a few days, then escorted back to their own village fully clothed. No one—not even the police—disputed the excellence of their farming and the dedication of their daily labour. They would be needed back in their fields.

"Did you know," my Henry Wadsworth Longfellow–loving father would say later, "that there is a famous writer in Russia who writes *everything* in that indecipherable alphabet! And it was he who arranged for these people to be sent to the northern Great Plains? He did that rather than see them continue to be persecuted."

I did not know this yet and would not truly know it until Doctor Angel told me. But I was curious about the persecution. I remembered, for example, that Jesus had been persecuted and, according to our minister, was better off for it.

When pressed, my father could not recall who exactly had been persecuting them. "Imagine all the writing that author did," he said instead. "Books and books and books of it, I've been told—in that incomprehensible alphabet, that language no reader will ever understand."

After crossing the room to examine Sophie while cooing terms of endearment such as "sweetheart" and "precious," which made Friedrich and I lift our eyebrows in surprise, Doctor Carpenter left the ward.

Eli called out, "Next week, this week will be last week!" But Doctor Carpenter just laughed and said, "Enough of your philosophy for today, Eli." Then he went on his way.

Humming a bit, and in harmony, the Doukhobors remained quietly by Tatiana's beside for the better part of three hours. (Sister Philomena stood guard for at least half this time, but as no one had taken off anything except their overcoats, she eventually gave up and strode away with as much dignity as possible.)

Just before they turned to leave, Tatiana said three more words. "Mama," she said, in barely more than a whisper. "Papa," she said. "Peter." And then, with great effort, she repeated the word "mama."

With this, we, the rest of the children, knew there was a mother in the room. We felt this maternal presence deeply. Though we had each had visitors, there were no mothers among them. When the Doukhobors walked sadly into the hall that led to the rest of the world, all of us burst into tears with the sudden recognition of loss. My own mother rose, lost and beautiful, in my mind. I remembered every part of her arm then, and the feel of the hand that had so often held mine. I remembered her face when she was distant from me and absorbed by her one important letter, and then her face when I was hurt or sick and she was absorbed only by me. And my father, how he had worked so hard to give us a new life, and how that life had shattered. And then the sound of his voice as he lifted me up towards the arms of Mr. Porter Abel, who had come running from a car near the front of the train, and who had pulled open the sliding walls of the boxcar and hoisted himself into position inside it that he might receive me on my white door.

"This child needs to go to a hospital," my father had said.

Sophie was crying loudest of all. And she talked while she cried, which none of the rest of us did. "My mama," she sobbed, "walked beside the wagon all the way from Oklahoma. My papa drove the oxen." She cried and cried about those oxen and about her parents. She told us the name of the oxen while she sobbed. "Jeremiah and Kaziah," she said. "My papa named them from the Bible."

"Kaziah was the second of Job's daughters," Eli informed the room, even though there was still a catch in his voice.

Sophie did not answer him. She cried and cried. And called for her mama. But then, she was the youngest.

I once asked Sister Editha why my own parents never came to visit me. Nor Danny either. I remember tears in my voice when I cited Danny.

"Oh, darling," Sister Editha answered. "They live hundreds and hundreds of miles away and have the other children to think of. But like Friedrich, you have at least one special visitor."

I had not seen a special visitor for Sophie yet. Nor for Eli. "Nobody's parents come," I said, ignoring my knowledge that Friedrich didn't have parents. "Not even Sophie's parents come, and she is only six."

"Fathers cannot leave their farms," Sister Editha pointed out. "They have to look after the animals every day."

"Tatiana's mother and father had left their farm," I countered petulantly.

"Tatiana is a special case." Sister looked at her now. She appeared to float like the sheet that was suspended over her.

My own special visitor, Mister Porter Abel, returned one day, shortly after the Company had entered the ward in full *Midsummer Night's Dream* costume. He was heading west. They were heading east.

"There is next to no north and south in this country's timetables," he remarked, "except for the spur lines of the railways of Saskatchewan, which are diminutive when compared to the transcontinental trains." He was squinting in Sophie's general direction, having never seen her before. "And the east-west touring shows," he said, tipping his hat to the members of the Company.

"No north, no south," the porter had assured me. "Not for me," he said. And then, pointing his finger at the company, he added, "Not for them either." Then he started across the floor.

"Don't count on that," the daily coordinator said to no one in particular. "We'll go anywhere. Even if we are required to hitch-hike to get there. We take the Dream everywhere because . . . well, why not?"

"He means *Midsummer Night's Dream*," said Mister Porter Abel over his shoulder from Sophie's side of the room. I had seen him do a double take when he looked at her, then he had made a beeline for her bed. "Hello, little sister," he had said. I knew he wasn't really her brother, but the affection in the greeting made me jealous. I was a bit put out, me being the one he was meant to visit. But I was warmed as well.

Friedrich waved his arm sleepily to get my attention. "Mister Porter Abel is likely her uncle," he said, "or maybe even her *grandfather*."

That is stupid boy-thinking, I decided. Why wouldn't Mister Porter Abel be as charmed by Sophie as anybody else? Then I went back to wondering about this Dream the Company was eager to perform.

I of course would not have known which play the Company was outfitted for had Mister Porter Abel not told me. I had heard of Shakespeare—my father had compared Longfellow to him while my mother rolled her eyes—but I knew nothing of the Bard's comedies or tragedies.

"Here's the gin," Porter Abel explained, standing now at the end of Sophie's bed, wanting, I thought, to amuse her, not me. "It happens on one summer night. The world is at sixes and sevens. Everyone falls in love with the wrong person—and there is a theatre troupe *in* the play not unlike this troupe here." His thumb motioned over his shoulder, where the members of the Company were cavorting. "There is quite a lot of grassy banks and flowers, a character name of Titania, which is the English version of Tatiana." He nodded in the direction of Tatiana's bed. "Oh, and fairies called Peaseblossom and Mustardseed, and the king of the fairies. There is a character name of Nick Bottom."

Friedrich and I laughed, and he did too.

"I played Mustardseed," said Friedrich, who, despite all the attention he was getting from a man wearing donkey's ears—the same man who in the past had brought him two books (*Tom Swift and His House on Wheels* and *The Radio Boys with the Forest Rangers*)—had been eavesdropping on our conversation.

"So did I," said Porter Abel.

This information almost silenced the room.

Sophie clapped her hands and laughed and said, "No you never!" But I could tell that while she didn't quite understand what Mister Porter Abel was talking about, she believed and was delighted by him.

But Mister Porter Abel continued speaking while walking back towards me, though turning around, now and then, to include Sophie. "And I played it with the great Richard B. Harrison, who was young then and came to our Halifax school with his touring company. He, himself, was playing the role of Puck. I was just a little kid, of course, and we did only one night." He looked vague and sad, remembering his childhood with affection and something resembling regret. "But my mother was absolutely thrilled that I was chosen by Harrison, and out of my whole class." He paused, then leaned forward. "Chosen to be Mustardseed," he confided, settling into a chair, to my relief and joy, on my side of the room. "I only had four lines, and a bunch of other children were chosen to be various sundry characters, of course." Shaking his head, he confessed that he was nearly paralyzed with stage fright. "'Every man look o'er his part,'" he said, quoting his favourite sentence in the play, "'for the short and the long is, our play is preferred.'"

This prompted the members of the Company, in order to gain his regard, to run over to the part of the ward where Porter Abel and I were situated. Once they were gathered at my bedside, they performed the whole woodland scene in which Mustardseed speaks. Mister Porter Abel enjoyed this, and laughed quietly and clapped his hands together. There was much giggling and stage whispering among the players of the Company. Also, some scampering and some leaping. I began to drift, though I was very aware of Mister Porter Abel chuckling softly as the Company high-stepped around him. And of Sophie laughing her small, high-pitched laugh, which sometimes sounded like a lamb calling for its mother.

I tried to picture Mister Porter Abel as a child in a play but found this to be impossible. As a primary rescuer of me, he would forever be a responsible adult in my mind. Instead, I visualized him with wings sprouting from the epaulettes on his uniform and a sword like Saint Michael's, rescuing me again, but this time from the Conductor who was chasing me on a dragon. The daily dog barked a few times in the dream I was having, but he had the head of a donkey. I heard someone far away say, "My mistress with a monster is in love." When I opened my eyes, everyone was gone. Except for us. The children.

Silence had re-entered the room. Sophie was awake, but she was solemn and withdrawn and appeared to be whispering to herself. "Daddy" was the only word I caught. And then the word "church." She sang a little bit, but I could not make out the words.

Friedrich was asleep. He had slept through the whole play, which was completely unlike him, especially because there was some singing, which he relished, and which gave him the opportunity to applaud, then criticize, and then instructively perform the whole set himself the "right" way. He also liked to give advice about the scenes the Company was acting out. "Leave it alone for fifteen minutes," he would say. "Then come back to it with some *emotion!*"

Only now, at the end of a long teaching career, do I understand the humanity resident in a group of individuals like those in the Company, who would encourage a sick child such as Friedrich to be the expert. And the kindness of those people when they made a show of taking his advice.

When I told Danny about this, he just smiled and shrugged. "Book of Isaiah," he said. "'And a little child shall lead them.'"

But he understood completely. Because he had loved Friedrich as well.

I recall the chalk in Mrs. Robinson's hand, the muscle of her lower arm moving under her cardigan as she wrote the words "Master Stillwell"—in large capital letters—on the blackboard. I twisted around to lock eyes with my brother at the back of the room, then quickly turned back. When Mrs. Robinson had finished writing the name Stillwell, she placed the chalk on the ledge in what I though was a deliberate kind of way, then she slowly pivoted to address the class.

"Master Stillwell will be returning to our classroom on and off during May and June, and he might even arrive as early as mid-April." She remained silent for a minute or two, allowing the information to sink in. "He is very important," she told us, "and we must be on our best behaviour when he is here."

It was then early March of our second year in the northern Great Plains. There were miniature snowdrifts on the mullions and sashes of the large windows, and dramatically high piles of snow on either side of the road we took to school.

The information about Master Stillwell caused quite a stir among the children in the classroom. Was he still an inspector? they wanted to know. Mrs. Robinson, whose mildness had relaxed us all—even the big boys at the back, who, according to Danny, would never be interested in staying still—said yes, that was what he was. She wrote the words "Provincial Inspector of Schools" on the board, but this time she used her own cursive handwriting—not capital letters—and it didn't take her very long. But he was also writing a book about the schools of Saskatchewan, she told us, and how they "performed" for children who had not been born into English-speaking families. "The children of foreigners," she qualified.

There were two children in our class who carried the faint traces of a previous language in the rhythms of their speech. English was not their first language, and I sensed their shame and felt sorry for them. Mrs. Robinson had begun to pay a great deal of special attention to them. This attention was humiliating for them, I thought—I knew I would have been humiliated by it as well.

"It's because of Master Stillwell that she's paying so much attention to Doroata and Fedir," I said to Danny when we were walking home from school over snow that was rapidly changing from wincingly white to soft shades of mauve. "They will be made to recite," I told him. "And their voices will be all wrong for true stanzaic order."

Our parents seemed unfazed when we burst into the kitchen filled to the brim with the news of Master Stillwell's imminent arrival.

They've known all along, I thought, and I felt put off by adult secrets that interfered with my ability to deliver such surprising and shocking news.

My mother simply shrugged. "He has a new job in the prairies." She was building two identical piles of small pants and shirts on the pine table. "Has been in the inspector position for close to a year," she added, moving Timmy and Patrick's clean laundry to a wicker basket near the door that led to the rest of the house. "And I suppose he is working on another book."

"A book, is it?" said my father, not bothering to disguise his disdain. "Has the man done one day of honest labour in his life?"

On the morning Master Stillwell entered our school and was fawningly introduced by Mrs. Robinson who then went home, I knew he had changed. He had "filled out" as was said then, and there were only vague traces of the handsome young man we had known only a few short years before. His remaining hair was cut short. His curls were gone.

Like Mrs. Robinson he paid particular attention to the two students who spoke with slight accents. Did they speak their other language at home? he wanted to know. Could their parents speak English? We all listened to his questions but did not turn around to look at the children under interrogation. We knew what their answers would be, and we pitied them to the bottoms of our souls. But despite these sentiments, we also knew that we would avoid them at recess. All of us understood that there were no correct answers to Master Stillwell's questions, and did not, by association, wish to be questioned ourselves.

Sometimes, in the following weeks, this king of inspectors would leave our classroom at lunchtime and not come back. "In order to work on curriculum," he told us. The first time he did this, he had called Danny and me to his desk mid-morning. "I will leave you two in charge," he told us. "You are the most responsible students, and of course, you come from Ontario." (This was delivered with a complicitous, knowing look that telegraphed Ontario's undeniable superiority.) He handed us the lesson plan. "Danny," he said, "you take grades five to eight."

Danny had nodded, solemnly. I could tell he was proud to serve.

"And, Emer," our teacher added, "you can handle the little ones? Read them some stories if necessary?"

"What about picture study?" I asked, boldly, though I liked the idea of the stories.

"No," he said. There had been disputes over which three children would get to hold the three books, he reminded me. "It's just too complicated," he said, never once looking up from the book Mrs. Robinson kept: the one that was filled with our grades.

I didn't love him anymore. I had gone neutral. He was just the same as all the other teachers now, but more powerful than them, and therefore more frightening.

I wonder now how a well-placed, highly educated—and sentimental—teacher could mutate into the politically persuasive man he later became, his mercuriality galloping alongside his need to control. This may have been invisible to my mother, or perhaps, this mutant was the man my mother knew he would be from the start. She would likely have recalled his compelling sternness as he presided over her attainment of that third-class certificate, his ambivalence and then his certainty. How he came to Saskatchewan not so much to be near her, as she would have wished for and dreaded, but to position himself in the foreign-speaking districts, among the recent immigrants from unimaginable lands, lands that until recently would have been far out of reach of the long arm of the British Empire. Those with the foreign tongues whose education—and modification—he was so obsessed by, those who wore ridiculous clothing and head coverings. Those who would need to be changed.

"For what is education," he wrote in that second letter to my mother, "but an enormous transformation? We take the ignorant and cleanse them and dress them in fresh new garments. We give them the gift of the English language. We make them into a reasonable facsimile of ourselves."

"Because who," he might have added, "has a cleaner, more reliable life-version than we ourselves?"

"And they will thank us," he wrote, "for this cleansing and modification. They will be forever grateful."

But no amount of gratitude satisfied him, and ultimately, when he was met with resistance, the anger that was hidden deep within him rose to the surface. They had turned against him. They had turned against everything he stood for by clinging to their peasant origins, or by wanting to speak their own languages, or by believing that true scholars could spend their lives interpreting the Torah. They had betrayed him by ignoring Milton and Thackeray, taking off their clothes, and throwing the books into the river, claiming that, like life, Christ was in the everyday, and was a constantly changing manifestation, and that no rules, no certainty, could—or even should—capture this manifestation. Even some of those who spoke English clung to Latin rituals and popery. "The correction of these people, the ones most like us," he wrote to my mother—did he forget that she had been raised a Catholic?—"is often a thankless task."

When the Doukhobors began to burn the schoolhouses provided for them by the men of government, he would have said to my mother, "Let's fight fire with fire. Let's gather money for the cause." And then he would have made love to her, for somewhere in the sentimental side of him, he knew that love was the most reliable transformer and persuader of them all.

She was in his thrall. She loved her children and husband, but she was in his thrall. She would have done anything for him. She began to ridicule the religion of her forefathers. "Catholics!" she had said in exasperation in our own kitchen, surprising our father, the Protestant.

"What of them?" he asked.

"They are as bad as the Jews, or all those other different foreign people," she answered, "with their costumes and candelabras. Their trinkets."

My father shook his head and went back to reading Longfellow— "My Lost Youth," "The Children's Hour"—and there was silence in our kitchen. He was bewildered by her. "She says the damnedest things," he once muttered under his breath after one outburst or another. "Where these crazy ideas come from is anybody's guess." He would throw his hands up in exasperation right in front of the uncomprehending four-year-old twins.

But I knew where they came from. By the time she began to say "the damnedest things" aloud, I had read the letter at least a hundred times and had committed it to my memory. And it remained there in the company of everything I had memorized: "The Wreck of the Hesperus," Gray's *Elegy Written in a Country Church Yard*, *The Rime of the Ancient Mariner*.

And then one day, when Master Stillwell had moved on to another school or had returned to the government offices in the city, I located the key and eased open the drawer. There was now a newer letter beside the stained and tattered previous ones. This version contained but few of the affectionate phrases that had dignified the first two. Instead, there were declarations, and instructions for something called the women's branch—instructions so firmly stated, it would not have been an exaggeration to call them commands. "You will do the sewing," it read. "You will make the women's robes." And then a bit later: "You must be absolutely certain of the loyalty and fidelity of those you choose to participate in the women's branch. And no one else can ever know."

There was another difference as well. This letter was signed with the initials that I was familiar with, W.S.S. But beneath this was another signature, in the same handwriting. The second name might have come from the stories of *The Lady of the Lake* or *Ivanhoe*. It sounded knightly and dignified. But at the same time, it made me want to laugh behind my hand, though I couldn't say why. The name was Exalted Cyclops.

The writer, as I would come to understand, was skilled in using political mystery and poetry—the poetry of chivalry, the poetry of the state. I knew from the first letter that he had read "The Lady of Shalott" aloud to my mother once when they were alone together. She had been living in a tower, looking at the world through a warped mirror. But in some strange way, she had also made three paces across the room, just like the woman in the poem, and then she had looked down to Camelot. Either way, from his point of view, she was wrong. Things would be different, he wrote, now that she would be at the centre of something important. She would be part of a New World correction.

I would hear her weeping and weeping when I ran home from school, away from Master Stillwell's classroom. And once I did not come into the house at all because I heard a different kind of deep crying, an irrational sharp sob, the sudden intake of breath. It would be years before I admitted to myself that what I'd heard, and instinctively knew not to intrude upon, was the sound of physical love.

There was something new, as well, in the letter's salutation. "Dear Laura," it read, then underneath was the name "Commander and Kladdess of the Women's Branch." My mother was now a "Commander." She was now a secret "Kladdess." I did not then know what the word "Kladdess" meant, but much later, in the Provincial Archives, I would discover that "Kladd" was translated as "Conductor in charge of initiating new members and collecting fees."

I couldn't understand this. It felt to me like play, like what we children sometimes organized when we went to the woods to build girls' forts and boys' forts. We always had our roles and functions, because of the pretend wars we were waging between us. Most Imperial Empress, we called the oldest, smartest girl. The Great Spear Header was what the boys called the oldest, smartest boy. We raided each other's forts, and took back booty, a jackknife from the boys' fort, a teacup from the girls'. Danny stayed away from all this. But I had entered it with whooping enthusiasm.

"We cannot be seen to speak," read one of the sentences in M.S.S.'s third letter. "It would be very difficult for you if we were discovered. And as for me, I am hoping to ultimately enter the political realm in these parts and cannot afford the scandal."

W hen the doctors made their rounds, they sometimes did so together. While their main purpose was to consult each other about our condition, they occasionally stood at the ends of our beds and talked about other things. Baseball or politics, sometimes even women.

"When you see those two docs together," Friedrich had told me, "keep your eyes and ears open. They hardly know we exist when they start in on the grown-up stuff. Or at least they think we don't have ears and brains." He was languidly tossing a yo-yo out in front of him and reeling it back in. "Anyway, it doesn't matter. You can get a lot of good information that way. You don't even have to be furtive about it." The yo-yo sang out and snapped back. "They don't think the sisters hear them either. But they do," he said.

I had not yet learned what the word "furtive" meant. But I was unwilling to admit this. Friedrich had swivelled his head to look at me and was smiling angelically. He palmed the yo-yo, made a theatrical gesture with his hands and lower arms, shrugged, and said, "That's how I found out I am going to die." Then he picked up the yo-yo again and threw it up and down in front of him, performing a complicated move. "Over the falls," he said, naming the trick.

I laughed, loving the way he had total mastery of the toy.

This eavesdropping on the adult power system was also the way, two weeks before, I had heard the important teacher's name for the first time since the big wind. "Stillwell's been turfed as director of education," Doctor Carpenter said. "Something to do with the handling of the burned schools." He inclined his head in the direction of Tatiana's bed as he said this but did not look directly at her. "They say he will go into politics."

He was rapidly flipping through the charts on a clipboard. My charts. I remember he often had a pencil behind his ear that he never to my knowledge made use of. "Conservative politics," he said.

"Back in Ontario?" Doctor Angel had asked.

"No," Doctor Carpenter replied absently, without lifting his eyes from the board. "No, here. Here in the prairies."

The yo-yo session had been an aberration, and soon the toy lay abandoned in the folds of Friedrich's top sheet. Truly he was seldom awake now, but when he was, he sometimes had these brief bouts of energy. Still, mostly he slept while members of the Company crept in and out of our room, as discreet and as nervous as mice. Certain of them even gave up touring, stayed in town, and therefore visited every day. They no longer cartwheeled into the room. They no longer made us laugh. Even the dogs were subdued, wagging their tails in a sorrowful, repetitive manner. Not with the usual circular abandon.

One night I asked Doctor Angel why Friedrich slept all the time. He shook his head and said some poetry. He told me stories from his medical life before he was a hospital doctor. He visited children in houses, he told me, and he had tried to make them well. "Some of their families," he confided, "the adults in them, were poor: most of them were poor, in fact. But I can assure you," he said, "everything was otherwise the same."

The children still played and ran in and out of the door, I thought, in those families. "I'll bet the door banged," I said. "The screen door." Doctor Angel didn't answer. We were both silent then, considering Friedrich. Or even me. How neither of us could run in or out of any door.

After a while Doctor Angel sat up straight and explained Friedrich's disease to me. Something I didn't fully understand, and which I believed had to do with Saint Pancras, one of the child martyrs my mother remembered from her old religion.

It was why, Doctor Angel said, Friedrich had only one foot.

I assumed, then, that martyrdom had been part of Friedrich's story, and was surprised that he had never boasted about it. Then Doctor Angel told me that Doctor Carpenter had had to take Friedrich's foot off in the operating room in order to save his life. But his life, alas, was not fully saved.

The Conductor laughed his rasping, breathy train laugh in my mind, and I began to cry.

"There is something . . . some hope," Doctor Angel said, patting my shoulder. "No, honestly. Some real hope."

I sensed he was talking to himself, as well as to me.

"A doctor I know, or more accurately knew—I went to school with him in Toronto—has cooked up a miracle in his laboratory," he said. He looked down at his own foot, then placed it on his opposite knee and proceeded to untie and retie the laces. Far away down the hall, someone shouted a swear word in their sleep. Neither the doctor nor I reacted to this.

"Do you mean there is hope because of martyrs?" I asked.

He didn't answer, but sighed, turned his head, and stared across my nightstand at the sleeping child that was Friedrich.

It was then that Eli had his burning cross nightmare for the second time. "Cross on fire!" he yelled, bringing in Sister Editha from her night desk and her work on the saints. Doctor Angel and she went over to Eli's bed, and both spoke in soothing tones while they held him in place. He was, as my father would have said, hell-bent on escape. I could hear Doctor Angel say the word "sedative." By now I knew that would mean a needle.

Earlier that evening something on my nightstand had caught Doctor Angel's attention. "Doctor Carpenter has left his table of bones," he said, lifting a small leather book from the circle of light made by my lamp.

Everything Doctor Angel said to me was mysterious. The hagiography of the pancreas, the table constructed out of bones, the word "sedation." There were only brief moments of clarity brought about by the word "hope" and the word "miracle." Those faint chances of things not turning out badly, the futile attempts, the grasping at straws. Or perhaps just one straw. That, I knew, even as a child, was the poetry in him. After Doctor Angel said the word "miracle," however, I knew what the score was. Both he and Doctor Carpenter had always known that Friedrich was going to die. The nursing sisters knew it; Friedrich himself knew it. The only one who didn't know was me.

Just as until now I had not known that my mother's sewing could lead to the repetitive nightmares of a child she had never met.

"Eli," said Sister Editha, gently, "all is well. It's all in your imagination, child."

"No, it's NOT!" cried Sophie from her end of the room. "It's NOT! I saw it too! Those men. That fire."

"Fooled you!" said the Conductor, winking in my mind.

The man I loved guided me up the long flower-bordered walk that led to the front entrance of the Saskatchewan School for the Deaf. We were squinting for the first third of our approach in the face of the setting sun. But then we entered the enormous towering shadow of the building itself.

All over the empire, governments were constructing public buildings like the one that loomed in front of us. Though huge, such architecture had something in common with the little paper European houses with snowy roofs my mother had placed on the shelf above the stove at Christmastime. Like that miniature fakery, monsters such as this school had no business being on the northern Great Plains, making architectural declarations about power in a beaux arts style. And yet, here it was, an institution, so like all the other institutions put up in the name of some monarch or another: schools for the blind, schools for the deaf, residential schools in which dwelt stolen and grief-stricken Indigenous children, jails, madhouses, colleges, poorhouses, workhouses, palace hotels.

By the time we were inside the entrance rotunda, which doubled as a grand reception room, I could hardly bear the new high heels. My hip ached, and I was worried that perspiration was ruining my makeup. Harp was heartily welcomed, of course, by dignitaries and politicians who droned around him in groups like bees around a hive. I needn't have worried about anyone noticing my limp or my deteriorating makeup, as no one paid any attention to me at all. Except for one man, who asked if I was Harp's secretary. "No," I replied, "I'm his—" I broke off in embarrassment; it was the first time I had tried to explain my relationship to Harp to anyone but Danny. "I'm a teacher—" I began to say, but the man who asked the question had already moved away from me.

There were no deaf children at the gathering. Had they been banished to the farthest recesses of the farthest wings of the palace? No one seemed aware that they existed. Much later I wondered if the poor quiet children were merely an excuse for imperialistic development. On the prairies, such sparkling new architecture shone in sepulchral stark relief against the minimal landscape—memorializing something, someone, echoing the pomp of the mother country, but having little to do with deaf children.

I stood in my good dress and high heels in a sea of flannel suits. A small group of men hurrying from one side of the room to the other jostled me and I almost lost my balance, having left my cane in the hotel in deference to fashion. Harp caught my elbow and whispered, "Careful." Then he guided me towards a man with closely cropped hair and a thin moustache who was holding court near a marble staircase with gleaming brass railings. At the landing of this staircase, there was a stained-glass window featuring Saint Jerome, his book, lectern, and lion. Sister Editha had told me about the lion. She felt that Jerome should have been made the patron saint of veterinarians, rather than librarians.

"Emer," Harp said, "meet the former provincial premier and current director of this place. My old pal Walt."

The man stepped closer to us, and a circle of his admirers broke apart to give him passage.

"Emer is an educator," my love explained to his friend. Then to me he said, "Walt used to be the director of education. That would have made him your boss."

"Before your time, I'm sure," said the old pal, bowing slightly.

I stared at the grey-haired dignitary in his grey suit. He was raincloud-coloured all over, faintly tinged with blue. Ghost-like, thin bluish-grey hair, black towards the ends of it, dusty black shoes. We did not shake hands but mumbled greetings instead, nodding our heads as we did so.

"How many students do you have here?" I asked, trying to make polite conversation. I had seen no sign of a play yard anywhere near these walls. No sign of a ball diamond.

He said vaguely, "Oh, we get them from all over," then gave me a description of the architecture instead. "We had the experts come in from Toronto to do the stained glass," he explained. "Also," he added, "the foundation is stone, not cement."

There was something in the voice and the long fingers, nervously fingering his pocket. Then he emerged from the mist of my muted concentration, which until that moment, I have to say, was mostly focused on the pain of my high-heeled shoes. Out of the fog and the shaft of sunlight that had burned into my eyes through a stained-glass Saskatchewan rose, causing me not to examine the speaker, there he was, my important Master. Twenty years older, he had now completely lost his grace. But the confidence that attended his presence was still firmly intact. Amplified, it would appear, by career successes and an enlarged sense of certainty.

I could see that he would never be brought to tears by poetry again.

He didn't recognize me. I was always of little importance to him. Added to this, the big wind had altered my physiognomy to such an extent that, even were I still the child he once knew, I would have been unrecognizable. He laughed at what Harp said about being my boss, but he was otherwise distracted. He scanned the room like an anxious searchlight, making sure that everything was in its proper place on the podium. After wincing at someone's attempt to tame a microphone, he excused himself and hurried away to correct the glitch.

He returned after the political speeches and for a moment stood possessively beside the man I loved, before escorting him to the stage. Then he walked back to where I was standing.

We both stared at Harp arranging his papers on the lectern. I touched the arm of my former teacher's jacket, now, right at that moment. I told him that I had read the letters he wrote to my mother.

He took in what I had said and looked at me then more closely. A ripple of bewildered recognition passed over his face before he turned back towards the stage. His expression suggested that he was afraid something was about to go terribly wrong; the lights might go out or the microphone wasn't going to work. Something that he, as grand master of ceremonies, would be held accountable for. He looked back towards me, finally, with a puzzled, anxious smile. "I'm afraid I don't know what you are referring to," he whispered.

I read all three letters, I told him. I read them so often, I assured him, that I could repeat them word for word.

After a long and unmemorable speech, Harp thanked the audience and stepped down from the podium. He struggled towards us through overwhelming applause but was held back by several people who were hoping to have a word with him. He was made uncomfortable by this, the sense that people in the room were hoping—through him—to cure friends or relatives, or to be cured themselves just by tugging on his sleeve. His old pal Walt excused himself politely, left my side, and went to intercede, which he did by shaking Harp's hand and thanking him for his support, then ushering him back to where I stood.

Then he winked at me and said to Harp, "Emer, here, your Irish friend, seems to think I knew her mother." He smiled benignly at me. "God help you and keep you, Mother Macrhea," he chanted.

I noticed that his hands, which he had kept so carefully at his side all evening, or fingering his pockets, were now raised and open, giving him the odd look of someone who was explaining, almost begging.

Harp raised his eyebrows. "Irish?" he said. There was a pause, after which Harp added ironically, "'Went Papist himself and forsook the old cause / That gave us our freedom, religion, and laws.'" Then both men bent with laughter and sang together, "'Oh, a bunch of the boys made a comment upon it. / And Bob had to flee to the province of Connaught. / He left with his wife and his fixings to boot. / And along with the latter the Old Orange Flute.'"

The setting sun had now penetrated the room by way of one of several ordinary, unstained windows on the west wall. Saint Jerome had grown dim at the top of the stairs, but the large reception hall in which we stood had brightened. I could see the postage stamp–sized bristly patch—missed by the morning razor—on my former teacher's cheek. I could see the red veins in my lover's laughing eyes. I realized I had not even asked where my mother's body had fallen after the wind had stolen her. Where she was found.

I thought of Danny. *Went Papist himself.* I recalled my own mother, her face half lit, reading and rereading those letters. I already knew where she had fallen.

I don't recall the moment of my decision to withdraw, but one minute I was talking to a banker and his wife who apparently always attended such fundraisers, and the next minute I found myself descending the front steps alone with one high heel in each hand.

Harp came back to the palace hotel late that night. None too sober, he nevertheless placated and made love to me. "Those rhymes we quoted were from 'The Old Orange Flute,'" he said.

I said I was aware of that.

"Harmless nonsense from Northern Ireland," he insisted.

Nothing is ever as final or as tidy as it should be, even when the blue-tinted Conductor isn't in the room.

"What on earth could be offensive about Walt?" Harp asked with great tipsy jocularity. "He is the most ordinary man I know. Boring, in fact."

"My mother," I told him. "He was very involved with her. I think she loved him."

"Loved him? It is impossible for me to imagine such a bland personality inspiring romantic love." He swayed across the room to an ashtray that stood on a pedestal, tried to deposit a long ash there, and failed. "Also," he said, "and importantly, wasn't your mother Irish? And a Catholic?"

"Yes," I offered, "though she had—"

"What?" he interrupted, with just a hint of anger in his voice. "Gone Proddy?" This was an aphorism, much used at the time, to refer to the conversion of Catholics to Protestantism.

"Anyway," he assured me, "you've certainly got the wrong man."

He was laughing now. He sat down on the edge of the bed, reached under the covers.

When I shifted away, he said, "Walt would rather shoot himself than be involved with an Irish Catholic." He punched my arm, softly, playfully, and added, "Even a former Catholic. Though to be fair"— he looked thoughtful, perhaps searching for the words—"here in the prairies, he would be even more put off by a Uke or a Jew." He rose to leave the room, but before his exit, he added, "Or a Doukhobor, in spite of all that nakedness."

Sister Hildegard came quietly into the ward pushing a small trolley with a basin, some folded linens, and a collection of bottles on the top of it. Because of the snow and the clear blue sky, the room was full of prismatic light, and our sister looked as if she were surrounded by the kind of delicate burning swords that I had seen on the picture of the Sacred Heart that was kept, along with the beads and brooches, in my mother's jewellery box. Sister Hildegard had not been associated in my mind with the Sacred Heart, so I was surprised by her sudden spiritual elevation. She took all of herself and the swords of light over to the curtains and the screen that surrounded Tatiana's bed. Then she disappeared behind those curtains, that screen.

Early the previous morning, before the first light, Tatiana—always so patient and so quiet—had begun to whimper. As the day dawned, she started to cry out as if someone were twisting her arm up her back, then stopping for a few minutes, then twisting again. By mid-morning she was roaring with pain, and two sisters I did not know and a strange doctor were in the room. They had pulled the curtains around Tatiana's bed so we could not see what was happening. But we could hear. One sister was talking softly to Tatiana in another language, which I knew must be Russian. The other sister and the doctor seemed to be talking to each other, or perhaps they were both speaking to Tatiana. Sometimes a nursing sister would come fluttering out of the curtains looking grim as she scurried out the door. When this happened, Tatiana's screams became louder, as if the curtains were walls that had been parted long enough to let the sound get free of them. She called for her mother. "Mama, Mama," she shouted, as if warning her mother about some imminent danger. Not one of us tried to make eye contact with the others. We were terrified by the chaos in the ward. We were all terrified except for Friedrich, who was silent and asleep. Towards nightfall, Tatiana became as silent as Friedrich. Then, suddenly, the oppressive silence was filled with the sound of a baby crying.

Sister Editha walked quickly through the hall door, slipped in behind the curtains, and emerged with the crying baby. At last, we had found a baby! Not one of us asked to hold it, however. We instinctively knew we were not permitted to touch it or even smile at it. We were certain we could not be happy about it, even though we noticed the look of tenderness on Sister's face as she walked out the door with the infant in her arms.

Eli and Sophie were neither moving nor speaking. I could hear the peculiar slapping sound that Doctor Carpenter's leather shoes always made in the hallway. He swung around the corner and into the room, pulling a pen out of his lapel pocket as he did so. "He's going to examine Tatiana," I whispered, without turning to the sleeping Friedrich, "to see what kind of interventions he needs to use to fix her."

Through the curtains I could hear the scratch of Doctor Carpenter's pen. He would be making his doctor notes, I figured, so he would remember in the morning which parts of Tatiana needed to be cut open and changed, then sewn back up.

Eli heard the pen, too, and when he did, he began to cry. Sophie wept as well, as she always did once one of the older children started.

"He's making his doctor notes," I called across the room to Eli, "so he can fix her."

"No, he's not," sobbed Eli. "He's . . . he's signing her death certificate."

"Tatiana has died!" Sophie called out in alarm, her small arms rising from the bed as if she wished to be picked up. "The blue man came to take her away," she yelled.

Sister Editha floated to her bedside, sat down, and stroked her hair.

There was an acid blue fog in the room. It moved around the legs of our beds. Out the window the sky looked acid blue as well.

. . .

Before the terror of Tatiana's trouble, Friedrich had been asleep for the better part of two days. He was now sleeping once again; I didn't have to look at him to know this was true. Even though there was crying of all kinds in the room—even though the baby had made such a big noise from such a small bundle of cloth, out of which flailed tiny fists and feet—none of this was enough to pull Friedrich from the sleep that had been his partner for days, and from whom he had not been separated even by the ferocity of Tatiana's pain.

I whispered his name. "Friedrich," I said, "I think that baby is the one that was carried off by the big wind. I think that now that baby has come back."

I remembered the birth of the twins, then, in faraway Ontario. But the memory was blurred by time.

"Friedrich," I said, wanting him to respond. "Friedrich, at last there is a baby." I turned my head and looked at him sleeping to the left of me. "A crying baby," I said, though it seemed to me that this was obvious.

The sound got fainter and fainter as Sister Editha progressed down the hall. She took the baby with her to a different, unknown part of the hospital.

Tatiana was twelve when she began to go to school. Gentle Sister Editha told us this when she came to quiet us after Tatiana's body had been removed. She had learned English swiftly and was soon reading and writing in that language, Sister said. Most of the schoolroom was filled with boys, some a little older, some younger. Peter, fourteen, was among the oldest in the room. They had walked side by side on the road that went from the settlement to the school.

We remembered Peter from the visit of the people who sang.

The community was deeply suspicious of schools, I now know, but had finally allowed a dozen or so to be built. They never completely overcame their fear that education was a tool of indoctrination and stasis. But they knew, also, that some of their children should learn how to read.

Beyond Sister Editha's words we heard the sounds that we knew were associated with Tatiana's bed being remade by Sister Philomena. The *bumph, bumph* of the plumping of pillows. The snap of a starched sheet being unfurled. And so, in this way, we learned the disturbing truth that the ordinary tasks of life continue after someone dies. Sister Editha was partly there to tenderly distract us. But only partly. She wanted Tatiana's story to be told.

"She always wore a head covering—a kerchief, I think they call it," Sister Editha said, touching her own wimple as she spoke. "Nevertheless, she had a sweetheart," she said, as if wearing a head covering could protect you from longing.

"Few of the boys attended class with any sort of regularity," she continued. Wanted at home for chores, she offered, and for field work, they often missed entire months of schooling. "But Peter was there more often than most."

And so, Sister Editha told us, he and Tatiana, both eager to learn, had the lion's share of their teacher's attention. Soon, I imagined, they were learning the things we had all learned and memorizing what we had all memorized.

"They became very close," Sister Editha said, "without, sadly, the sacraments of the church." She fell silent then. She's praying, I thought. "But they joined with all good intentions," she assured us.

I was amazed by this. Not knowing children could marry.

"They were little more than children," Sister Editha said, as if to echo my thoughts. "But they already knew they needed to make the baby." She touched her own stomach as she said this. "And they were sweethearts," she said again, with a certain shyness in her voice.

I now understand that Sister Editha was making up a good deal of this story. It was in her to want to make a fairy tale out of dark, unimaginable circumstances, to make these circumstances palatable for her audience, which, in this case, was a roomful of damaged children. The child that she was in the convent had never disappeared, as Mister Porter Abel would have said.

But now the baby seemed to be the reason for everything. For becoming sweethearts. For the sharing of poetry.

"Evangeline," my father would have said.

Who are we, I wonder now, without such romanticism? What is the point of us? I remember the man I loved bending down to pick up a blue jay's feather from the ground once he finally consented for us to walk outdoors together. I remember him handing it to me. It was a rare enough moment that I should have been grateful. Instead, I was embarrassed, and mostly for him because it was so out of character. I could barely look at his face in full daylight. We had been cloistered that long. On other occasions, I remember his skeptical expression, not fully trusting, but engaged, curious. Edging nearer in order to discover something hidden in me—or in anyone, for that matter— then moving quickly away. The long list of his terrible departures, those of the flesh and those of the spirit, the anxiety that accompanied him when he returned, something both otherworldly and evasive in his features, tension in the room. The enormity of his enthusiasms and the tenacity of his dislikes; feuds that went on for years without the subject of his distaste even being aware. I was fascinated by the physicality of him, by his obsessions, even by his rages, which I knew about, and which were sometimes, but not often, directed towards me.

I was also fascinated by every mercurial, and not always pleasant, aspect of my own character that, often without my permission, leapt into being when I was in his presence. I remember all the anger and eagerness associated with him, how visceral it was, how life-enhancing. And in the end how disappointing and ultimately impossible.

The child that Friedrich was then did not care, or so he claimed, did not care about romance. Doctor Angel had given him so many needles that he finally awoke and lifted his head to seek out his nurse. But despite the colour that had returned to his face, he was making no effort to get out of bed.

"Who cares about that romantic stuff?" he said. "They were only playing parts."

Like my brother Danny, whom he would come to know and love, Friedrich would grow into a man who cared deeply about romance, even though it would be so hard for him to do so. A sentimentalist at heart, he would have taken any risk for love, if that love had remained available to him.

But now, having slept through the moment of Tatiana's terrible suffering and her departure, he knew nothing about what had happened. "I need a urinal," he said to Sister Editha, who dutifully left the room and quickly returned with not only a urinal but also a set of clean sheets. Friedrich was now wetting his bed so often that he was in diapers. But even these could not completely hold the copious amount of liquid that kept pouring out of him. All the children in the room looked the other way when he was being ministered to. Though only children, we tried to allow one another the dignity of privacy.

Even Sophie learned to do this, though her curiosity about the continual changing of white bedsheets was palpable in the air. And you could tell she longed to ask questions.

Just after the tidying up, from far off down the hall, Friedrich heard the very faint sound of the baby crying. He quickly looked around the room, searching our faces for fellow amazement. Eventually, he noticed the empty bed and the partly opened curtains. For the first time in days, he sat bolt upright. "Where is Tatiana?" he asked.

That night the crying baby kept me awake. Sometimes the baby was crying in my dreams, and other times the baby was at the end of the bed, crying pitifully, but no matter how I tried, I could not reach down to comfort it. I was concerned that it would fall off the mattress and be broken on the tile floor below, which seemed to me to be a long, long way down. I was convinced that the hospital was only a whistle-stop in the travels that the big wind had planned for this baby. I called and called for a nurse to help, but Doctor Angel came instead, and sat right down on the part of the bed where I believed the baby was crying.

First, he let me know the baby was fine. "She is in another part of the hospital"—he pointed down—"one floor below us." He lifted one leg and pulled up a surprisingly red sock that emerged from one white shoe. "You could barely hear her even if she were crying"—he put his leg back down—"which she is not."

I was completely awake now. Both the baby and its cries were gone from the room. "She?" I asked.

"Yes. It is a girl."

We both remained silent for a few minutes after that. Then I said, "Well, Friedrich heard her too. Not just me."

"Tatiana's people will come for the baby," Doctor Angel told me. "And they will be good to her. They will come for Tatiana—to bury her—and for the baby, to look after her."

Then he told me the story of why Tatiana was burned.

She had memorized poems in the classroom and then performed and translated the poems she had memorized in the kitchen, and her parents, distressed by the militaristic tone and insistence of allegiance that poet Walter Scott had telegraphed, pulled her from school. Other Doukhobor parents were either fully in disagreement with the whole concept of education (and always had been) or appalled by the sentiments in the memorized poems, which none of them had read but all of them had heard about. In each of their villages, one or two children were reciting in kitchens.

There were no books at home. Books were stasis. Or worse, they were filled with directives Tatiana's parents could never support. The state, they maintained, was promoting itself. Empire encouraging human sacrifice in wars for the expansion of empire. Their people bore no allegiance, they told her, except an allegiance to Christ, who spoke to them through their souls, not through a book filled with printer's ink. They did not endure this journey to a new land to be loyal to anyone but their own people and to God. In the old country, they had burned the weapons sent to them by the tsar when the state wanted their sons to be soldiers. They could never condone the taking of human life for any reason. Now the weapons of state came disguised as poetry. And as novels. The weapons of state came disguised as wooden buildings with school desks bolted to the floors.

Tatiana had wept in the kitchen. Her little brothers, who also attended the school, were crying as well.

The fires started soon after what the villagers would come to call the Great Recitation of Wrongs. One by one, the dozen or so schoolhouses burned to the ground. Tatiana's school stood for several weeks after the others were gone. At first it looked as if it might be spared. But ultimately it too was set alight.

Tatiana was outdoors, pinning a white sheet to her mother's clothesline. She had fastened only one corner when she saw the smoke. There was a small book that had meant a great deal to Peter and her when they were just beginning to read, and she knew where it was on the schoolroom shelf. She must have believed that the school was near enough that she could rescue the book and keep it hidden so her parents would not find it.

Years later, I would learn that not even the most extreme member of the extremist fringe that was the Doukhobor Sons of Freedom would admit to burning that one school. They, who happily took responsibility for the destruction of all the others, denied they were even in the vicinity. Some said that this denial was because a child was so gravely injured and later died. But others said that the Sons of Freedom had purposely left the one schoolhouse standing because they needed a headquarters, and because the master of that school was a Doukhobor himself. The schoolhouse in which Tatiana was so badly burned, they said, must have caught on fire in some other way.

The white sheet remained partly pinned on the line for many days after. The book—miraculously unburned, and in Titania's hand when they found her—was *A Child's Garden of Verses*.

Though our season was long, I saw the man I loved infrequently.

And during the months when I didn't see him, I dreamt his life without me. The long journeys to destinations I would never visit, indefinite locations and commitments—at least indefinite to me. All the cumbersome paraphernalia of greatness. He was weighed down by all that, he told me, sweeping his arm across his body as if pushing clutter out of the way. Responsibilities, appearances, he was burdened by them, carrying a buzz of calendar-related anxiety with him everywhere he went. He pointed out that he had carried a camp stove on his back when he fled to the wilderness with his painter friends. "A camp stove *and* an easel and two jugs of water, one in each hand. And I didn't feel burdened by any of that," he boasted.

"Well," he added, smiling, lifting the glass in his hand, "it's true that one jug was filled with whisky."

I told Harp that Mister Porter Abel said that everything up close was all clutter and chatter, that you had to pay attention to the landscape in the distance. Speaking about this, I realized that he, Harp, was the landscape of distance for me. Not the clutter and chatter. The pause in all that for him was as close to love as I was ever going to get. But still I longed to see just one French cathedral, an English moor, a valley where an ancient monastery had stood. It was Harp who pointed out to me the nearness of Saint Peter's Abbey, its glorious cathedral-like church, and the wondrous empty prairie on all sides.

Somehow, the sojourns with the painter friends did not enter my imagination to the extent that the other journeys had. I knew how important and present these excursions seemed to him, how he hoped to redefine himself in his own consciousness as a result of them, to remove the increasingly cadaverous public skin. In the life he was living, those days apart were a rare privilege, could simply never bring him the burden of greatness. Because I loved him, I often feared that his connection to me, with all its secretiveness and denial, was simply an effort to dodge public life. This proclivity was certainly among the ingredients of the recipe that bound us together. My resentment of this was partly, I suspect, because more than I knew or would admit to, I wanted access to that public life, its ceremony and social placement, all the things that he claimed to abhor but nevertheless took part in vigorously and voluntarily. Occasionally, I pictured myself on his arm. But the people and surroundings were blurry. I had never known and would never know such things, so I had no details with which to conjure them.

Later I realized that the instantaneous accomplishment itself was partly what I wanted from him. The awakening annunciation before dawn, the brief number of words jotted down on a scrap of paper, the extraordinariness. All that Harp may have been trying to escape from by being in my arms.

My mother would have wanted something similar. Those stations we were not born to, and could never aspire to, always seemed magical to the sons and daughters of an agricultural world. But few of her generation walked away from the fields to which their ancestors had pledged allegiance, and almost none who did so were women. The presence of a man who had known cities, speakers' halls, and crowning glories would have enlarged and brightened the thinness of my mother's life. To be the subject of such a man's attention would have suggested that all along the potential for such things had lain dormant inside her, and were it not for circumstance, she might have stood by his side. She was drugged by a kind of worship that circled back to the self. And in some respects, so was I.

...

I was lazily riding Bruno home from the school my important temporary Master had left me in charge of when I saw that same Master, the man my mother worshipped, walking away from the house. I first glimpsed him from the road and knew, with a child's instinct, that I wished neither to acknowledge nor to be regarded by him. I pulled on Bruno's reins and walked us both into the camouflage of what my father called wild birches, the same wild birches through which he and my brother would—not many days later—walk with the wounded burden that was me on the beautiful front door. Then I waited until the Master passed by.

No longer a tall, slim man with an elegant build, he telegraphed anxiety in his extremities: a working of the fingers as he walked, a fiddling with cuffs and their links, and an irregularity in his gait. Once he stopped outright halfway down the lane and almost turned back, as if he had forgotten something. But then he pressed on, as if that which he had forgotten was of a consequence so minor it was not worth the extra steps. He strode quickly on towards his motor car, which was parked in a clutch of wolf willow at the end of the lane, where it could not be seen from the road. Everyone is hiding, I thought. I remember him fighting with that wolf willow, swatting it aside, only to have it come back into his face. So undignified for a master and book-writer with a city university postgraduate degree. Still, it wasn't all that long before I heard the purr of his motor, the crunch of the wheels as they met with the gravel on the road. I did not move Bruno forward until I could no longer hear the noise of the engine.

How long would it have taken my mother to convince others to donate the dollar bills that refused, like all meaningful evidence, to be scattered out of existence by the arbitrary storm, instead wrapping themselves around the only available tree. What other sad farm wives would have given her that money? Would have contributed to her cause? How angry they all were! How suspicious! How desperate to hang on to their own desperation! Those little plots of garden—surrounded by pickets—where they planted flowers indigenous to neither the landscape nor their stiff, unused parlours. "Those flowers weren't meant to be in the house," my mother had said. "I've joined a women's organization," she had said, bent over her sewing machine, the white costumes for the women's branch coming into being under her hands.

Years later I was shown the drawings for such a uniform at the city archives. It was filed under "The Invisible Empire" and included such statements as:

"68. Should any members of the Ladies' Klan wish to discuss any matter of Klanscraft with Klansmen, the Excellent Cyclops shall request the Exalted Cyclops to appoint a delegate or arrange for a joint meeting of the two organizations for such purpose."

Men obsessed by power operate separately. They keep women at a distance, even when they want those women to join them in acts of evil.

I discovered that Klecttoken was the name of the membership fee for the women's branch. This church collection–like offering of a few dollars per person was supposed to be gathered by the Kladdess until it reached a certain amount, then forwarded to the Imperial Headquarters. But because of the big wind, my mother never got the chance to send the money on.

Imperial Headquarters. Excellent Cyclops. I remembered the conical pure white dunce caps my mother was making, which required the use of posterboard as well as the sewing machine.

No child establishing a fort in the woods would be unfamiliar with such jargon, such get-up and gear. It is as infantile as it is heinous. I thought of the colonist cars, how my mother demanded *something better* and how the people in them had looked like a bundle of rags to Danny and me.

And I felt ashamed.

As I've suggested before, Sophie had quickly become the pet of the room. Even Friedrich spoke to her with tenderness, something I envied from my side of his bed, though I knew she was the littlest among us, and we were all meant to make her feel loved and protected. She was, she said, from a big estate with orchards of full peaches and cherries, and cotton as well. I knew that this could not be true because I had never seen an orchard on the prairies. Or cotton, whatever that plant looked like. I'd only seen fields of grain, Missouri currants, and Saskatoon berries growing close to the ground, and my mother's one little tree with its scant blossoms in the spring and small wrinkled apples in the fall.

Once, when Sophie was safely asleep, Friedrich said it was likely her grandmother's family estate she was talking about. Or her father's. Maybe her mother came from an estate in the southern United States. "They have cotton fields down there, millions of them, just like we have wheatfields here," Friedrich assured me.

Sophie was asleep with her back turned.

Friedrich was exercising his one good leg in an unbecoming way. "I can see your bum," I said.

"If her mother did come from there," Eli offered thoughtfully from his side of the room, ignoring my comment about Friedrich's lack of modesty, "her family would not have *owned* one of those estates." He appeared to mull this over for a while, then announced, "Those owners would have had to high-tail it out of there lickety-split once any kind of revolution happened. The imprisoned workers would have had enough." He thumped his cast with his fist. "Those landowners had to be held accountable!" he insisted. "They *enslaved* their workers. Their workers were slaves!" He was silent for a few moments. Then he said quietly, "Real slaves."

But apparently, neither of the boys could quite figure out Sophie's story. "I think," Eli said, after a few moments of thoughtful silence, "I think that Sophie's grandparents would have *been* the enslaved workers. But she is right about the principle. They owned the profits that the owner made. They *made* those profits! They owned those profits. They just never *saw* those profits."

"You could be a film star, Sophie," Friedrich always said. "You are that pretty."

I thought this was going too far, but Sophie seemed to take it in her stride. And I could see that it was true.

"Do you want me to read to you, Sophie?" Eli often asked, hoping to coax her to his end of the room.

I had learned from Doctor Angel that Sophie had something called leukemia. I had also learned that it was incurable. I had shared neither of these facts with my compatriots, only because I could not figure out a way to do so with Sophie out of earshot.

She talked about her church, called Shiloh. She talked about her parents and baby brother. She was homesick, we knew, for all that. Sometimes she cried and cried.

But on the other hand, unlike the rest of us, she was often up and running around the room laughing. At least once or twice during the day, though, she would creep sadly back to her bed, lie down, turn her back to us, and go to sleep. One of the sisters would come in at times like these and take her temperature in a way that I thought was undignified. I knew exactly what they were doing, for in the early days, my own temperature had been taken in just such an undignified manner. We would all pretend to be busy with something—a book or toy on our bed—or gazing off in another direction while this went on. We would all pretend that nothing undignified had ever happened to us.

"Did Sophie come from the southern United States?" I asked Sister Editha.

"No," she answered. "Maybe her mother and father, but not her. Her parents have a farm here on the prairies. They knew she was poorly, so they left her in our care." She sighed. "Good farmers," she said. Then added, "They have gone back to their home and fields."

Not too long ago, one day in summer, I made the drive to see the Shiloh church that Sophie had so often talked about. Made of logs, as our own early churches had been, it stood in the middle of window-high prairie grasses. A wind moved everything except that church and the few white crosses—some of them small—placed near it. The ghosts of lost children were in that wind. Not just children like Sophie, but the children who had wanted to play inside me. And also, the children who had been here before, and who were pushed off this land by the clutter of avarice and insatiability. They were, all of them, crying for their mothers, as Sophie so frequently was. And as I myself had on so many occasions.

There was talk among the doctors about a brand-new kind of medicine for Friedrich. And about how they could get their hands on some of it, and when it might arrive if they did. Doctor Angel was pressured to get in touch with the person he had known at medical school in Toronto (though really not well, he demurred). Sister Philomena said, pointedly, that she was *praying* that Doctor Angel would get in touch with his medical school classmate.

"He wasn't a classmate," said Doctor Angel. "He was in a different year altogether."

"God doesn't care about dates of graduation," Sister Philomena announced before walking huffily out of the room.

I wasn't supposed to hear any of this, of course, but as instructed by Friedrich before he fell into a long sleep, I was paying attention to the talk among the adults. Often, I pretended to be asleep myself in order to do this. But I soon discovered that the adults thought the children had no ears or were unable to understand English. In no time, I was even able to watch them and read their expressions while they talked without them noticing I was paying attention.

There was lots of talk about a box of vials. At first, I believed the adults were referring to bad people, as Eli had always done when speaking about vile capitalists. But it gradually became clear to me that these vials had something to do with needles.

Meanwhile, Friedrich was sleeping. Nobody liked this even though he was quiet. Sophie cried about it. The sisters rolled him around on the bed while they changed his sheets, and even so, he did not wake up. The word "coma" was used. I had no experience with this word, but I knew it had something to do with Friedrich's not being able to open his eyes.

One day Doctor Angel, who had been given the cold shoulder by Sister Philomena, was told by this same person that he was a candidate for sainthood. "Beatification at the very least," she said, flinging her arms around him in a completely uncharacteristic gesture of affection. She assumed, and I did too, that he had got in touch with the friend from medical school, whose name was now being bandied about in the ward. But Harp claimed later that the arrival of the drug had nothing to do with him. There were others involved, he maintained.

"Half a dozen of them," he would tell me later, "all jockeying for position. I never met your Doctor Angel." Then he asked if I was absolutely sure this "Doctor Angel" really existed.

Each morning Doctor Carpenter walked in the room with a needle, and each afternoon Friedrich became a little more animated than he was the afternoon before, waking up for an hour or so before settling into his long sleep. On the fifth day of the needles, he woke up and was filled with energy. "Back to himself," said Sister Editha. He immediately started bragging, claiming to be in a genealogical line descending directly from Mozart. "I am his fourth cousin," he announced, "seven times removed. I have no other relatives but him." (Years later, reading a biography of Mozart and learning a little about his character, I thought of Friedrich's assertion and wondered if it might not have been true.) He was still often asleep and wetting the bed, but I could tell that there was a change in him from what I had been witnessing the past two months.

The doctors, both Carpenter and Angel, were spending a lot of time observing him between needles.

"Early days," they said.

Friedrich was often busy with bird-like arias from *The Magic Flute* and being very instructive when it came to the opera's narrative. It was all mixed up with *A Midsummer Night's Dream*, in my view, and also with *Peter Pan*: Titania, Peter, Papageno, Queen of the Night, Tinkerbell, Puck. Something mysterious was afoot. Weren't they all the same story? Friedrich said they were not, then went on to explain why. He kept singing and talking about all this. Triggered by his voice, everything spun busily in my inner theatre, but I was a happy, if dizzy, recipient of everything he passed along. And glad he was awake.

Sophie sometimes joined him. Just for the pure joy of singing: she did not sing the same songs. She tired quickly, however, and sometimes she would stop mid-trill and trail sadly to her bed to lie down.

The members of the Company had burst back into creative life once they knew that Friedrich had been saved. They were working on a musical about the doctor who had discovered the serum that saved him. No daily dogs were in the production, however, because, as one of the principal actors told me, the dog part of the story, though noble, was far too sad. Instead, they were focusing on goings-on in the lab, the set for which they were collecting at the city dump. They had performed two songs for us in the ward. One began, "Eureka, I've found it / There is no way around it!" And the other, I recall, was called "Beakers" and had a line in it concerning "seekers." Though there were no dogs in the musical, the company cat had a cameo role: he was encouraged to walk across the stage in the song "Beakers" when reference was made to the "labby tabby" who spent much of her time in the "laboratory taboratory," where a bowl of milk always waited.

Once I knew him, I, of course, told the man I loved all about this. I witnessed him laugh aloud for the first and next-to-last time. "It's all been worth it just for that," he said, still choking with laughter and leaving me wondering whether he meant the play or my story about the play. Or Friedrich's miraculous recovery. I myself found the Company's response to Friedrich's resurrection touching rather than amusing and was glad that Harp did not often laugh aloud. I could see the silver fillings in his molars.

One of the odd things about love is that it is irrelevant details such as this that temporarily stop it in its tracks, whereas his insensitive comment about Doctor Angel's existence did not. The molars put me off, but only momentarily. My love was a healthy beast. Almost nothing could weaken it, and absolutely nothing could kill it. I was back in his arms in half an hour.

The Company members were going to take Friedrich out of the hospital and off on the road with them soon, he told us. They didn't care that he had only one foot. He could deliver fireside chats! He could do the parts of soldiers returning on crutches from battle! He could sit at the piano and perform Mozart's Piano Sonata no. 16 in C Major! "K. 545!" In short, he could do everything except dance, and even that would be a possibility once he had mastered his prothesis.

Outside, spring was hurrying towards the northern Great Plains in the form of wind-driven, towering clouds. They mushroomed up over the horizon and raced along the train lines towards the hospital. Then they flung their shadows, along with a scattering of brief sunlight, through the window glass, which was clear of frost (though sometimes peppered with rain), and onto the floor of the room.

I recalled it had been late spring when the big wind came to our farm.

When I told Harp about the new season and the billowing, shadow-causing clouds, he brushed my hair back from my forehead. I was uncomfortable when he did this.

"You must have been in the hospital for almost a year by then," he said. He ran his finger softly down the scar that bisected my forehead. He did this with tenderness, as if giving me absolution. He lay back on the pillow, and I placed my head in the soft curve of his shoulder and curled myself around his warmth, feeling safe, feeling protected. Soon we were both asleep.

It was often like this with us. And I should not forget this. There were long periods of time when we both were tender. And innocent.

S ophie was lying on her side with her knees up and her eyes scrunched shut. Her small fists were clenched under her chin.

"Sophie!" Eli, who was the nearest to her, called her name, then asked, "Sophie, what are you doing?"

She neither moved nor opened her eyes. "I am getting better," she said. "You have to work on it and work on it."

Friedrich and I were sitting side by side on hard-backed oak chairs. Eli, who was eager to join us, couldn't get out of bed because he was still in a cast and in traction after his foot-correcting operation, which, according to Doctor Carpenter, had been a great success.

But we two were sitting on hard-backed chairs. I have seen those oak chairs since, at the teacher's desks in schools where I have taught, in the offices of accountants, and in important-looking government buildings. Wherever and whenever I see them, I think about Friedrich, so hesitant—as was I—about entering the world we had left behind many, many months ago. We blamed those chairs for their complicitous role in trying to make us leave the hospital. After more than a year of being bed-bound, we had been encouraged—then commanded—to take the few steps from those beds to the now despised chairs. Miraculously, we had risen and done so. But like many miracles, this one did not receive the recognition it deserved, and we were already irritated and bored. Friedrich said so to plump Sister Hildegard, who passed by on her way to Eli's bed.

"Bored, are you?" she answered. "Why not get up and walk, then?" She swung her thumb over her left shoulder in the direction of the hallway. "You too," she added, nodding in my direction.

Friedrich had been forced to wear his new prothesis for a few days at this point. But he hated it and raged against it. It chafed his skin, apparently, and turned in every direction except the direction he wanted. "I'm not going out there with this thing," he said, with what I saw as a great deal of self-pity.

"Out where?" said Sister Hildegard. "To the hallway? Nobody cares about fashion in a hospital, particularly not this hospital."

Still, he refused.

"Would you prefer the alternative?" Sister Hildegard asked, "because that alternative is a wheelchair." She paused. "Or worse." She was looking in the direction of Sophie, who was sound asleep. "You're the lucky one," she said to Friedrich. "You and your needles! Get up and walk!"

Both of us would have preferred the alternative of the known territory of our beds. We were never bored there. Friedrich had his hidden booty, provided by the players of the Company. I looked at the wall and saw railroads, fashion, my mother's life. Friedrich sang and bragged and got all bossy about telling us things. I watched sunlight play with the room or, later in the evening, listened to Doctor Angel's poetry or Sister Editha's stories of her childhood. Friedrich would have marvellous arguments—shouted from bed to bed—with Eli, who would refute whatever it was that Friedrich had been trying to impart. Long debates ensued. A great pleasure for the boys, and not unpleasurable for me, in that, confined to the nest of my bed, I could take or leave whatever was offered, was able on occasion to maintain a private ironic distance, and was never asked to assume the responsibility of having to participate.

Those two boys could make Sophie laugh and laugh, and often did. She woke up, now, and laughed out loud at something Eli had said. Everyone in the room smiled then. Such love we felt for her, for the smallness of her frame, and for the largeness of her struggles to get well. Even when she was deeply asleep, we all knew that she was working and working. It was her job to get well, and she made that her life's vocation. Laughing now, she still held an expression of concentration on her little child's face. I knew that she didn't for a moment lose that focus—trying to get well. The laughter was part of that focus. Her alertness to others was another part.

Even though I was in a separate bed, I knew I always had Friedrich near me. He was my first hospital companion, almost spousal in his unselfconscious attentiveness.

We knew those chairs were the first part of the journey that would take us away from each other, and what followed would be the resumption of what was left of our previous lives, with all the complications, triumphs, and sorrows therein. We knew this in a nonverbal way, as children always know such things. There was already breakage in our short lives; we were fearful of being broken apart again. We had our little community in this collection of sick beds, in those who occupied them, and in those who visited them. The Company, Mister Porter Abel. The sisters and doctors. No other community would ever be so completely ours. And a part of us knew that as well.

And so, we resisted Sisters Philomena and Hildegard and their mandates. At first, we refused to get up and walk. It was too much of a commitment to the plans of others beyond the region of ourselves. But after gentle coaxing by Sister Editha, abrupt demands by Sister Philomena, and ironic remarks from Sister Hildegard, we relented and, filled with fear and resentment, sat side by side, as I've said.

Mister Porter Abel still visited twice a month and was always his warm self, but he seemed older and looked tired. He said one of his legs had got shorter from all the balancing in the aisle of the train. He said this as he offered me his arm so that he might escort me up and down the hall outside the door. Even though at this point I hated walking, it seemed mean to refuse. As we stepped through the door of the ward, I could feel his shoulder moving towards the floor with each stride we took. We made quite a pair. I had my own new and irregular gait to contend with; my cane in one hand and his strong arm in the other. "That's right, Buttons," he would say. "You are getting stronger every time I see you." He squeezed my arm with his free hand. "Next time I visit, I'll have to run to keep up with you."

When we re-entered the ward, Sophie ran up and hugged Mister Porter Abel's knees. He laughed and patted her head. "You'll be the last one left in here, peaches," he said to her. "Last one."

Sister Editha floated through the door and escorted Sophie gently to her bed. She looked at her for some time after she had tucked her in. "I remember," she said. "I wish," she added, not finishing the sentence.

I have said that the Company was coming soon to take Friedrich away. But that is not quite accurate. There were many plans in the works for him. Sister Editha, having been told something astonishing, had come in wide-eyed to his bedside one late afternoon at the beginning of her night shift. After she had given him his needle, she asked him if he knew that there was a large hospital in Toronto entirely full of children. "Only children," she announced. "Hundreds of them."

"No babies?" Friedrich asked. We both firmly believed that Tatiana's baby would live forever, and remain a baby, in the nursery of this hospital. Only I thought that Tatiana's child was the baby that had been blown out of her mother's arms by the big wind. I also suspected that this thought would be blown out of my life, were I to utter it. So I remained silent, and kept the baby close and happy.

"Oh yes," Sister Editha laughed. "Lots of babies. Dozens of them."

"I won't like it," said Friedrich. "I'm not going, and you can't make me."

I tried to imagine Friedrich in a society of children where there would be no worshipping adults. I found myself unable to picture this.

"Friedrich," said Sister Editha quietly, "you'll be near the laboratory where your medicine is made. And you will meet other children who have your condition.

"And it won't be forever," she added.

"The Company doesn't perform there," he said. His voice was trembling. "Toronto is too stuck up for the Company. They have theatres there where all they ever do is spend money painting the ceilings gold. The Company has never even been there." He was close to tears now. "How will they find me?"

"I've been there!" This was Eli, calling out, unhelpfully, from his end of the ward. "I have an uncle—no, two uncles—there! One has a fish store in a place called Kensington Market."

Sister Editha ignored this. She was silent for a moment. Then she lifted Friedrich's chin in her soft hand. "Look at me, Friedrich," she said. There was a silence. "Look at me," she repeated when he didn't respond. He finally regarded her with tears in his eyes. "Your Company will always find you, no matter where you go. You can be certain of that."

"They work only the smaller places," he whispered.

I began to cry. For the Company. For the smaller places.

"They will find you."

I still don't know why, but Sister Editha's remark put me in mind of the end of *Peter Pan*, where Mister Darling thinks he remembers seeing something like Peter's flying ship once before, in his own boyhood. I stopped crying once I had that thought. Now, though, my eyes fill with tears at the mere remembered reference to a distant parent with his formal clothing somewhat askew, attempting to resurrect his own childhood.

"Is she being sent there too?" Friedrich asked sulkily, pointing in my direction but not looking at me.

"No," said Sister Editha. "No, she is not."

I wondered why that was, and worried about what was going to happen to me instead. Looking suspiciously across the room to the sixth bed, I was happy to note that no one was near it. Not even a blue miasma lingered in its vicinity.

Sophie, who had come awake, jumped off her bed at this point and ran over to Friedrich. "Take me with you," she said. "I want to see the gold ceilings."

I kept looking at the sixth bed. Nowadays it wasn't always that reliable. Sometimes it was there when I looked. Sometimes it wasn't.

Now it was there, all right, and suddenly the Conductor was sitting cross-legged on its mattress. He had his ticket punch and was pretending to be absorbed by perforating tickets. He stopped doing that, however, when Sophie went back to her own bed and lay down again. Then he put his chin in his hand and stared at her. I closed my eyes against what I knew was eventually going to happen. When I opened them again, both the Conductor and the sixth bed had gone, and Sophie was sleeping peacefully in the fifth bed.

"Why can't I go to Toronto with Friedrich?" I asked now.

Sister Editha smiled brightly. "Oh, I meant to tell you your good news today at lunchtime. But now that you've asked . . . I've written to your father, and he has written back," she said. I could hear the happiness in her voice, but it carried a bit of sadness as well. "He and your brother—Danny, isn't that his name?—are coming to get you Thursday morning."

I was so startled by this news I couldn't tell whether I was feeling joy or fear.

Friedrich was refusing to look at me, but Eli was staring, and even little Sophie woke up and turned her attentions from Eli to examine me more closely. I, who had been so broken when I was admitted, was being summarily discharged. Had I done something wrong? Was I guilty or innocent? None of us knew what this meant. So far, the only one of us who had left the ward was Tatiana.

"Thursday is only two days away," said Sister Hildegard, steaming into the room. "Get up and walk."

T he man I loved was *un grand personage*, a great man, a great beast of a man, and as so many great men do, he devoured every room he entered. Even when he was silent, he was not quiet. The Chippendale furniture was nothing compared to him. The art on the walls was nothing compared to him. It sprang to life only as a result of his gaze. It withered under his disregard, and it died with his disdain. The whole history of art, which had been in his purview for only a few years, started to look shaky and unreliable if he glanced at it dismissively. Rococo, German Expressionism, the Pre-Raphaelite period—any one of these could vanish with a wave of his hand. There were certain poets, as well, that he felt confident enough to disapprove of; he who had not read any poetry until recently—beyond that which, like me, he had been forced to memorize in grade school. Henry Wadsworth Longfellow was one of the disparaged poets. He laughed at my descriptions of my father's devotion. And I laughed, too, traitor that I was.

The thing about love is that we don't choose it. It is imposed upon us. The Greeks knew this; even the Anglo-Saxons knew this. The

Romans blamed the gods. The Cornish blamed love potions delivered to the wrong address. The Irish blamed the love talker or the changeling. One way or another, they threw down their spears and admitted that love was inconceivable, unkillable, and beyond their control.

We continue to believe, however, that the good or bad character of the one we love will enable our attachment to them, or at some convenient moment, destroy it. Nothing could be further from the truth. Love is uninterested in a crack in the character of the beloved. And even at its most conventional, it is the enemy of rational decisions. I no more decided to love Harp for the fact that his research and great discovery had saved Friedrich than I decided not to love him for his pal Walt's appalling political associations.

It took everything in me—all my energy, my stubbornness, the mystery of Doctor Angel's poetry, the memory of my damaged mother and father, Tatiana's fire, and some previously unrecognized inner combination of self-preservation and morality—to walk away. As I knew that night at the School for the Deaf that I must. "Walt?" he had said. "What on earth could be offensive about Walt?"

But love—the tormenter—was still there. A few months later, had Harp been able to ask me to, which he was not, I might have begun again. Yes, I am certain of that: despite my age, and despite a firm knowledge of all that had remained, and would continue to remain, disturbing, shadowy, and unclear, I might have begun again.

As it was, Harp would not live to see his "old pal" ascend the political ladder to a place of power in the right-leaning party of this country. Always denying his former associations with a group as filled with hate as the one I knew him to have embraced, the old pal, Master Stillwell, nevertheless showed—to my mind, anyway—a proclivity for just such divisiveness and hatred. Disguised as prudence. Disguised as love of country. Disguised as concern for the very groups he meant to re-educate out of existence.

I am alert to every news item, every rumour about this man. I mean to follow his ship with all the tenacity of Captain Hook's crocodile. The letters I had read in my mother's dark drawer were scattered and torn apart by the big wind. They will never be found. But thanks to this specious politician, this most important, most educated teacher, this Master, I will never again forget one word of what I have learned, never forget his insistence on the true stanzaic order. As it turns out, I am a child of memory work and recitation after all.

Harp, who was too old to be called up, responded to the war, like so many men over the centuries have done, as an opportunity. Unlike most opportunists, however, he did not see it—or anything else, for that matter—as an opportunity to make money because, simply stated, he had never been and never would be interested in anything as banal as that. Ever since the great discovery, he had wanted to return to the spontaneity that was lacking in his more recent life (except in the company of the *plein-air* painters and their campfires), and in his heart, he worshipped not empire or the greater good but intuition. Because his great discovery was intuitive, he believed that intuition could take him anywhere, and would be there on arrival to solve any problems that might come up in the new terrain. During the war, he thought he would like to fly to Britain on a Canadian Air Force flight. He was discouraged from doing so. But great men generally get their way.

Hardly anyone I have loved remains alive. The exceptions are the famous tenor Friedrich, who is constantly on tour, and whom I see every year or so at a concert in a prairie city; my brother Danny, in his nearby cloister; and the twins in their distant separate cities. But most of the others are gone: the other children who were like family to me for that whole year we were ward mates, my parents, and my Ontario aunts and uncles—my friends and cousins, even some of the younger Ontario cousins I never knew. It is the natural way of things, of course. You think you will greet these catastrophes philosophically. But let me warn you, you do not. The light grows dimmer and dimmer with each removal, and the busy world itself, and everything natural and unnatural in it, becomes something unreliable and lost. The man I loved died in middle age, so was spared the view of all the lights around him being put out one by one. I, on the other hand, have not yet died in middle age.

"I know how to fly," he told me towards the end. "Suddenly, I think I understand aerodynamics."

"Just like that?" I asked.

He snapped his fingers. "Just like that," he said, laughing. Then he crossed the room towards me.

I often go to the monastery to see Danny after my mornings in the schools. Driving up the lane, I am escorted by a grove of trees planted fifty years ago by horticulturally ambitious monks. The bare branches—and their shadows on the snow—are an anomaly. There is brightness everywhere on the prairie in the full winter sun. To be a figure of any kind, in such a landscape, is to be inaugurated into a state of grace. There is no season anywhere like a winter season on the northern Great Plains. Even though I am writing this on a summer evening, with the window opened (though screened because of mosquitoes), I cannot mentally conjure the word "prairie" without seeing the colours white and blue and yellow, the pure dazzle of it all.

The day I am remembering was a Wednesday. Danny, his choir, and I were to meet at the abbey's college. For Danny is choirmaster as well as guest-master, and chicken-, duck-, and beekeeper, while I am merely the accompanist. The choir is almost entirely secular now, made up of townspeople and farmers. They sing the chants and hymns of religious music, but also songs relating to life on the prairies: "They Call the Wind Maria," for example, or "Red River Valley." "For you take with you all of the sunshine that has brightened our pathway awhile."

Danny loves the idea of the human voice making music. And this was part, I imagine, of what attracted him to Friedrich. I have never asked Danny about this, and I never will. I have never asked Friedrich, either, though on the few occasions he is in the prairies, I take the unimportant branch line to the city to listen to him sing and to have a meal with him. We speak of our childhood. But never about Danny.

This day, Danny and I had planned to go to the abbey church to practise Bach's *Jesu, Joy of Man's Desiring* for the spring concert. All that glorious noise beneath the painted saints so lovingly chronicled by Sister Editha!

I had never been able to look at those painted figures without thinking of the wandering saints and prophets from the hospital, and how we the children knew they were not just people from the old persons' floor but saints and prophets as well. How could they be assembled in one dormitory and be manageable? They had too much wisdom to be forcibly held in place. And too much desire to impart that wisdom. Even those who had been for years unable to speak. I recall them murmuring by my bed. One of them had asked me if Sophie was "going," and I said that yes, I thought so. Maybe.

I pretended to myself that I was unaware of where Sophie was going. But I knew. In my heart. I knew.

Then three of them hugged me. And one, the most silent of them all, did not hug me but said, "Bless you."

I arrived early because Danny had suggested I do so. I assumed this was because I needed to practise the complicated Bach accompaniment, to raise it to the level of his acceptance. But he met me at the church door, instead, and suggested we go for a walk.

He had a pail of seed with him. "Must feed the chickens," he said. "They need more food in this cold." I went back to the car for my hat and stick, and as I again walked towards him, I realized that under such an extremity of light, he was a radiant star, perfectly at home in this mad illumination.

I also knew, by his white hair and lined face, that he had graduated to a different plane. He was becoming one of the saints, one of the prophets. *Then shall the righteous shine forth as the sun in the kingdom of their Father.*

"Danny," I said, "you look perfectly marvellous." I was almost certain my own wear and tear would not hold up under such scrutiny.

"So do you, Emer," he said. Ever courteous, as was his way.

But as we set out, he became silent and serious. This was one of those confusing winter days—bitterly cold, but without the wind—and in the presence of this crazy and magnified sun, the air felt as if there were no reason to call it cold at all. People in the prairies had now and then frozen to death in the company of just such a winter-trickster sun.

"Emer," he said, and as he said my name, I looked at him and saw with surprise that there were tears in his eyes. We experience plenty of wind tears and sun tears in this region, but as I have said, there was no wind.

And I knew instinctively that Danny's eyes were not sensitive to the sun. Not today.

He took my gloved hand and then linked his arm in mine. "Emer," he said again, "I had a visitor earlier this week."

I sensed his need to tell me more, so I said nothing. Our footsteps were causing the snow to make a creaking noise, more noticeable in the silence.

"Our former Master, the former politician," Danny said, naming the former Master/politician in question. "He is very old now—ninety-one, he told me—but he still has his wits." Danny said this with an uncharacteristically ironic laugh.

I had not told Danny about my meeting with this man. I did not tell him now. I asked instead why he had come to the monastery. "Seeking absolution, I imagine," I said, matching Danny's ironic tone. By now, everyone in the prairies had at the very least heard rumours concerning the unsavory company he once kept.

"Sort of," Danny answered. "He was seeking absolution of some sort. But he was also looking for me." He unlinked his arm, stepped away from me, and looked me straight in the face.

"Emer," he said, and there was a hoarseness in his voice. "Emer, he said he was my father."

I remained silent. Had I always unconsciously known this was the case? I took Danny's arm again. I loved him so much. I loved even the sleeves of his wool overcoat.

"This cannot be," I said, though I believed it was true. "What did you say?"

Danny did not respond right away, but finally he said that the man had refused to pray with him. "I told him I forgave him anyway," Danny admitted, "with or without prayers."

Danny opened the chain-link gate to the chicken yard and took off one glove to be better able to grab a fistful of seed. "But, Emer," he said, "what am I forgiving him for?" With the birds all around him and his footsteps in the snow, he looked like a combination of Saint Wenceslas and Saint Francis.

I was glad that the educator-politician had not knelt. I could not imagine, did not want to imagine—there was something obscene in it—these two men kneeling together. "Abandonment," I immediately said. "Betrayal. Manipulation, then abandonment and betrayal. But not of you." I rubbed his arm and hoped the touch travelled through the padding of winter clothing. "Of our mother."

"Is it true?" Danny was asking me now. "And what of her, our mother?" He looked towards the horizon, which carried a thin snow cloud on the edge of a pristine cerulean sky. "Possible blizzard tonight," he said.

The chickens had come out to squabble over the seed he had tossed in their yard. We both watched this for a while, then turned back in the direction of the church and stepped away from the noise of the angry poultry.

Danny was silent. Shadows thrown by the grove of bare winter trees were grey stripes on the snow.

I told him then about the one important letter, and then the others. How I had read them. "There was no mention of you in them," I said. "But yes . . ." I paused here, letting my own sense of multiple disloyalties run into and then out of my mind. "Yes," I finally said, "she was in love with him. From the beginning, I think. Right from the time of the examination for the third-class certificate." There was more silence. "Or at least that is how I explain it to myself," I added, knowing now that this last remark, my part in it, was true.

Danny held the door of the church open for me. "We'll be frostbitten if we are not careful," he said, motioning me inside.

"Our father never knew about any of it," I said. "I'm certain of that." My heart was alarming, beating as if there was immediate danger in my path.

Danny's face relaxed then, and he embraced me. "Our dad," he said, smiling. "He is the only one for me." Then he laughed a bit and pointed upward. "Except the other one," he whispered conspiratorially. "The one in heaven."

I have spent a lot of time, now, measuring seduction against the world's larger catastrophes. What does something so small, so intimate, and involving only two people mean in the face of the larger, noisier tragedies that visit the innocent of the world? My mother would marry my father, have an early baby, and be grateful for her husband's lack of questions, though now and then she might have confused this failure of inquiry with lack of curiosity, or of care.

But over the years, as her daily life unfolded, the father of the baby would continue to inhabit her mind, her dreams. In her vanity, she would mentally deny the abandonment and betrayal, as if it were a mistake, an inaccuracy that could be corrected and elevated into something more meaningful. Something "better," like the system of classes implemented on a passenger train. In the decades that followed Danny's birth, my mother would take on the mental, and sometimes the physical, task of trying to make this past—and sometimes current—relationship more acceptable to her palate. She would never turn the important teacher away because of her need for revision, for these few desperate and brief opportunities to get it right. She would work on it and work on it, this imaginary house that sheltered her love affair, her one or two glimpses of castle hotels. She applied herself to it with almost the same fervour that poor innocent Sophie—small sick child, granddaughter of slaves—would work and work at trying to stay alive.

But my mother would not deny the seduction. The important teacher, the keeper of the keys to the rural third-class certificate, would dismiss it and hide it. Almost to the end of his life. But when my mother walked through the rooms of her inner life, she would not deny it. For seduction is a soft thing. It fills your rooms with golden light, sings your praises, makes you feel elected. Sainted.

Abandonment, however, is not to be endured, because it provides proof that—no matter how he made you feel when he was, now and then, in town—you are ordinary after all. And so, until the storm came, she held to the notion that if she could only just please him enough, he would return to her once and for all.

And what became of those letters? That almost-proof of who knows what? Torn by the storm, soaked and bleached by winter snow and sun, they would be irrelevant to the wind on the prairie, as would the faint smell of my mother's hand soap that inadvertently scented them. And the white costumes she had angrily sewn at that devil of a machine? If they were ever found among the broken remnants of our household goods, they were likely taken for bed linens or window dressings.

"Changed by white curtains!" Doctor Angel always said when noisily pulling the bleached drapery, with its ringing metal hooks, all around my bed. I was sometimes in distress and needed privacy, and he would provide it. Shutting out the Conductor, who was moving, bed by bed, across the room.

Then he would say some Doctor Angel poetry. I never understood the meaning of the words. But they soothed me, nevertheless, and calmed the anxious bird in my chest.

One night I confessed to him that hearing the baby in the distant parts of the hospital had made me feel safer, better.

Then he said another newer "piece," which is what he called those things he composed and sometimes wrote down. This one was filled with verbs that were alarmingly imperative. "Sweep!" he commanded. "Hurry!" As if he were a drill sergeant. And right in the middle of the poem!

"'Changed utterly,'" said Harp, quoting Yeats while lying in white sheets. He said this twice. Once when he described his life after the great discovery, and once when I told him about my mother. But he might as well have used the imperative, too, when addressing me. "Change utterly!" he might have said.

But there would have been no need for me to obey. I had already changed utterly under his touch.

O nce we were reunited, my father and brother told me that after being flung there by casual weather, my pony, Bruno, was enjoying the new grass in that ninth field. "Further fields," my father said, smiling. "And of no mind to leave," he insisted. "Wouldn't even look at me!" My father shook his head. "'Bruno,' I said to him, though he didn't pay me any mind. 'Bruno, it wasn't me that tossed you into the air.'"

The pony was considered a wonder, and for several years, people from all over the prairies came to see him. Sometimes there were three or four wagons parked at the edge of the road, and adults and children near the fence. Danny said those people were probably hoping for a miraculous assumption. And true to his character, Bruno accepted any apples offered to him, then bit the gift-giver as they turned away.

"Always a backbiter," Danny said.

Then we all laughed, as we could sometimes manage to do by then. Timmy and Patrick didn't remember Bruno from before the storm, but they laughed anyway with the true delight of young children.

Tomorrow, if the weather is settled and clear, I will drive the old car out to Maplewood School, as I always do two Tuesdays a month. And I will step into the classroom where I first met Harp. The children now are not much different than the children were then—some of them are the offspring of the pupils who had enthusiastically greeted him when, smelling of the previous evening's campfire, cigarettes, and whisky, he entered their schoolroom. I am no longer the young full-time teacher who appears to be a child herself when looked at from the age I am now. I am the change that occasionally happens in the midst of routine. And as I have said before, they love me better for being so brief, so temporary.

These days, only a handful of the children know anything at all about Harp's achievement. His great discovery has been refined, packaged, absorbed by corporate interests, and taken for granted. The class writes to newer famous men now—not one of whom, to my knowledge, has accepted the invitation to visit, and few of whom have even taken the trouble to reply.

There is official talk of busing the students to larger centres where, as one politician put it, "They will have the benefit of a gymnasium and a football field."

I know what this means for me, and for my music.

And so, our little lights go out. Somebody changed the world. Somebody taught a child about the treble clef. Another sowed a field and built his house. Three nineteen-year-old nuns told to embark on a long journey started the fund that would eventually build a hospital. A young man in Nova Scotia whose name was Abel got a job on the railway. Two young men met each other at my suggestion, and they fell in love. Both had vocations. One entered a monastery. The other, a tenor, began to travel the world. Perhaps one day there will be hope for a public expression of love like theirs. Alas, there wasn't then, and there still isn't now.

Even the anthem has changed. As I previously observed, we now sing "God Save the Queen." As my mother and father would have done as children in their own schoolrooms.

I want my father to visit me tonight, in the same way I wanted him to visit every day and every night in the hospital when I was torn and broken and given over to the mercy and kindness of strangers. He is gone now, but still, I want to turn back to him. I want to see his light, the warm light his lantern poured over the whitewashed walls and pine floorboards of our brand-new house, built by his hands. Sometimes, when he came back from the morning barn, he stopped at my bedside, touched my shoulder, and rumpled my hair to make me rise for school. I would often pretend to be asleep in the hope that he would try to wake me.

He didn't always pause in his chores to light my morning in such a way. But now and then he would. Often enough that I felt loved.

ACKNOWLEDGEMENTS

This book has been almost a decade in the making, and during those long years many people have helped and encouraged me.

Great thanks go to my loyal friend and agent, Ellen Levine, who was understanding when I stalled, and generous when I made decisions based on emotions.

I am also very grateful to this book's brilliant editor, Jared Bland, whose warmth and clarity had a calming effect on my scattered thoughts and words, and to Janice Weaver, who saved me from myself more times than I can count. Thanks also to the perceptive Stephanie Sinclair at McClelland & Stewart, who made sure she was always available to lend a helping hand. I am indebted to the meticulous eye and hand of Heather Sangster of Strong Finish, who has often come to my aid over the years, and to Kimberlee Kemp who was tireless in her efforts to see this ship into an eventual safe harbour.

Those who shared stories about the northern Great Plains of the 1920s include the late Clifford Quinn, who wrote about the prairie tornado in his Ontario memoir; the late Frank Quinn of Saskatchewan, whose tornado story was transcribed by Donall Wigmore and sent to me by Betty Quinn Plonka; and other members of the extended Quinn family who provided scraps of narrative (Roseanne Quinn and Jill Robinson Quinn come to mind). I owe them all an immense debt of gratitude. My novel was unruly fiction, however, and ran away from their truth and into my imagination. Any inaccuracies, therefore, are mine alone.

I have read dozens of books and articles related to my subject, and they have inspired and informed my novel in direct and indirect ways. The most important of these texts were: *SickKids: The History of The Hospital for Sick Children* by David Wright (University of Toronto Press, 2016); *My Name's Not George: The Story of the Brotherhood of Sleeping Car Porters in Canada* by Stanley G. Grizzle (Umbrella Press, 1998); *The Education of the New-Canadian: A Treatise on Canada's Greatest Educational Problem* by J.T.M. Anderson (J.M. Dent, 1918. Reprint Legare Street Press, 2023); *Banting: A Biography* by Michael Bliss (McClelland & Stewart, 1984); *St. Peter's Cathedral: The Inside Story* by Marcella T. Hinz (St. Peter's Press, 1995); The Company of St. Ursula; *The Erwin Story* by Patrick Donohue (P. Donohue, 1982); *The Doukhobors* by George Woodcock and Ivan Avakumovic (Oxford University Press, 1968); and the delightful *The Prairie Does Flourish: Sisters of St. Elizabeth, 100 Years of Blooming on Canadian Soil* by Joan Eyolfson Cadham (Sisters of St. Elizabeth, 2011).

Among the many articles that I read while writing this book, two in particular caught my imagination: Lisbet Koerner's fascinating piece "Goethe's Botany: Lessons of a Feminine Science," published in *Isis* 84, no. 3 (September 1993), pp. 470–495; and Mavis Reimer's enchanting "Soliciting Home: The Cultural Function of Orphan Girls in Early Twentieth-Century Canada," published in *L.M. Montgomery and Gender*, edited by Laura M. Robinson and E. Holly Pike, 119–151. (McGill-Queen's University Press, 2021).

I am grateful to the copies of the *Prairie Messenger* (the former weekly newspaper published by the Benedictines of St. Peter's Abbey and printed by the St. Peter's Press) for a look inside the monastery, The

Provincial Archives of Saskatchewan for well-organized files on a dark subject, and to Catherine Hobbs at Library Archives Canada for a file I lost and she found.

The lines on page 135 are from the poem "Between Walls" by William Carlos Williams, from *The Collected Poems of William Carlos Williams: Volume I, 1909 to 1939,* edited by A. Walton Litz and Christopher MacGowan (New Directions Publishing Corporation, 1987).

Friends helped with my research. Among these were Mia Woodburn and Ann Dobby, who shared their knowledge of pediatric nursing; Michael and Oonagh Phillips, who visited St. Peter's Abbey and brought back books, papers, and a full report on the many wonders to be found there; and Phyllis Ketcheson, who loaned a book to me about her father's prairie life as a travelling player.

I was enormously grateful for my friends (some of whom are tragically no longer here) during this past decade, and for my family. I cherished the love and support of my dear friend Mieke Beverlander (1946–2022) and my lovely brother, John Carter, who sadly died on April 7 of last year. My treasured friend and editor, Ellen Seligman, died in 2016. She is sorely missed.

JANE URQUHART was born in Little Longlac, Ontario, and grew up in Northumberland County and Toronto. She is the author of eight internationally acclaimed novels, which have received Le prix du meilleur livre étranger (Best Foreign Book Prize) in France, the Trillium Award, and the Governor General's Award, and have been finalists or longlisted for the International IMPAC Dublin Literary Award, the Rogers Writers' Trust Fiction Prize, the Orange Prize, The Giller Prize, the Booker Prize, and the Commonwealth Writers' Prize for Best Book, among others.